# HIS CURVY SUNSHINE

A SMALL TOWN CURVY GIRL ROMANCE

BOOK BOYFRIENDS WANTED
BOOK 18

MARY E THOMPSON

# BOOK BOYFRIENDS WANTED

What's not to love about a quaint small town? Nothing for her, but there's nowhere else he'd rather be. How can the place that's perfect for her be all wrong for him? Maybe there's a compromise. Or a misunderstanding. Or some ghosts that need to be evacuated from the closet. Whatever it is, there's sure to be some drama, some steam, and a happily ever after.

Never miss a thing when you sign up for Mary's newsletter. *Romancing the Curves* comes with subscriber exclusive freebies, sneak peeks, and a first look at everything Mary has to offer. Be the first to know about new releases and sales and all the curves ahead!

**SUBSCRIBE NOW AT MARYETHOMPSON.COM**

Happy reading!

*Never stop looking for your light...*
*And always let it shine*

# 1

## KINGSLEY

PICKUP LINES WERE INVENTED BY SOME ASSHOLE WHO WANTED to watch others squirm. Who was looking to piss off as many people as possible, all at once.

I drummed my fingers on the steering wheel and resisted the urge to honk at the car ahead of me.

Pickup lines in a bar were so much better than the ones outside an elementary school. Especially on the last day. You would think they had their shit together by the last day, but no. It was worse.

Not that I blamed the school. It was all the fault of the parents in line. The ones who wanted to talk to other parents and hold up everyone else. The ones who didn't follow the damn rules and pulled up in the middle of the exit lane instead of staying in the pickup line and waiting their damn turn.

Because their precious child was more important than all the others who were waiting to get picked up.

"Asshole," I mumbled as yet another parent drove right on by the rest of us and stopped to get their kid, blocking all the traffic that was trying to leave while their super special student took their sweet-ass time getting in the vehicle that was too big to climb up in alone, making the shithead parent put the vehicle in park and walk around to help their kid in. Delaying the whole process even more.

I rolled my eyes and inched forward, one car making their way out of the endless line while I searched for Isla.

I moved another inch, almost able to see the door where the teachers kept the pre-k students until they could see the parents, when my phone rang.

A glance at the dash showed my mom was calling. "Hey, Mom. I'm about to get Isla. You can say hi in a minute. How are you today?"

"Kingsley?" The word came out as a breath, barely enough of a sound for me to hear it.

"What's wrong?" Adrenaline spiked in my bloodstream. My hands tightened on the wheel. I searched the crowd of students, ignoring the asshole parents and preparing for a fight if I needed to have one.

"Your dad had a heart attack."

Air rushed into my lungs, relief and anger fighting for presence. *I hope he died* raced through my mind, the words filtered by a long ago grudge I would never let go of.

But I couldn't say them to my mother.

"Did you hear me, Kingsley? Your father is in the hospital."

So not dead.

"Sorry, Mom. I just spotted Isla. Are you okay? What's going on?"

She sniffed and sucked in a shaky breath. I felt her pain from three hundred miles away.

"He's... He collapsed at work. Sheila called nine-one-one, and they got to him in time, but the doctor is talking about surgery and medication and a new diet and—"

"Mom, take a breath." Panic was setting in. For both of us. I knew what was coming next.

"Hi, Daddy!" Isla said, opening the back door with the help of her teacher.

Mom sniffed on the phone, the sound loud through the speakers of the car.

"Hi, sweetheart. How was your last day? Hi, Mrs. Dickson."

"Hello, Dr. Harris. Have a great summer."

"You, too!" I waved as she closed the door and went back to the school to get other kids and send them off for the summer.

Mom whimpered as I eased away from the curb, double checking Isla was secure in her booster seat.

"What's that noise, Daddy?" Isla asked.

"Hello, Isla, honey. How are you?" Mom said, alerting my daughter to her presence on the phone.

"Grandma! Hi! Did you call to tell me happy summer? Everyone has been saying it all day. I'm so excited for summer. It's going to be great. Daddy is going to take some days off because I'm home all summer, and we're going to have fun. Are you going to come visit us?"

I made it to the end of the parking lot and waited for traffic to clear before I turned onto the neighborhood street the school was on. The majority of traffic was parents getting kids, and I felt bad for the families who lived in the neighborhood. They probably thought it was great at first, but having a thousand extra cars in your neighborhood every day would get old in a hurry.

"I'm not going to be able to visit you, Isla. But maybe you can come here to see me. Grandpa is sick."

"Why is he sick?"

"His heart isn't good, and he might need surgery."

"We should definitely visit then. Daddy, can we go?" Isla asked, looking up at me in the rearview mirror.

"I don't know," I said, balancing the conversation I didn't want to have in front of my daughter and the one I couldn't have with my mother.

"Kingsley, I can't run his practice. You know that. There's no other doctor around. I need you. Isla just said you're off some of the summer. Can you come here? Please? I can't do this all by myself."

Her soft sobs squeezed at my heart. My mom was the only reason I had any contact with my parents. It never felt right to cut her out of my life, or Isla's, but I didn't speak to my father.

"We have to go, Daddy. You always say when people need our help, we should do everything we can to help them. Grandma is not just people. She's Grandma."

The logic of a four-year-old was hard to argue with, especially when she wasn't wrong.

But I still didn't want to do it.

"Please, Kingsley. I know this is a big thing to ask you. Please."

I drew a breath and knew I had no choice. Not when she was asking. "We'll pack up when we get home and be there tonight. If that's okay."

"Yay!" Isla shouted from the back. She clapped her hands and looked absolutely thrilled with the idea of visiting her grandparents.

"Thank you, Kingsley. So much." Mom sucked in a sob and released another shaky breath. "It means a lot to me. You can stay here. With me. Your father is going to be in the hospital for at least a week, maybe longer."

"We'll find somewhere else to stay by the time he gets home." I would not stay under the same roof as that man.

Not if I could help it.

"Okay. I understand," Mom said.

"We're going to grandma's. We're going to grandma's," Isla sang in the backseat. "Yay!"

Mom laughed softly. "I'm looking forward to seeing you, my sweet girl."

"Me, too."

At least someone was excited.

By the time we made the ten minute drive home, Isla was planning her entire summer out. She missed the part about me working, but I didn't have the heart to tell her I wouldn't be able to take much time off if I was running my father's practice. It wasn't like the one I'd joined when I finished veterinary school. There were seven other doctors with me, and time off was fairly easy to come by.

Not when I was the one and only vet in town.

But I owed my mother. More than I could ever repay, I owed her.

"Can I bring my swimsuit, Daddy?" Isla asked as she scampered into the small house we rented, almost leaving her backpack behind.

"Yeah, grandma has a pool in the backyard."

"Yay!" Isla took off down the hall to her bedroom across from mine.

I headed for the bathroom, knowing she'd empty her drawers into the suitcase that was in her closet. The house was small, but we didn't need more than we had. We were a team, just the two of us.

It wasn't supposed to be that way. The one person who would understand how I was feeling about going back to my hometown was gone. Stolen from me by a careless driver who was too impatient to wait for her to pass before turning in front of her.

"I'm ready, Daddy!" Isla called, dragging her suitcase from her room.

"What do you have in there?"

She shrugged, her brown eyes that matched her mother's at the floor instead of my face.

"Isla Elizabeth Harris, what did you pack?"

She sighed like a teenager instead of a preschooler and released the handle of the suitcase. "Just the stuff I need."

"And what do you need?" I stepped into the hall and peeked into her room, noting her completely stripped bed and closed drawers. "Did you pack any clothes or did you just take your bedding?"

"But I need that!" The whine was one of exhaustion, exhaustion I knew was the main reason she wanted her bed. She crashed most days when she got home.

"You do need that, Isla, but you also need clothes. Let's go back in and pack some clothes for you in the suitcase, then you can bring your pillow and blanket out onto the couch while I finish packing everything else."

"And Sabie?"

"Yes, you can bring Sabie."

Her smile returned, her prized sabertooth tiger revealed from behind her back. It was the last thing Faith bought for Isla before she died. A gift for her first birthday. A birthday Faith never got to celebrate.

We went back into Isla's room and opened the suitcase. She grabbed her pillow and sat on her bed while I packed her things for the summer. There was so much to do. So much to think about. But we had to go.

I finished packing Isla's things, then turned on a show

for her in the living room while I focused on what I needed to do. I'd already taken the rest of the week off so I could spend it with her before the summer camp she was supposed to attend opened. My first call was still to my boss, the managing partner of the clinic.

"How was the last day of pickup?" Harry asked as he answered.

"Those parents are horrible," I told him.

Harry chuckled. A father himself, he knew well the hell of a pickup line for elementary kids. "Yep. Last day is the worst. You should be spending time with Isla. What's going on?"

"My dad had a heart attack."

"Oh, shit. Are you okay? What do you need?"

"My mom asked if I could handle his clinic for the summer."

"Is he a vet, too?"

"Yeah."

"Oh. I didn't realize. Why aren't you working with him?" Harry's question was asked with levity, but I wasn't feeling light.

"We don't get along."

"Shit, I'm sorry. Um, yeah. Take all the time you need. Keep us posted on how things are going, and we'll cover for you until you can get back. Don't worry about a thing."

"Thanks, Harry. Means a lot."

"Of course. Hopefully you can spend some time with Isla, too."

"I hope so."

Harry hung up, and I made the next call to the summer camp program to put a hold on Isla's spot. I told them we might be back in a few weeks or not at all, and they agreed to let us go week by week, considering the circumstances.

My last call was to our landlady. She agreed to pick up the mail until I could get it forwarded or put on hold. And she said she'd watch the house while we were gone, and take the trash and recycling to the curb in two days so things weren't left in the house to stink.

"Drive safe," she told me before we hung up.

I always do. I would not lose someone else to a car accident.

Isla was sleeping on the couch by the time I packed my suitcase, loaded the back of the SUV, and emptied the fridge. I didn't like rushing and felt like I was forgetting something, but I couldn't come up with what it was.

Anxiety.

I didn't want to go.

But we'd find a place to rent once Dad came home. It was a small town, but there had to be places to rent.

Isla woke up an hour into the drive. She cried that she was hungry, so we stopped for dinner at a fast food place that had a small play area where she could run around.

An hour later, we were back on the road, her steady chatter my sole accompaniment until she fell asleep again.

The second half of the trip was quiet, but the closer I got to my hometown, the more tense I felt. I always planned to build my life in MacKellar Cove. Faith and I met in college, and she fell hard for my hometown. We knew it was the right place to raise our family. A perfect small town for all of us. A place where neighbors knew each other and watched out for each other. Safe and simple and home.

Before I started veterinary school, we would walk around town and pick out houses we would buy one day. A starter home for just the two of us, a bigger one for when we had kids, then a ranch for when we were retired.

Leaving town for vet school was tough, but making the

choice not to come back was even harder. Faith didn't fight me on it. She knew I couldn't stay. Not after what happened.

We thought it would be fine. I found a job in a great practice, we had Isla, and we were talking about other kids.

Then Faith died, and everything changed. All the plans we had for the future, all the things we wanted, were gone just like when we left MacKellar Cove.

Driving north along the Saint Lawrence River, past the small towns that dotted the banks, and heading into MacKellar Cove brought back all the pain of loss I felt. Faith wasn't there. Isla didn't know the town. The life we were supposed to have was gone.

But we were back. For a little while.

I pulled into the driveway of the house I grew up in. The paint on the front was peeling. Mom's car sat in the cracked driveway. The landscaping had seen better days, one half-dead bush the only thing in the flowerbed in front of the house.

A lot had changed.

I parked the SUV and turned off the engine just as the front door opened. Mom waved from the porch, stepping carefully in the darkness without exterior lights to help her down the steps.

I got out, checking Isla was still asleep before I closed the door. "Hi, Mom."

"Oh, Kingsley. Thank you for coming." She threw her arms around my neck and pulled me in close. She trembled, a sob escaping as I hugged her. "I was so scared."

"I know, Mom."

She sniffed again, then pulled back. "What can I help you with?"

"Anything you can grab. I brought a cooler with food from my fridge that I didn't want to throw away, and we have too much stuff, but Isla didn't want to leave anything behind."

"We will make it work. Is she going to be okay in the spare room?"

I nodded. The spare room was Dad's office, but Mom put a twin bed in there when Isla was born. We'd never stayed there, but she wanted to make sure there was room for us to visit. Instead, Mom stayed with Isla and me when Faith died, bunking with Isla and helping take care of my toddler when I could barely get out of bed.

Yeah, I owed her a lot.

Mom and I worked to bring all our stuff into the house, leaving Isla for last. I unbuckled her seatbelt and scooped her up, holding her close as I carried her inside.

I went down the hall to the spare room, setting Isla on the bed that I'd already set up with her things. She smacked her lips a few times, then snuggled up to Sabie and kept sleeping.

"She's so precious," Mom whispered.

I nodded, looking back at my daughter. "She is."

"I really appreciate you coming here."

"Of course, Mom."

"Your father is having some more tests tomorrow, and the doctor is trying to decide a course of action by the weekend."

"Really? They're taking that long to figure something out?"

Mom chuckled. "Your father said the same thing. He's ready to get out of there."

I grumbled something I hoped she would take as agreement. The last thing I ever wanted was to be told how similar I was to my father.

"I'm sure you're exhausted. I know I am. And it's late."

I nodded. "Yeah, it is. What time do I need to be at the clinic tomorrow?"

"Dad usually starts his day at seven."

"Okay, then I need to get some sleep."

"Good night, Kingsley. And thank you. You'll never know how much this means to me, and to MacKellar Cove. I know you don't want to be here, but this town is special, and your dad is the only vet for a hundred miles. He helps people."

"I know, Mom," I grumbled. The last thing I wanted was a lecture about how great my father was.

Mom squeezed my hand and let me close the door to the spare room so Isla didn't wander. I went across the hall to the bedroom that was mine growing up. The only thing that had changed was the twin bed became a queen after Faith and I were married. Otherwise, it was the same room with the same memories that haunted me for years.

Memories I had to live with for the summer.

**2**

---

DAISY

I UNLOCKED THE BACK DOOR TO MY FAVORITE PLACE ON EARTH and flipped the switch to illuminate the room. I stepped inside and closed the door behind me, locking it again to avoid any eager parents from trying to get in before I was open.

Lincoln Toys was my dream come true. The place I'd always wanted when I was a kid. A magical store where kids could be kids and parents could breathe.

Not that I understood what parents needed, but it seemed to work. Families loved coming to Lincoln Toys. They could play with toys before they bought them in the massive all-inclusive playroom that was safe for kids of all abilities or in the quiet playroom for kids who needed a space with less activity and fewer distractions.

That second one was inspired by my best friend and favorite person, Natalie. Nat loved kids, but she sometimes needed quiet and calm, and she was far from the only one. She cried when I told her she inspired the space.

Natalie understood what Lincoln Toys meant to me, and why I created a space that would allow me to live out the childhood I missed out on. Why I needed a place where play was the focus, and where every kid mattered.

I moved through the warehouse space at the back of the building toward my office when I realized there were new boxes near the loading dock that never got put away. Thankfully, the boxes were inside and not left out in the overnight rain, but they were in the middle of the walkway.

I grabbed a utility knife and sliced through the plastic wrap holding the boxes onto the pallet, then cut the tape on the top box, smiling when I saw the footballs I ordered.

Natalie's summer camp was holding a Grand Opening over the weekend, and she invited local kid-focused businesses to attend and meet local parents and families. The footballs were part of the swag I ordered to hand out at the event.

I set the box of footballs on the floor and opened the next box. Flattened colorful beach balls were in the next two boxes. Stickers were in one box. Temporary tattoos were in another. Then there were five more boxes of footballs.

I couldn't stop my grin as I looked over all the supplies. One thousand of each would be plenty for the kids attending the Grand Opening, I hoped. If I had any left over, I was going to keep them at the register as giveaways for the summer.

The only thing bothering me was that the boxes were left and no one bothered to put them somewhere out of the way, or to let me know.

"I need an inventory manager," I mumbled to myself. I'd been fighting that truth for months, but I was done resisting it. Since the holidays six months earlier, I saw it coming. Keeping up with everything was only getting harder for me.

It was a good problem to have, though. My store was growing. People were shopping every day. Lincoln Toys had become a destination for families all around the Thousand Islands. And if I wanted to keep it that way, I needed help.

A key slid into the lock on the back door, and I turned to see who was there early. The store opened in an hour, so I assumed it would be the manager on duty for the day since the associates usually showed up only fifteen minutes before their shifts started.

"Good morning," Penny said with a smile before she locked the door. She'd been with me since day one and was my first store manager.

"Hey, Penny. How are you?"

She looked at the boxes and tsked. "I'm so sorry. Those were delivered at the end of the shift last night, and I wanted to get here early to put them up. I hoped I'd beat you here."

"It's okay," I told her. "I figured something like that happened. They're for the Grand Opening at Mountain View Retreat. Want to see?"

"I do. It's going to be such a fun event." Penny walked over, leaving her handbag and keys on a shelf.

"I think so, too. Natalie has been working so hard on getting everything set for the summer." I handed her a football.

"This is so cute. My nephew is going to the camp. He's so excited. It's huge for my sister, too. She was really stressing about what to do with him. She and my brother-in-law both work full time."

"That's why Natalie fought so hard to get it open and running this summer. She saw the need last year. It's exciting he's going there. Will they be at the Grand Opening?"

Penny nodded as she set the football back in the box and reached for a sticker. "Ooh, I love the stickers. Good touch with the Lincoln Toys logo on everything. Then parents will remember where they picked up the items."

"That was my thought, too. The tattoos are the same as the stickers. But I thought some families might prefer one over the other."

"Good thought. This is going to be fun." Penny put the sticker back and looked around. "I wasn't entirely sure where you wanted the boxes. Since you're going to need to take them to the event in a few days, I didn't want them too far away, but I also figured they should be a little out of the way." She pointed to a corner of the warehouse. "I was going to put them over there, but it's up to you."

I looked around the space and didn't have a better idea. "That makes sense. The biggest issue I'm going to have is getting all of this to Mountain View Retreat."

"I can help you, if you want. I'm going to be there anyway with my sister."

"Yeah?"

Penny nodded as she picked up a box. "Absolutely. Are you going to come here Saturday morning and load up your car?"

"That was my plan." I carried a box to the corner and set it next to the one Penny put down.

Penny grabbed another box. "I'll meet you here, and if we need to put stuff in my car, we can, then I'll just go to the Retreat with you to unload."

"That would be so great, Penny. Thank you."

"Of course."

We finished moving the boxes and set the pallet near the door so we could take it outside for recycling once we opened. Penny moved through the store with me, turning on lights and checking the displays. I went to the back and retrieved the cash box to stock the registers for the day. When I met Penny at the front, she had a notepad out.

"What's that?" I asked her.

"Oh, I noticed we're running low on some things. Sorry if I'm overstepping, but I figured I'd let you know so you could get them on order."

"Thank you," I said, accepting the sheet of paper she tore from her notepad. "This is really helpful."

Penny smiled and blushed.

"Hey, I was thinking this morning that I need an inventory manager. Would you be interested in the job?"

"Oh, um, I don't know. What would it require?"

I held up the list of toys we were running low on. "Things like this. Checking inventory and ordering new items that are getting low, sourcing new things that come out, evaluating sales of current stock and determining if we should stop carrying something or carry less of it."

"I could probably do all of that."

"I would hire a new store manager, so you wouldn't have the current responsibilities you have. I would ask you to manage all the deliveries so you know what's here, taking that task off the store managers. But it might mean more evenings or weekends."

"Oh. Can I think about it?"

"Absolutely. We can talk about everything, too. If you needed a weekend off, or couldn't work nights, we can make other arrangements as needed. But I think it'll be good for the store to have someone like you paying attention to the inventory. As we've gotten busier, I feel like I'm stretched thin and need the help."

Penny smiled. "I understand that. Let me think about it today and we can talk after the shift?"

"That works. Thanks, Penny. I really hope you say yes."

Her smile was less than joyful, but that was okay. She'd decide what was best for her, and what really mattered was not losing a good employee.

Penny unlocked the back door twenty minutes before we opened so the associates could put their personal items away and be ready for the shift to start. At ten o'clock, I opened the front door and welcomed in our first customers of the day.

It was going to be a good day.

I GOT a start on inventory and accounting early in the shift when it was a little quieter. When things picked up, I went out onto the floor and helped out.

By the time Penny's shift was over, I was really hoping she was going to take the job. I hadn't finished the orders for the day, and I knew if I didn't get help soon, I would have bigger issues. Especially if the Mountain View Retreat Grand Opening brought in new business.

Penny nodded to me as she headed to the back, and I followed her so we could speak without anyone else around. She walked to my office and smiled when I walked in behind her.

"Yes," she said.

"Yes? You'll take the job?"

She grinned. "I will. There will be times when I can't work a weekend or night shift, but if we can work that out, I think it'll be good."

"Oh, yay! Thank you so much. I'm so excited."

Penny's grin widened. "Me, too. When do you want me to start?"

"Whenever you can," I said. "I'm working on new orders

right now if you want to look over my shoulder and see how that side of things works, and I can get your official title changed, too."

"Today?"

"It's up to you. If you can't stay, we can do all of that during your next shift."

"What are you going to do for the store manager position?"

"I'm thinking about promoting Jeff, if you think he'd be interested. He's great with the families, and he has a good handle on how things run around here."

Penny nodded. "I think that's a great idea."

"Good. So, today or next shift?"

"Um, let's do next shift. I need to head out today."

"That works for me. Thank you, Penny. I think this will be great."

"So do I. See you Friday, Daisy."

"Oh, you're off until Friday?"

"I am. Is that a problem?" Penny paused and looked closely at me.

I shook my head. "It's fine. I just didn't realize you wouldn't be here the rest of the week."

"I'm helping my sister out. Like I said, she and her husband both work full time. My brother-in-law works a rotating shift and is on nights this week. They don't have anyone who can watch my nephew. Today is his last day of school."

"Oh, that makes sense. Um, okay. We'll talk Friday, and you're still good to help me on Saturday?"

"Yep. Thanks, Daisy. Bye!"

I waved as she rushed out the door, the slam of it making me jump.

It was going to be fine. Penny was a good store manager, and she was conscientious. She would be a great inventory manager. We just had to figure a few things out. It would be fine.

I finished the order before I went back to the floor, meeting a new family and helping a stressed out toddler to get out his energy by throwing a stuffed chicken at the wall until he laughed.

It was a great day.

THE GRAND OPENING of Mountain View Retreat was a huge success! Penny came through and helped get everything to the Retreat, and I gave away nearly all the toys I brought with me, leaving the handful of extras at the Retreat instead of bringing them back to Lincoln Toys.

I met so many families, and all the parents said they were going to stop by the store soon to check it out. Moving Penny to inventory manager was the right move. If even half of those parents bought something, we would be ordering new stock quickly.

I headed for home with a smile on my face and exhaustion seeping in. Natalie and Omar invited me to have dinner with them, but I wanted Natalie to be able to celebrate her success with Omar. I loved them both, and I was so damn happy Natalie found her perfect match. One day, I'd find mine.

After checking in at the store, I went home and changed into comfy clothes and started dinner. My second wind hit, and I danced around the living room while my dinner cooked.

A ding on my phone drew me back to the kitchen. I checked my food before I looked at the alert on my phone.

A new match. I smiled as I opened Book Boyfriends Wanted.

"DrGrumpy? Who would call himself that?"

His profile was new, but it was intriguing. A single dad who clearly adored his kid. Widower meant there was no messy ex drama to deal with, but made my heart squeeze for the husband and kid who lost their person. Smart, clever, a little odd based on some of the things in his profile, but weren't we all?

"What's the best that could happen?" I smiled and typed out a message saying hi. I'd had plenty of matches that hadn't worked out, but one would. Maybe he was the one that would.

I set my phone down and retrieved my dinner from the oven. The one-pan meal was perfect for me and would be amazing for a future meal. It smelled great and had my stomach growling as I got a plate and served myself a good portion of dinner. I was starving.

I grabbed my phone to take it to the living room just as it dinged with another alert. Before I checked it, I turned off the music and started a movie. A rom-com I'd been saving for a night when I had no other distractions.

I settled on the couch, then remembered the ding and checked my phone. "He already replied?" That was new. And it made me tingle. He was a single dad and no doubt busy, but he replied quickly. I liked that.

DRGRUMPY

Good evening. Thank you for accepting my match.

Very formal, but okay.

FOREVERPLAYING

> Hi. Nice to meet you. I'm happy we matched.

DRGRUMPY

> So am I. How are you?

FOREVERPLAYING

> I'm good. Thanks. Tell me something about you. That's not in your profile. If you could bring back one toy from your childhood, what would it be and why?

I set my phone down and dug into my ranch chicken and vegetables. I always asked that question when I was getting to know someone. It told me a lot about a person to understand how they played and what they enjoyed.

I would have brought back my favorite doll. Her name was Bella, and I adored her. She went everywhere with me when I was little. She looked like me, and she was my best friend when we would travel for hockey. My twin brothers played from the time they could walk, and they were good. So good that they were playing in games all around the state before they were out of elementary school.

Bella was left behind in one of the many hotel rooms. My parents insisted she was packed in a suitcase when I couldn't find her one morning as we were leaving one hotel to travel to another, but when we arrived at the second hotel, Bella was not in the suitcase. Or anywhere else.

It broke my heart. My parents bought me a new doll, but it wasn't the same doll. My mom called the hotel, but house-keeping didn't see her.

I chose to believe another little girl found her and loved

her, but at the time, it was hard to let go of my favorite thing in the world.

DRGRUMPY

I didn't have a lot of toys, but I would bring back my dog.

FOREVERPLAYING

Everyone would bring back their pets.

DRGRUMPY

Would you?

FOREVERPLAYING

I didn't have pets. My family traveled a lot and weren't home to take care of them. I tried to sneak a cat in once, it was a stray, but my mom was allergic and couldn't stop sneezing. That didn't last long.

DRGRUMPY

Do you have a cat now?

FOREVERPLAYING

No. But I've thought about it. A friend has a dog, and he's great. Life is busy right now, but hopefully it's something I can act on soon.

DRGRUMPY

There are always animals in need of a good home.

FOREVERPLAYING

True. Do you have pets?

DRGRUMPY

Sorry, I have to go.

I stared at the message. That was abrupt. And weird. But okay. He signed off the app, and I followed suit, starting the movie over from the beginning since I was paying more attention to our conversation than the movie I'd been waiting to see.

That was saying something. Hopefully I'd hear from DrGrumpy again very soon.

# 3

## KINGSLEY

I SAT IN THE CHAIR THAT SMELLED LIKE MY FATHER AND TRIED not to think about it. The first four days I spent working in his clinic were busy. After two days of cancellations because of his heart attack, I was on my feet constantly and barely had time to think about where I was, let alone sit down in the chair.

But I'd caught up, and I needed to review the transcriptions from the previous week to make sure nothing was missed. It was tedious work, but important, especially when I would be walking away from the practice before too long and someone else would be managing the care of the animals I'd seen.

A knock on the door brought my head up. "Yeah?"

The knob turned, and Sheila walked in. "Good morning," she said, stopping at the door. "Is there anything you need before you start seeing patients?"

I stood abruptly. "No." I brushed past her and out into the hallway, leaving her in the office.

"Okay, well—"

"I don't need you to tell me how to do my job. I'm well aware of how a veterinary practice works."

She bit her bottom lip and nodded once.

I glared at her as I walked away, ready to start the day, preferably with as little involvement from her as possible.

Unfortunately, I wasn't so lucky. The vet tech was on my heels as I met the owners of the first animal of the day. A young couple with a little girl adopted a new dog recently and brought him in for a checkup.

"Let's see how things are going," I said, mostly to myself and partly to the dog. He trembled on the metal table, working his way toward the little girl he'd clearly decided was his protector.

I got down low and spoke softly to the dog, Buster, including the girl in my conversation. "What's Buster's favorite thing to do?"

"He really likes to play fetch in the backyard. He's good at it, too. Always comes right back to me." She beamed like a proud parent.

"That's very smart of him. Not all dogs can do that. How long have you had him?"

"Two weeks," she said, looking up at her parents for confirmation. "He was at the shelter, but no one wanted him. Until I went there."

"Sometimes it takes a very special person to see how great an animal is." I smiled at her and checked Buster's paws.

"There are so many animals in need of good homes," Sheila said.

I lifted the dog's ear to peek inside and fought against my rage. I did not want her there. Interrupting my conversation with the family. "That's why it's important to spay and neuter your pets. And why the clinic I work at partners with the local shelter to take care of any strays that are brought in. Too many animals are neglected by people who don't care to think about their actions."

"That's why we encourage people looking to adopt to go to the local shelter. We do the same here. It's not as bad in this area as some of the cities, but we still have stray animals and animals that people struggle to care for that are turned in to the shelter." Sheila's voice grated on my every nerve.

I lifted Buster's other ear and peeked inside, not catching on fast enough that he picked up on my anger. The dog turned and nipped at me, catching my knuckle on his teeth. He yelped and pulled back, going to the little girl to protect him.

"Oh my God. I am so sorry," the father said quickly, stepping forward. "He's never been like that with us."

I checked my finger and shook my head. "It's not him. I promise. I'm fine. Didn't break the skin. He's just a little uneasy. It's expected when a dog comes in for the first time, or meets a new vet. They don't know what to expect."

"Do you think we need to worry?" the mother asked.

"Not at all. He's a wonderful dog, and he clearly adores your daughter. She's his protector, and he will be the same for her. He will be a very loyal dog. I have no concerns about his behavior," I told them.

The parents exchanged a look, but I focused on the dog again.

"What do you think, Buster? Can we try again?" I asked the dog.

The little girl pressed against Buster's side and rubbed his back. "He wants to help you, Buster. You should let him."

Buster looked up at her, then ducked his head toward me, giving me permission.

"He's a smart dog, too. He understood you," I told her.

"He listens really well."

"I can see that."

The rest of Buster's exam went well. I stayed focused on him, and Sheila stayed quiet. Buster was in great health, and the shots he got before he left the shelter were enough. I asked them to schedule an appointment for him to be neutered in a few months and thanked them for bringing him in.

"Is your finger okay?" Sheila asked when we walked toward the next exam room.

"Fine."

"I can look at it, if you want."

"I don't want you anywhere near me," I snapped.

"Dr. Harris, I'm not sure—"

"You're not sure? You really don't remember why I left town?"

Sheila took a step back, then cast her gaze to the floor. "I apologize."

I snorted. "Too late for that. Why don't you just stay out of my way while I'm here? Then when I leave, we'll never see each other again."

She nodded.

I inhaled and stepped around her to go into the next exam room. I was vaguely aware of her following me, but at least she kept her mouth shut this time.

I WAS DRAINED by the time I made it back to my mom's house that night. The work was the same as I did every day, but the tension in my body was so much worse. It was why I left MacKellar Cove in the first place. Nearly a decade away wasn't long enough.

Not when I had to go back to the clinic and be around Sheila every day.

"Daddy!" Isla cried when I walked in the door. She rushed over to me, throwing her arms around my waist and resting her head on my stomach.

I rubbed her head and smiled at her. She was my world. She had been since the day she was born, but losing Faith proved to me how fragile life could be. I worked hard to be around for my daughter.

And helping out at my father's clinic jeopardized that.

"How was your day with Grandma?" I asked her, scooping her up into my arms and propping her on my hip.

She toyed with the collar of my shirt and shrugged. "It was good. We didn't do much, though. Grandma doesn't have a lot of toys."

"I know. Maybe we need to get you some new stuff so you have things to do. Didn't you bring a coloring book?"

Isla nodded and kicked her feet. "Yeah, but that's boring."

"Okay, so what would be exciting?"

"You said we were going to go to the zoo and the aquarium and the park and the pool and do fun stuff."

I bit back my sigh. I owed my mother, but helping her out meant putting Isla second. I didn't like that. "We will still do some fun stuff. Did you swim today? You can jump in the pool anytime you want."

"Grandma said no. She didn't want to swim today."

I inhaled, realizing I needed to talk to my mother. She didn't know Isla was a great swimmer. She'd been in lessons since before she could walk. Obviously, she needed to be supervised, but she didn't need someone in the pool with her. "I'll talk to Grandma. Where is she?"

"She went to the bathroom."

"Okay. Well, what do you want for dinner? Maybe we can get started on something."

"Can we have enchiladas?"

"Sounds good to me. Let's make sure Grandma has everything we need." I opened the fridge, putting Isla down so she could open drawers and investigate with me. "What did you have for lunch?"

"A turkey sandwich."

"Was it good?"

"It was fine."

Time for a change. In less than a week, Isla was bored. I'd be fighting with her to stay if I didn't find ways to entertain her.

"Oh, Kingsley, you're home. Good. We had a good day," Mom said, joining us in the kitchen.

"Good. We were looking at enchiladas for dinner. Is that okay with you?"

"Sounds good to me. I should have everything in there. If not, check the freezer." Mom was looking at her phone, smiling at something. "Would that be your last supper?"

"My what?" Did I hear her right?

"It's this thing online. What would your last supper be if you could choose? Would you choose enchiladas?"

I narrowed my eyes at her, but she didn't pay attention to me. "I guess, maybe."

"What about your favorite dessert?"

"Chocolate cake!" Isla shouted.

I chuckled. She'd been a chocolate fan since before birth. Faith couldn't get enough chocolate when she was pregnant with Isla. Nothing had changed for Isla since.

"I like chocolate cake, too," Mom said. "You, Kingsley?"

"I think I'd go with turtle cheesecake."

Mom pursed her lips. "I didn't know that."

"Faith used to make it sometimes."

"Oh," Mom said, her gaze drifting to Isla.

"But Mommy liked chocolate best like me," Isla declared.

"Yes, she did," I agreed with her.

Mom smiled and slid her phone into her pocket. She washed her hands, then jumped in and helped us make enchiladas.

Isla was in charge of the process, instructing Mom and me every step of the way. She was a chef in the making, always choosing to get involved in the kitchen and paying attention to everything I did.

When I slid the enchiladas into the oven, I asked Isla if she wanted to swim after dinner.

"Yes!" she cheered.

"Good. Why don't you get your suit on, and as soon as you're done eating, we can jump in."

"She should wait thirty minutes for her food to settle," Mom argued with me as Isla rushed off to change.

"That's not actually true, Mom. There's no scientific evidence to support it."

"You always did."

"I know, but there's no reason to. She loves the water, and she said you didn't want to get in with her today so she didn't swim. She's a great swimmer, Mom. She doesn't need you in the water."

"I'm not going to let my four-year-old granddaughter swim by herself." Mom's huff of indignation almost made me laugh.

Almost.

"I didn't say sit on the couch and watch a movie while she's out there, but she can go in the pool alone if you're right there. She's bored, Mom. She can't sit around here all day."

"We went to the hospital today."

"You did what?" I asked, my voice low.

Mom pursed her lips. "I wanted to see your father, Kingsley. I had no choice but to take Isla with me. I didn't think it would be a problem for her to see her grandfather."

I ground my teeth until my jaw ached. And there was the issue. Mom didn't know why I hated my father. She didn't understand because she had no idea what he'd done. I owed her because I was just as bad as him and never told her about his affair.

I didn't want Isla around him. I didn't want to be around him. He wasn't a part of my life anymore. Not since that day. He never would be again.

"The doctor wants to keep your father in the hospital longer," Mom said, as though she was right and I was ridiculous for objecting to Isla seeing my father. "He's going to be there another week, so you and Isla can stay here longer."

"Okay," I said. I hadn't had time to look for a short-term rental anyway, so it worked out. But before he was released, I needed to find a place. "Any idea how long until he can get back to work full time?"

Mom shook her head and turned on the light in the oven.

"Well, when you know, let me know."

"So you can run off again?" Mom crossed her arms over her chest and glared at me.

"So I can go back to my job, Mom. I have a career, a life. I'm fortunate that my bosses were willing to let me take a leave, but it's not forever."

"I know. I've accepted that you never wanted to be here. I

just always thought you and Faith would settle down in MacKellar Cove."

The jaw pain was back. My teeth hurt from holding back the truth. How many times had I thought about telling her?

But did that make me just as bad? Telling my mother would only hurt her. Keeping the truth from her meant she was living a lie, but if it was a lie she was happy to live, then how could I blow that up?

Especially since the affair ended the day I found out. That's what my father said. He promised me it was over.

I chose to believe he was being honest. But I still carried the weight of the lie. A lie that destroyed all my plans for the future.

If my father hadn't cheated, I would have joined his practice. We would have moved back to MacKellar Cove after vet school. Faith could still be alive. But none of that happened, and my daughter was growing up without her mother.

"I'm ready!" Isla shouted, jumping into the kitchen wearing her bathing suit.

I smiled at her and nodded. "You are ready. Let's get this food out so we can eat and you can swim."

"Are you going to swim with me?"

"I was thinking about it."

"Yay! Daddy swim!"

I chuckled and waved for her to back up. I set the pan of enchiladas on the stovetop and reached down plates for all of us. Isla helped Mom fill glasses with water. We sat down at the table together and dug into our food, groans of deliciousness and scrapes of forks on plates the only sounds.

As soon as Isla was done eating, she jumped up and tugged at my arm. "Let's go, Daddy."

I laughed. "Give me a minute. We need to help Grandma clean up the kitchen."

"I can help."

"Good. Put your plate in the dishwasher, and your glass."

Isla did as I asked, then took mine and put them away, too. I left her with Mom while I changed into my swim trunks.

When I got back to the kitchen, Mom had the leftovers put away and was wiping down the counters while Isla wiped down the table. Isla finished her task, then pulled me toward the backdoor and outside.

Isla took off as soon as she was outside, running toward the pool and jumping in at full speed. She came up, a huge smile on her face. "Jump in, Daddy!"

I didn't run, but I did jump in after her. My cannonball splashed her and sent water over the edge and onto the pool deck. "Don't run anymore, okay? It's wet now. And so are you."

"Okay. Can I dive?"

"Sure. Go to the deep end."

Isla swam over and pulled herself out of the pool, her tiny little body limber and light. She stood on the side of the pool and put her hands in a triangle above her head. She stared at the water, then bent forward and half-flopped-half-dove into the pool.

When she came up, she scowled. "That wasn't good."

"It takes practice," I told her. "You know that. Try again."

She climbed out and tried again, getting a little better with each attempt.

"Try to bending your knees and pushing off with your feet a little. Like you're jumping," I suggested after a dozen dives.

Isla nodded, then stood at the very edge, her toes curling

over the edge. She bent her knees, then pushed herself up and dove in, going in more hands-first than her other attempts.

She rose grinning that time, scampering out and repeating the process another dozen times before she stayed in the water and swam around.

She was a water baby, always content to splash around in a pool or a puddle or anything that had water. She loved bath time when she was born and refused to take showers so she could sit in the tub.

The sun sank lower in the sky and the air outside the pool grew cooler. I didn't want to get out and go to sleep, though. I wanted more time with Isla. More time to be a dad instead of working. More time to see my girl.

As Isla slowed down, I knew we needed to go. "Are you ready for a bath?" I asked her.

She nodded, swimming to the side and climbing out without an argument.

I wrapped a towel around my waist and followed a very sleepy little girl to the bathroom. Mom hovered at the door, but Isla didn't take long in the tub. Not when she was falling asleep already.

I helped her get dressed, then tucked her into bed. "I love you, Isla. So does Mommy."

"So do Grandma and Grandpa," Mom said from the door.

"I love Daddy and Mommy and Grandma and Grandpa," Isla whispered, her voice fading as her eyes closed.

I turned off her light and closed the door to her room, forcing a smile for Mom before I went back to the bathroom and rushed through a shower and carried my exhausted self to bed.

Only to know I was going to have to do the same thing again tomorrow.

# DAISY

I SIPPED MY COFFEE AND READ THE LATEST MESSAGE FROM DrGrumpy. I couldn't figure him out. I liked talking to him, and he made me feel like he enjoyed it, too, but there was something strange that I couldn't put my finger on.

"Morning," Natalie grumbled as she joined me in the kitchen, going straight to the coffee.

"Good morning. How are you today?" I loved mornings. I was excited to start my day and happy to have a job that brought me joy. Natalie did not share my AM enthusiasm.

Her grumbled response made me smile behind my mug.

"How were the first few days of camp?" I asked. She'd stayed with Omar the first night, and I was at work late the second night, managing a delivery, so I hadn't heard how things were going.

A smile brightened her eyes. "Really good. The campers are so excited to be there, and the staff is amazing. Those kids are having fun and making it better for the campers."

"That's awesome. I told you it would all come together."

Natalie grinned and took a sip of her coffee. She closed

her eyes and sighed. "You know I'm not nearly as optimistic as you are."

I chuckled. "No one is."

Natalie laughed.

My phone dinged with a new alert.

"Is that Book Boyfriends Wanted? Do you have a match?"

I nodded and set my coffee down so I could read my message. "I do. He's a single dad, but he's pretty quick to message me. And he has very interesting answers to my questions."

Natalie snorted. "Favorite toy, last supper, and superpower?"

"Yeah." I read his reply, tilting my head.

"What?"

"I don't get him. There are some answers that make sense, but others feel like a totally different person is answering."

"His kid?"

I wrinkled my nose. "I doubt it. It sounds like the kid is young."

"Still."

I shrugged. "Doesn't matter. It's fun to talk to him. I'm enjoying it."

"That's what really matters," Natalie said. She found her own happily ever after through Book Boyfriends Wanted. She'd almost given up on meeting someone, but the connection she had with Omar was enough to bring her out of her shell and forced her to overcome the anxiety she struggled with. She would always have anxiety, but Omar was the solid support that she needed to prove she was more capable than she ever gave herself credit for.

"He said his superpower would be to heal with a touch."

"Aw," Natalie said.

"I know, right? How awesome is that?"

"That's really sweet."

I nodded and sent another question, then traded my phone for my coffee.

"Why are you up so early today?" Natalie asked.

"I need to open the store today."

"Okay, but not at six o'clock."

I rolled my lips in and debated telling Natalie what was going on. I knew what she would say.

Natalie crossed her arms and leaned against the counter, giving me one of her get-it-over-with looks.

I sighed. "Penny can't get there to oversee the delivery this morning."

"I thought she couldn't be there for the delivery last night?"

"Yeah."

Nat's brows shot up. "And this morning?"

"It's a change. She'll figure it out. She's been in the job for less than a week."

"And she's done it zero times."

I sighed. I didn't like fighting, and I definitely didn't like having to defend my choices. Especially when my choice meant giving someone a chance. "Penny is very capable. She will get her groove on, and she will be good at this."

"If you say so," Natalie said into her coffee. She finished her mug and set it in the dishwasher. She went into the fridge and grabbed her lunch bag, then pulled out a carton of eggs. "Breakfast?"

I checked the time on my phone and shook my head. "I need to go. I'll grab something after the delivery."

Natalie sighed but didn't argue with me. "Be careful."

"I will. It's all good."

"See you tonight?"

"Yeah, no late deliveries tonight."

"When do you go to Chelsea and Derek's?"

"Thursday night. They're taking off after work Thursday and home Monday by lunch."

"Are they excited?"

I nodded. "I think so. It'll be nice for them to get away."

"And nice for you to hang out with Dozer," Natalie said.

I laughed. "I love that dog. He's so great."

"Yes, he is."

"Okay, I gotta go. See you tonight."

"Bye!" Natalie called as I rushed out the door.

The sun was starting to light up the sky as I drove to Lincoln Toys. I parked in the back and hurried inside, even though I already knew the loading dock was clear.

Ten minutes after I arrived, the horn outside alerted me to the truck backing up. I waited until the locks engaged to secure the truck, then opened the bay door and unlocked the back door for the driver.

"Good morning," Dick said, waving when he stepped inside.

"Hi, Dick! How are you? I didn't know you were making the early morning run today." Dick was married to my friend's mom. Patrick struggled when his mom starting dating the truck driver, but they reconciled when Patrick realized how happy his mom was with Dick in her life.

"I saw your stop on the board and snapped it up. Anything I can do to help you out."

"Thank you. Means the world to me. You ready for me to unload?"

"I'll take care of it. I'm certified to drive your lifts."

"Thank you," I told him, squeezing his forearm. He

knew I wasn't always comfortable driving onto the trucks and helped me out whenever he was there.

"Anything for you, hun."

I smiled and signed the paperwork he had for me, reviewing the items he was delivering.

While Dick worked, I unpacked the delivery from the night before. It was going to take me all morning to get the new stock out onto the floor, but it needed to be done.

"You're all set," Dick said, approaching when I walked to the back to get another box. "Need a hand?"

"No, I'm all good."

"You sure?"

"I got it. Go home and see your wife. I'm sure she's missed you."

Dick winked. "Feeling's mutual. Have a good one, Daisy!"

"You, too! See you soon."

"Count on it!"

I followed behind him to the door and locked it once he was outside. He'd already closed the door to the loading dock. I listened for his truck to rumble to life, then pull away, a horn of goodbye as he drove off.

Silence followed. I sighed, then got back to stocking the shelves.

THURSDAY MORNING, the house was quiet when I got up. Penny was handling the delivery, so I had time to pack before going to Chelsea's for the weekend.

I picked out some new toys for Dozer and had them in a bag, ready to go. I debated on what to wear, but grabbed a sweatshirt and some cozy pajamas for the weekend since I wasn't sure how warm or cool the house would be.

Chelsea told me to make myself comfortable and that I could eat anything I wanted, but I was bringing my own food, and everything else I needed for the long weekend. Just so they didn't have to think about it when they got home.

I loaded up my car, then drove to work in time for the store to open. Penny waved and went to the front as I walked in the back. She was still working her store manager job for a few more days, but Jeff agreed to start as store manager the following week. The only thing I needed to do was hire a new store associate.

I made my way out onto the floor and straightened displays and checked on the toys in the playrooms. Families came through the store, shopping and playing and finding the perfect thing before leaving with smiles.

Just how I wanted things to be.

After lunch, I heard a little girl crying in the aisle next to the one I was walking down. I changed course and went to see if there was something I could do to help.

"Good afternoon. How are we doing?" I asked the girl, smiling at the exhausted woman next to her who I assumed was her mother.

"She missed her nap this morning. I'm so sorry about the noise."

I shook my head. "No apologies necessary here. It's a toy store. It's supposed to be loud and fun and a little crazy." I picked up the loudest toy on the aisle and hit a button so it would make a noise. "Toys can be loud, too."

The little girl stopped crying and looked at her mom.

Mom smiled at the girl, and my heart squeezed. "She

has a party for a classmate this weekend. We were hoping to find something."

"Same age? I'm guessing four?"

"Yep, turning five. Kindergarten next year."

"So fun." I crouched down so I was eye-level with the girl. "What's your favorite thing to play with? Your favorite toy?"

The girl looked up at Mom again, and Mom nodded for her to answer me. "I like my dolls."

"That was always my favorite, too. Does your friend like dolls?"

The girl shrugged.

"When I give someone a gift, I always think about what they would like, but if I'm not sure, I choose something I would like. That way, they know they're special to me because I got them something that's a piece of me. Maybe we can find a doll that looks like your friend."

She nodded, her smile brightening her entire face.

I stood and nodded to the next aisle. "There are a lot of dolls right over there. Should we go look?"

The girl tugged Mom's hand, and both followed me to the dolls.

"Wow." Her eyes were huge as she looked at the options.

It didn't matter how fancy the dolls were, kids liked dolls. We had soft dolls that were stuffed and good for the youngest kids or kids who didn't do well with harder toys. We had dolls that were more lifelike and solid. We had dolls that looked like monsters and dolls wearing costumes, dolls with colorful hair and dolls that looked like movie characters, and dolls that had different abilities. Every kid resonated with a different style, and I wanted them all to feel seen and loved when they walked into the store.

The little girl gravitated toward a doll with hot pink hair

and another one with glasses. She held both, lifting their hair and talking to them as if they were friends.

"Thank you so much," Mom said.

"You're welcome. I'm glad she found something that made her smile."

"I am, too. I wasn't sure how long she was going to last."

"Happens to all of us."

Mom chuckled and nodded. "True."

"If you guys need anything else, please let me know. Otherwise, I'll let her play."

"Thank you. I love bringing her here. It's such a welcoming place for kids."

"That means a lot. That was my vision."

"You're the owner?"

"I am. Daisy Lincoln."

"Oh, wow. I'm so sorry we took up your time."

I shook my head. "There was nothing more important for me to be doing. I opened this store so I could be here to enjoy childhood all over again."

"You must have had a great one."

I smiled, choosing not to dump my less than perfect childhood on a stranger. "Thank you for coming in."

"Thank you. Say bye, Michelle."

"Bye!" Michelle said, still playing with the dolls.

"Bye, Michelle," I told her. I waved to Mom, then left them to their playtime.

"You are so good with them," Penny said, catching up to me on the next aisle.

I smiled. "Kids just want to be heard. Parents, too."

Penny nodded. "True. So, the delivery this morning was good. I think we're all set to transition next week."

"Excellent. Thank you. I'm off tomorrow. Don't forget about the delivery before opening."

"Oh," Penny said.

I stopped walking and focused on her.

Penny shuffled her feet. "I didn't realize that. I was supposed to be off. It's Wendy's day to work."

"Are you available to come in and accept the delivery?"

Penny shook her head. "I really can't. I didn't know I needed to be here for that one. Um..."

I pressed my lips into a smile. "I'll handle it. It'll be fine. Next week, though, you need to be here to accept all the deliveries. You can schedule them whenever it's going to be convenient for you, as long as everything is getting here on time."

"It'll be totally fine. I can do it. I promise."

"Okay. I'm glad we talked or the delivery would have been missed tomorrow."

"I'll take care of the rest. I promise."

"Thanks, Penny. I know you will."

She smiled and walked away.

I nodded. It would all work out. I wasn't worried. Penny was capable, and we were working through the learning curve.

Dozer was used to being alone during the day. It would be fine to leave him for a few hours while I handled the delivery.

I GOT to Chelsea and Derek's house just as they were getting home from dropping off Derek's son, Jude, with Chelsea's parents. Her parents loved Jude like he had always been in their lives. Chelsea and Derek met at the beginning of the school year when Chelsea bought the house next door. It was not a great first meeting, or second, but they figured out how to get along and fell in love. They were married a few weeks ago. Chelsea planned to adopt Jude as soon as the paperwork could go through.

"Jude settled?" I asked as I met them on the sidewalk.

"Yeah. He's never going to want to come home," Derek said with a laugh. "I think Cathy and Ken bought your entire store."

I laughed. "They're going to have a great weekend. And so are you two."

Chelsea grinned, and Derek reached for her, wrapping her in his arms and kissing his new wife. They decided on a very small wedding in their backyard with family only, so I didn't attend, but they booked a weekend at Mountain View Retreat for a big reception at the end of summer. I was looking forward to celebrating with them. Everyone was.

"We can't thank you enough for staying with Dozer." Chelsea unlocked the door and walked in first, holding the door open for me to follow her.

"Yes, truly. I was not looking forward to sharing my wife with our dog and our son for our honeymoon," Derek said with a look at Chelsea.

That was her plan, one I interrupted when I volunteered to watch Dozer for them. "Hi, Dozer," I said, dropping to my knees in front of the beast of a dog. I rubbed his ears and down his body, and he wiggled for more attention. "I am looking forward to the weekend. I have to go to work tomorrow morning for a little while, but I'll be here the rest of the time."

Derek and Chelsea both shook their heads.

"You don't have to be here full time with him," Chelsea said. "He's completely fine home alone."

"I know, but I want to spend as much time with him as I can. I don't get enough of it." He nudged me, nearly knocking me to the floor. I laughed, pushing back against him. "You earned your name."

"He definitely did. Do you have anything you want me to grab?" Derek asked. He had a suitcase in each hand and was at the door.

"You don't have to do that. I can get it later."

He shrugged. "I'm heading out to pack our SUV. It's not a big deal to grab your stuff on my way back inside."

"Are you sure?"

"Absolutely."

"Thank you. Everything is in the trunk."

"Got it."

I loved on Dozer while Derek took their stuff outside. "Are you excited?" I asked Chelsea.

"I am. We don't have a lot of time just us. It's only a few days, but it'll be really good."

"It will. And Dozer will be fine. Natalie is going to spend Saturday here with us, maybe Omar, too. If that's okay."

"Of course. Dozer loves them."

"Good. I'm really sorry about work tomorrow. I need to help unload a truck in the morning, then I'll be back."

"It won't be a problem. He is pretty good about everything when we're gone."

"Good."

"Did you buy groceries?" Derek asked, carrying in my shopping bags with my suitcase and the bag for Dozer.

"I did. I didn't want to eat your food," I admitted. "And I bought some stuff for Dozer."

"You didn't have to do either of those things," Chelsea said. "You could have eaten all our food."

I shook my head. "I didn't feel right doing that. And I wanted him to have something new since his people are leaving for a few days. I know we'll be fine, but I wanted him to like me."

"He already loves you," Chelsea said, nodding to Dozer as he sprawled against my side and let me rub his belly.

Derek snorted. "Both our boys are going to be miserable when we come home."

"No," I told him, laughing. "They love you guys. I'm just making sure he's not miserable for me."

"I have no worries. We really appreciate you being here."

"Absolutely. Now, you two go, enjoy your weekend away, and don't worry about a thing. We will be totally fine."

I stood, dislodging Dozer from my side. He jumped up with me and barked.

"See? He said the same."

Chelsea and Derek laughed.

Chelsea dropped to her knees and hugged Dozer, whispering to him to behave and listen to me. He rested his head on her shoulder like he was hugging her back.

She stood, and Derek rubbed Dozer's head.

I hugged them both, then walked them to the door, closing it behind them and waving.

Dozer barked, and I turned to him. "Just you and me, dude. What do you want to do?"

Dozer ran to the backdoor and let himself outside to run around.

I followed him, laughing as he enjoyed his play place in the yard, a gift from Derek when he almost screwed everything up with Chelsea.

My phone dinged with an alert, and I pulled it out.

DRGRUMPY

Are you available tonight? I'd like to meet you in person.

My heart skipped. He wanted to meet me? We'd only been talking for a few days. That was really fast.

But I couldn't stop my smile.

FOREVERPLAYING

I can make that happen. Do you know O'Kelley's in MacKellar Cove?

DRGRUMPY

I'll be there at six.

FOREVERPLAYING

See you then.

Wow. I was meeting DrGrumpy. And spending the weekend with Dozer. Good start to my summer.

**5**

———

O'Kelley's was busy when I arrived. Hudson was behind the bar, and I headed his way. I was a grown woman and old enough to be smart, but I was also very aware that I was meeting a complete stranger and part of being smart was telling someone my plans.

"Hey, Daisy. What can I get you?" Hudson asked.

I looked down the line of men at the bar, all waiting for me to answer. "Um, what's going on?"

Hudson jerked his head toward them. "Guys' night. Omar's come a few times. Hasn't Natalie mentioned it?"

I shook my head and smiled at the men. I knew all of them, but mostly through their wives and girlfriends. Not a lot of single men shopped at my store. Thankfully.

"Are you meeting Natalie here? Omar didn't mention he was coming," Patrick said.

I shook my head again. "Nope. I'm meeting someone else."

"Who?" Hudson asked.

I smiled. "I don't know. It's a match, so I'm sort of flying blind here."

"So when I see a guy who looks confused, send him your way?" Hudson asked.

I chuckled. "Maybe not all confused men. I'd be busy all night."

The men to my left burst into laughter that made me realize what I said.

"Man, you guys act like you're still in middle school," I told them, laughing with them.

"We're always thinking about sex. Can't help it," Hudson explained. "But they could be more respectful."

"It's okay. I would have laughed, too."

"That's good. Because it was funny," Knox said.

I laughed.

"Drink?" Hudson asked, bringing the attention back to why I was there.

I nodded. "No alcohol, though. If that's okay."

Half the men held up drinks, showing me they weren't drinking alcohol either.

I smiled in thanks, grateful none of them were judging me.

Hudson pulled a tab and filled a glass. He added a lime wedge and a squirt of something red. "Hopefully you like it. And sit somewhere I can see you." He jerked his head toward the booths next to the bar. "Just to be safe."

"I was going to ask you to keep an eye out. Thanks, Hudson."

"You're welcome. You need anything, we're all here for you."

"I appreciate it." I grabbed my drink and sipped, realizing I didn't pay. "Can I open a tab?"

Hudson shook his head. "James'll cover you."

"Hey!" James shouted.

"Dude, it's your job to protect people," Ramsey argued.

"Doesn't mean I should pay for everyone's drinks," James grumbled.

"Hey, good idea. James is paying for everyone's drinks," Rowan said.

I laughed and carried my drink away, lifting it in thanks to Hudson before the arguing got worse.

My leg vibrated as I sat there, waiting and watching the door to see if I could spot the guy who was there to meet me before he approached.

A crowd of people came in and blocked the entrance, and I abandoned my staring contest with the door to focus on my drink and stop worrying about whoever was going to sit down across from me.

I checked my phone and was just about to put it away when someone stopped next to the table. I looked up and smiled. He was cute. A little young. But I liked most of our conversations, so I was going to be open-minded.

"Hi," I said.

"Hey. Um, are you going to be here long?"

"What?"

"I was just wondering if you're going to use the booth for much longer." He nodded to three others standing a few feet away. "We wanted to sit."

"Um..." Wow. How was I supposed to reply? "I..."

"Excuse me," another man said. His voice was deep, vibrating through the room above the noise of the other patrons.

The man wanting my booth turned and stepped away, his gaze locked on the new guy.

So was mine. He was gorgeous. Dark hair cut neatly in a short style. Dark eyes that met mine and stuck. Light brown skin. Probably close to my age with fine lines around his eyes and a nice suit that made me wonder what kind of doctor he really was.

"Are you ForeverPlaying?" he asked, that voice skimming over me.

I resisted the urge to shiver and nodded, smiling in a way I hoped was welcoming. "You're DrGrumpy?"

He cringed and nodded, sliding into the booth across from me. "Kingsley, actually. Which is why I'm here."

"I'm Daisy," I said, offering my hand and ignoring the fact that he didn't ask. Maybe he was nervous. I was nervous.

"Daisy. Sorry. Nice to meet you." He shook his head and clasped my hand for half a second before releasing me and folding his hands together on the table.

"You, too, Kingsley. How are you?"

He drew a breath and looked at me.

Those eyes were full of emotion and captivated me. I leaned in, feeling like I couldn't resist the pull toward him. I smiled, happy he asked to meet. It was fast, but it was the right decision.

"I wasn't the one you were messaging," he said.

"What?" A pitcher of beer spilled over my head would have made more sense. "What do you mean?"

"My mom created the profile for me."

"Your mom?" I shook my head. "Did one of those guys put you up to this?" I glanced at them, but besides Hudson, none of them were looking at me.

Hudson raised his brows at me, silently asking if I needed help.

I shook my head and focused back on Kingsley.

"I don't know them." He looked more closely at them. "I don't think. But either way, no one put me up to this. I'm in town visiting my mother, and she created the profile. She set it all up, and she was the one texting you. She didn't ask me."

"But you're here?"

"I found out about it earlier today. I was... It doesn't matter. I found out what she did and asked to meet you so I could explain in person. It didn't feel right to do anything else."

"So you're here to tell me I was having conversations with your mother over the last week. That you didn't talk to me at all. That all of this was some joke or misunderstanding or something."

"Yeah. Misunderstanding. My mother feels horrible. I guess she thought she'd find me the perfect woman and I'd drop my entire life and move up here for good, but that's not going to happen. And she dragged you into the middle of this, which she actually apologized for. Not that it makes all of this better. I'll compensate you for your time, and your drink." He leaned to the side to retrieve his wallet, opening it up and looking at me.

I shook my head. "My drink was free, and I don't live far. I'm not taking your money."

"Pain and suffering?"

"I thought you were a doctor, not a lawyer."

"I am."

"Okay, seriously, it's fine. It's a funny story, actually. I was catfished by your mother. It's only been a few days, and I'm good. It's all good."

"But what she did was wrong."

"She loves you. She wanted you here. I think that's pretty special for a parent to go that far to have time with their child. Even if you're an adult and have your own life."

"Yeah, but—"

I put my hand on his and smiled. "Kingsley, it's okay. I

promise. I'm not mad. I'm not going to say anything bad about your mom or you. It was an innocent misunderstanding. A very sweet gesture. All good. Have a good night."

He opened his mouth to say something, so I stopped. "You're not angry?"

I shook my head. "I promise you, I'm not. There's nothing to be angry about. Your mom is pretty great. Enjoy your visit."

"Thanks?"

I smiled and walked away, heading for the bar.

Hudson met me at the side, away from the other men. "Everything okay?"

I nodded. "All good. Just not who I thought he was."

"Did he say or do something?"

"No. He was nice. Just not going to work out. I'm heading to Chelsea and Derek's to spend the weekend with Dozer."

"Nice. Have fun."

"Thanks. Good night, Hudson. Bye, guys!" I waved to the others and headed for the door.

They all said goodbye, and I headed out, ready for my pajamas and some cuddles from the best dog ever.

Dozer was waiting for me when I got to Chelsea and Derek's. He jumped and barked and told me how happy he was to see me.

It was nice after DrGrumpy's admission. I had to give the guy credit for apologizing when he did nothing wrong. It was pretty great of him, but he obviously wasn't the right one for me since he wasn't looking.

Dozer ran outside and did his business in the yard before we settled on the couch. I changed into my pajamas and checked in with Natalie, letting her know I was at Chelsea's and in for the night.

Dozer and I watched a movie, then headed upstairs to

the spare bedroom. Dozer's bed was next to the twin bed in the guest room. He laid down while I brushed my teeth and climbed into bed.

I set my alarm and rubbed Dozer's head, then snuggled under the covers and went to sleep.

I WAS MOSTLY awake by the time my alarm went off in the morning. Different space and different sounds made it harder to sleep than I expected. But it was worth it to spend time with Dozer.

"Do you need to pee first thing in the morning?" I asked him as I headed for the bathroom. "I always do."

He sat in the hallway but watched me use the bathroom.

"That's weird, dude," I told him as I washed my hands. "But at least you're not judging me. I'm going to watch you in a minute, so I guess it's fair."

Dozer barked, then led the way to the back door.

I unlocked the doggy door and started the coffeemaker while Dozer wandered around outside. When he came back in, the coffee was done, and I was starting breakfast.

Dozer shared my breakfast, Chelsea approved of course, then followed me to the bathroom for my shower. It was a little uncomfortable to strip in front of him, but I had no choice but to get used to it.

After my shower, I gave Dozer one of the new toys I bought for him and told him I'd be back soon. He happily chewed on the toy while I let myself out into the early morning light.

I got to the store ten minutes before the truck and was able to get it unloaded without any issues. I was just finishing putting the stock away when Wendy walked in.

"Hey," she said, setting her things down. "I thought you were off today."

I nodded. "I am. I had to meet the truck, though."

"You should have told me. I could have done that."

"It's not your job."

Wendy shook her head. She was a terrific employee. Always on time and eager to learn. It was an easy choice to promote her to store manager. She was seven years younger than me, but age had nothing to do with skill. People doubted me my entire life, and I refused to do that to anyone else.

Plus, Wendy was more than capable of anything I'd ever asked her to do.

"We are all in this together, Daisy. I love working here, and I would do anything to help you out. Next time, let me know."

"Hopefully there isn't a next time. Penny is going to be managing the deliveries starting next week."

"Well, then I'll tell her to let me know. I wouldn't have minded."

"Thank you, Wendy. I appreciate that."

"Of course. Is there anything I need to know or can take care of so you can get out of here?"

I shook my head. "I was actually just about to leave. I have a hot date this weekend."

"Ooh, that's fun." Wendy toyed with her wedding band. "Hot dates are always good."

I chuckled. "He's a dog, literally, but I adore him."

"Um, okay?"

"I'm dog-sitting for friends. I always wanted a dog, but never had one growing up."

"You should get one. We have a terrier mix we got two

years ago. Hyper little thing, but I wouldn't trade him for anything. I can't imagine not having him."

"Aw, that's awesome. I've been thinking about it. I was talking this week…" I stopped when I realized my conversation was with Kingsley's mom.

"This week?" Wendy asked.

"Sorry. Um, yeah, just thinking about getting a dog. Maybe one day."

Jeff came in, interrupting us. "Hey. Daisy, why are you here?"

"She's not!" Wendy said, stepping in front of me to hide me from Jeff. "It's just me."

I laughed, and Jeff nodded. "Sounds good. Nice to not see you, boss!"

"You, too!"

Jeff walked to the break room to put his things away, and Wendy turned back to me. "Head out before anyone else arrives and you get pulled into something. Enjoy your weekend."

"Thanks, Wendy. You, too."

Wendy waved, then followed Jeff.

I stepped outside and exhaled deep when no one else was there yet. I could get back to Dozer without more delays.

I sang along with the radio as I drove back to Chelsea's house. I was excited to play with Dozer for the day. I'd seen his play space outside, but I'd never gotten a close look at it. I was excited to have him show me around.

I parked in the driveway and locked my car, heading to the house. I was surprised Dozer wasn't barking, but I thought it was good that he was used to me.

Inside, the house was quiet. No paws or barks or anything. It was definitely not like Dozer. I searched the house, wondering where he was. I went outside, figuring he was playing, but the yard was empty.

My heart pounded as I raced back inside and upstairs. He wasn't in my room, or in Chelsea and Derek's. He was in Jude's, in the middle of Jude's bed.

"Oh, buddy. You miss your friend?"

Dozer whimpered and put his head back down.

"You doing okay?" I asked, as though he could answer me. "Do you want to go outside?"

He lifted his head and looked at me, then put his head back down.

"What's going on?" I went over and sat on the bed with him.

He rested his head on my lap and sighed heavily.

I rubbed his head. "This isn't like you. What's going on, Dozer?"

He didn't answer me, of course.

"Let's go downstairs, buddy. Want something to eat? Hungry?"

I knew that always got a reaction out of him, but I got nothing.

I was starting to seriously worry. It was not like him. It could be sadness from Jude being gone, but it could be so much worse than that.

"Come on, Dozer. Do you want to call Jude?"

He lifted his head, then put it down again.

Something was not right with him.

"Okay, we need to go to the vet, Dozer. Can you walk? Can you get downstairs?"

I tugged on his collar, and thankfully, he jumped off the bed and followed me downstairs. He sank to the floor when we got to the living room. I debated calling Chelsea, but she was on her honeymoon. I could handle Dozer. And if I needed to call her, I would.

I clipped on Dozer's leash. He stood and moved toward the door with me. We went outside, and he laid at my feet while I locked the house. He followed me to my car and climbed into the front seat and laid down while I hurried around to drive.

I kept one hand on him while I drove, my heart pounding the entire time. I knew where Dr. Harris's clinic was, but I'd never been there. When I parked, I was relieved to see they were open and there were only a few cars in the lot.

Dozer jumped out of the car slowly, then followed me inside, not moving very fast. I went straight to the desk, and he laid down at my feet.

"Can I help you?"

"Yeah, I'm dog-sitting for my friend, and her dog is not acting like himself. He's usually really hyper and a little too much, but he's just laying here." I looked down at Dozer.

"Okay, we'll get you back soon. What's the dog's name?"

"Bulldozer. My friend is Chelsea Bailey, maybe Moss. She just got married, so I'm not sure which name it would be under."

"There it is." She clicked a few more things and looked up at us just as the door to the back opened. "Oh, Sheila, can you take Bulldozer to an exam room?"

"Bulldozer?" Sheila looked around. "There can't be a second one. Where is he?"

"He's here," I told her, pointing to the lump of a dog on the floor next to me. "I think he's sick."

"You must be Chelsea's friend. She called last week and said someone would be with him while they're out of town. Daisy?"

I nodded, feeling better that someone knew him. "Yes. Thank you so much. I don't know if he's just missing Jude or if something else is going on."

"Definitely better to take a look. Let's get you two into a room and Dr. Harris will be in soon."

"Thank you so much."

Dozer walked with Sheila, slowly following behind her. I stared at him and worried. He had to be okay.

Sheila took Dozer's vitals and talked to us for a few minutes. "Did he eat anything he wasn't supposed to?"

I shook my head. "Not that I know of."

"Okay. We'll be back soon. We'll figure out what's going on. I promise."

"Thank you, Sheila."

"Of course." Sheila walked out, leaving me alone with the world's most pitiful dog.

I rubbed Dozer's head and tried to calm both of us down. I scratched his ears. I talked to him.

And I waited.

And waited.

And waited.

Nearly an hour passed, and Dr. Harris still hadn't come in.

We didn't have an appointment, but I still thought we'd be seen quickly. My cheeks flushed. We weren't important. The dog was sick, but no one cared.

I cared.

I was about to leave the room to find someone to look at Dozer when I heard a voice outside. I wasn't sure what he said, but if he didn't come in, I was going to go out there and find him.

The door knob spun. The door opened.

And my date from the night before strolled in.

# 6

## KINGSLEY

I looked up from the tablet and stopped. The blonde from the night before, the one I almost didn't confess to, the one I thought about all night, was there.

Was she real? Was I having a stroke and conjured her?

I shook my head. No. She was there. And she was hugging a dog.

The dog.

I cleared my throat. "Um, hello. It says here Chelsea?"

She pulled back like she was startled. "No. I'm Daisy. I'm dog-sitting for Chelsea. This is Dozer. And he's not doing well."

I closed the door and tried to balance what I knew so far. The woman I met the night before was in my office. And I made her wait for an hour because Sheila tried to get me to go in there, and I refused.

Not because I didn't want to help, but because we had other patients. Ones with appointments. And Sheila was not going to influence me.

But there was a very worried woman that I made wait because of my pettiness.

"I apologize for taking so long." I moved toward the dog, and she held up her hand.

"What are you doing here? I was supposed to see Dr. Harris."

I stopped and took a minute. I'd already been through this multiple times, but my brain went haywire when I saw her. "Sorry. I am Dr. Harris. Well, I'm one of them. This is my father's practice, and I'm covering for him. He had a heart attack last week."

"Oh. I'm so sorry. I didn't know. Um, so you are a vet?"

I nodded and moved closer to the massive dog laying on the floor and looking particularly pitiful. "I am. Are you okay with me seeing him?"

Daisy nodded and turned her focus to the dog at her feet. "He's usually very active. Friendly and a little wild, to be honest. I've never seen him like this. I don't know what's wrong."

"Okay, well, we'll take a look at him and maybe run some tests." I sat down on the floor in front of the dog and offered him my hand.

Bulldozer sniffed my hand, but he didn't move to do more than that.

That wasn't good. Even dogs who were anxious would react. He wasn't aggressive, and the notes in the file said he was a playful and active dog. This dog was neither.

"What's going on Bulldozer? Did you eat something you weren't supposed to?" I asked the dog.

He whimpered, the sound making my heart twist. I loved my job, but I knew the sound of pain. And when it came to animals, that sound was worse because they didn't have ways to say how they felt until it sidelined them.

"He's never made that sound." Daisy sat on the floor

next to me, rubbing the dog's back. "He has to be okay. I promised them I'd take care of him."

The tears in her voice sent a surge through me. I wanted to protect her. To take her pain away.

But I couldn't. Not yet. I needed to focus on the dog, not the blonde woman who had me in knots for more reasons than one.

I looked in Bulldozer's ears and mouth. I checked his paws, then I felt his body, waiting for a yelp. When I squeezed his stomach, he growled.

"He's never growled at anyone," Daisy whispered.

"He's in pain. I'm guessing he ate something. I'd like to get a quick X-ray to confirm and see what is bothering him."

"Oh, no. Is he going to be okay?"

"Most of the time, dogs will pass whatever they eat. Did your friend tell you he likes to eat weird things?"

Daisy shook her head, that blonde hair dancing around her shoulders. "No. She never said anything. I don't know what he ate. I didn't... I bought him some new toys. Could he have eaten one of those?"

"It's possible. We'll take a quick look and go from there."

"Okay. Thank you, King—Dr. Harris."

I nodded, wanting to correct her. I wanted to hear my name on her lips.

Which meant I needed to get away from this woman. Fast.

I vowed to love my wife for the rest of my life. It didn't matter to me that her life was cut short. I still loved Faith. I didn't have space in my heart for another woman.

I led Bulldozer out of the room, thankful he could walk. It was a good sign that he wasn't just laying there and refusing to move. The X-ray room was empty, so I guided him onto the table and took a few quick images.

I sighed, feeling better and worse. He definitely ate something. Most likely a toy. But the good news was it was passing through his system and would likely be out by the end of the day.

"Let's go back to Daisy, Bulldozer." The dog got up when I picked up his leash and followed me out of the X-ray room.

"Dozer!" Megan gushed, dropping to her knees in front of the dog as soon as we stepped into the hall. She'd been at the clinic for years, first as a volunteer and now as a tech. She was still learning, but was smart and great with the animals.

Bulldozer's tail wagged when she rubbed his head. It was the first sign of life I'd seen from the dog.

"X-ray? Is he okay?" Megan asked, not looking at me as she focused on the dog.

"Ate a toy. It will come out."

"Want me to take him outside for a minute?"

Bulldozer danced a little, a nearly sure sign he was looking to use the bathroom.

"Yeah, that's a good idea. Thank you, Megan. We're in room two."

She grabbed the leash and stood. "Be right back." She headed for the back door, Bulldozer following closely behind her.

I knocked on the exam room door, then let myself in.

Daisy lifted her head. She quickly wiped the tears streaking down her cheeks and looked past me for Bulldozer. "Is he okay? Please tell me he'll be okay. Where is he? Oh my God, is he that bad?" Her pretty brown eyes went wide and panic settled over her. Her lower lip trembled, and I lost all ability to resist her.

I stepped into her space and pulled her into my arms. She shook, her arms tight around me. She fit there. Her head was just below my chin, her soft curves molding to my body. She smelled like fresh air and cardboard boxes. And fear.

"Bulldozer is going to be fine. One of the techs took him outside to see if he'd use the bathroom. I didn't mean to worry you."

"He's fine? Are you sure?" She stepped away from me, the loss of her a swift punishment for holding her in the first place.

I cleared my throat. "It looks like he ate a toy, something plastic or rubbery, maybe?"

She swallowed and nodded. "There was a hot dog. I thought he would like it."

"He clearly did. A little too much. Unfortunately, I see this a lot with toys that look like food. The animals sometimes don't process that it's not food."

"It didn't smell good."

"Dogs roll around in dead animals and feces. They don't always make smart choices."

She snorted. "Point taken."

I smiled, then stuffed it down. "Anyway, he'll be okay. It looks like it's moving through his body, and it'll come out. Likely today."

"And then he'll feel better?"

I nodded. "He will. He should be back to normal."

A knock on the door stopped our conversation. Megan brought Bulldozer in, praising him for being good. "He didn't get rid of the toy, but he did pee. That's a good sign."

"Good. Thank you. I left him alone last night..." Daisy glanced at me, then quickly focused back on Bulldozer. "I had to go to work for a little while this morning. I don't know when he ate it."

Megan shook her head. "We've seen all kinds of things.

Last month, Dr. Harris had to do surgery on a dog that ate a pair of sunglasses, a dishcloth, and an infant's onesie all within a few hours. Eating a toy is nothing."

Daisy laughed, shaking her head. "I feel better that Dozer only ate a toy. But he's not mine, so I still feel bad."

"He'll be okay," Megan said. She handed the leash back to Daisy. "Sorry. Almost forgot. Bye!"

"Bye. Thank you!"

Megan waved and let herself out of the suddenly small exam room.

Daisy looked up at me. "Is there anything I should do to help him?"

"No. Unfortunately, you just have to wait it out."

"I need to tell my friends, don't I?" Her face twisted with pain and regret.

That urge to make everything okay for her came back. I wanted to comfort her. To ease her pain, even though I wasn't the cause of it. She made it clear the night before that I wasn't important to her, that my presence didn't matter to her. That bothered me. More than I cared to admit or examine. Which meant I had to keep things professional. "They should know, but I don't know the situation and if telling them now is the right call. That's entirely up to you. If they're far away, waiting until they come back is okay. There's nothing they could do if they were here."

"I feel bad waiting to tell them. They trusted me and less than twenty-four hours after I go there, the dog is barely functional."

"He's okay. You did the right thing bringing him here. I apologize for taking so long to get in here."

She narrowed her eyes at me. "I get it. I mean, if I'd known you were here, I probably would have delayed coming in. It's a good thing I didn't, but I don't blame you for avoiding me."

"It wasn't that. I didn't realize you were here."

"Oh." She rolled her lips in and rubbed Bulldozer's head. Her throat worked as she swallowed. Tears filled her gaze once more.

I put my hand on her shoulder. The shot that went through me was entirely unwelcome. I needed to get away from this woman. I'd never been tempted. I wasn't going to be now. But for some reason, I didn't move. "I shouldn't have made you wait. I apologize for that."

She inhaled sharply, my hand lifting with her body. She looked up at me, her brown eyes drawing me in. She leaned forward.

I did the same. An invisible pull drawing me closer.

A dog outside barked, and we both jumped.

I dropped my hand from her shoulder.

She took a step back, plastering herself against the wall.

I cleared my throat. "I would suggest a follow-up. Maybe next week. If you can do that."

"Chelsea and Derek will be home by then. I'll tell them when they get back from their honeymoon so they can schedule an appointment."

"Honeymoon?"

She nodded. "That's why I don't want to bother them. If it was anything else, I would."

"Do you need to go back to work, or will you be with Bulldozer the rest of today? He can stay here if you need someone to watch him."

She shook her head before I finished talking. "I took the rest of the day off. The weekend, too. He won't be alone again."

"Okay. Well, if you need anything..." I reached into my

pocket and realized I didn't have any cards. "Um, the receptionist can give you a card. Actually, I'll write down my number for you. In case you need to call after hours."

"We'll be okay. Chelsea has the emergency number on the fridge. I'll call if I need to. Thank you, Dr. Harris." She tugged gently on Bulldozer's leash, and the dog followed her.

I wanted to do the same.

"Bye," she said as she turned toward the front.

"Goodbye." I watched her go, hating myself for it but unable to resist. I wouldn't see her again. I couldn't.

"Dr. Harris?" Sheila said from behind me.

I turned and scowled at her.

"The patient in room three is ready for you."

I nodded and brushed past her. Back to work.

I DEBATED REACHING out to Daisy all afternoon and into the evening. It would be an overstep, but I couldn't stop thinking about her.

She cared about Bulldozer, even though he wasn't her dog. She was a good person, and she deserved better than she'd gotten from me in our two interactions.

When the day was finally over and the animals of MacKellar Cove were safe and healed and home, I sat in my father's office again. I promised Isla I would take the next day off, so I was doing everything possible to finish all the paperwork for the week.

The office was quiet, which made it easier for me to think. The busyness of the day was good, but the quiet of the night was better. Especially when it came to the tedious work of files.

I finished everything much faster than I'd expected, happy to find most of the files had been updated during the day without my intervention. Sheila's name on them was enough for me to double check her work, but I couldn't find fault with any of it.

That was good, right? It should have been good. Instead, it left me feeling frustrated and annoyed as I locked up the office and made my way to my SUV.

Isla and I had been in town for ten days. Ten days of exhaustion and painful memories I didn't want to relive. Not enough time in those ten days was spent with Isla, but I struggled to go home and see my mother after spending all day with Sheila.

I decided to take a drive along the Saint Lawrence River before I went home. It was a nice night, and the weather was perfect for a drive with the windows down.

Life as a single parent didn't allow much time for me to be alone. I couldn't take a drive or go out of town or do any of the things most people didn't think twice about doing. My continuing education classes were all online so I could complete them when Isla was sleeping, or when I took time off work.

Summer was supposed to be a fun few months for us. She was starting kindergarten in the fall. Another milestone Faith would miss. Another milestone Isla wouldn't have her mother around for.

Faith would have known how to handle the summer with my parents. She would have been able to bridge the gap. Being there for my mother was the right move, but being back in MacKellar Cove brought back so many memories. Good and bad.

But the memories weren't the only thing being in MacKellar Cove brought. Daisy. I couldn't stop thinking about her. As I drove, I wondered what she was doing. I wondered where she lived. I wondered if she was thinking about me.

I shook my head and dragged my thoughts from her. I didn't know why she was the one woman since Faith who caught my attention, but it didn't matter. I had Isla to think about. I wasn't sticking around. There would be no point in getting to know Daisy.

No matter how tempted I was.

I turned the SUV around and headed back toward my mother's house. Maybe being busy was for the best. It meant I didn't have time to think about Daisy or my father or any of the other things I was avoiding. It meant I was focused and getting things done.

I parked in the driveway and grabbed my bag. Isla's laughter was the first thing I heard when I walked in, followed by my mother's voice. In the kitchen.

I set my bag down and headed that way, wondering what I would find. I was not prepared for a flour covered child standing on a stool with a rolling pin in her hand. "What is going on?"

Isla squealed and jumped. Mom's arm wrapped around her before she could lose her balance.

"It's a surprise," Isla declared, sticking her lip out to tell me I ruined the surprise.

"Does that mean I need to leave?"

"Yes," Isla said.

"Your daddy doesn't have to leave," Mom said.

I shook my head. "It's okay. I need to shower anyway. Is that enough time to finish my surprise?" The strawberries and rhubarb on the counter were enough to tell me what the surprise was, but I wasn't going to spoil it for Isla.

Isla looked at Mom, and Mom nodded. Isla turned back to me. "Yes."

"Okay. I'll be back soon. Then you have to tell me what the surprise is."

Isla went back to work, all her focus on the task at hand.

Mom winked at me, knowing I already knew what they were doing.

*Thank you*, I mouthed to her.

She smiled and nodded toward the hallway.

Yeah, I got the message. Get out before the four-year-old caught me standing there. I went down the hall to my room and found clean clothes. I carried them to the bathroom and turned on the shower to warm up while I undressed.

That was what I needed in my life. Time with my favorite person. Isla would erase all thoughts of Daisy. Just like I wanted.

## 7

## DAISY

Trip number three outside. These were the not-so-glamorous parts of owning a pet that no one told you about. I imagined it was the same if you had a potty-training toddler, to a certain extent, based on the conversations at book club.

Since I had neither, I was not prepared to chase Dozer around the backyard and examine his poop. Wow.

But I signed up for the task, and I was the one who gave him a toy that he ate, so I had to deal with it.

Dozer looked up at me from his squat.

"I don't want to be standing over you either," I told him.

He whimpered, then grunted.

"Oh, please tell me this is it."

He made another noise, one I wasn't sure I'd ever heard before, then took off. Straight for the house.

"Shit," I hissed. Did I chase him down or examine the poop first?

God, what a question.

I crossed my fingers that he didn't make a mess in the house and shined my phone flashlight at the pile of poo he left behind. Complete with a formerly bright yellow and red hot dog.

"Thank God," I breathed.

I would have liked nothing more than to leave the pile there, but I had to make sure he didn't do something even more disgusting and eat it. Again. I had no idea what he would do, so I turned the plastic poop bag inside out over my hand and grabbed the toy.

"Yuck," I cried as I held the warm, poo-covered toy. I flipped the bag right-side out and tied it up. I went straight to the trashcan and deposited the prize, then ran inside to scrub my hands clean. Three times.

When I was done, I went looking for Dozer. He wasn't downstairs, which made me a little nervous. I headed upstairs and looked in the bedrooms until I found him on the floor next to Jude's bed.

"We're going to see him tomorrow," I told Dozer. "Do you want a treat for being a good boy?"

His ears perked up at the word treat, and he jumped up. It was the most life I'd seen from him all day. I let out a sigh of relief.

"You're so good," I told him as we walked back to the kitchen. I grabbed the container of treats and held one up.

He sat down, patiently waiting, just like he was taught.

I couldn't make him do more tricks after what he'd been through, so I gave him the treat and praised him for pooping out the hot dog.

He followed me to the living room, where I was watching a sappy movie about two people falling in love over the years of their friendship.

"It looks so easy," I told Dozer. "Falling for your friend. I've never found love to be so simple. But it'll work out one day."

I thought about Dr. Harris, but shook my head. He was a very nice man, and attractive, but he made it clear he wasn't looking for a relationship.

Someone else would be.

I logged into Book Boyfriends Wanted and checked for any new matches. There were two, but neither of them had the same pull as DrGrumpy.

I put my phone away and watched the movie. I didn't want to date someone just because he was available. It had to feel right. I'd find that person one day.

DOZER WAS TOTALLY BACK to his usual self when Jude and Chelsea's mom came over the next day. I confessed to Cathy what happened with the toy, and she laughed.

"Oh, you poor thing. You should have called me," Cathy said.

I shook my head. "I couldn't drag you into it. We went to the vet, and he said all we could do was wait."

"I thought Dr. Harris was in the hospital."

"What? He is?" I blurted. I just saw him the day before.

"Oh, you met Kingsley," Cathy continued. "I forgot he came to town."

"Yeah, sorry. I didn't think. I've never met his father."

"Kingsley grew up here. He graduated with my niece, Elise. I haven't seen him in years."

"I didn't realize he was a local," I said, trying not to be too eager for information about the man I was absolutely not going to obsess over.

Cathy nodded. "He was. Nice boy. Always helped out in his father's clinic. Adored his father and went to vet school.

Then, a year before he finished his schooling, he and his fiancée stopped coming back here to visit."

"Was she from here, too?"

"No, they met in college. Beautiful woman. So nice. Always friendly and kind. They seemed so perfect together."

"What happened?"

"Car accident is what I heard."

"Oh." My heart ached for the grumpy man I'd met. The man who was not interested in dating and was likely still in love with his wife. I couldn't compete with that. I didn't want to try.

"It's been three years, maybe four. His mother and I were friends once upon a time. Been years since I've seen Tina. I've been thinking of checking in since Gregory's in the hospital. See how she's doing."

"I would imagine it's hard, and I'm sure she'd appreciate a visit from a friend."

Cathy nodded. "I think you're right. Maybe next week when Jude's at camp. Natalie has done such a wonderful job with that place. Jude absolutely loves it there, and loves Natalie."

I grinned. My bestie was amazing. "What's not to love?" I laughed.

Cathy smiled. "I agree. And so does the mayor. I'm so happy they found each other. Are you next?"

I laughed. "I hope so. But I know it'll happen. I'm always on the lookout."

"Good. If I see a good one, I'll send him your way."

"Thanks, Cathy."

"Grandma, can we have a snack?" Jude asked, racing over with Dozer on his heels.

"Of course. If Ms. Daisy doesn't mind."

I stood. "It's his house. I'm just borrowing it for a little while. Don't let me stand in the way of anything."

"Thank you, Daisy. Do you want a snack, too?" Cathy asked me.

"I always want a snack. Let's see what we have."

The four of us went inside, escaping the warm summer heat.

NATALIE SPENT Saturday night with Dozer and me, making herself at home on the couch. Sunday morning, she went to see Omar, and for the rest of the weekend, Dozer and I were alone.

It was a perfect weekend. We went for walks, I met his neighbors, and I figured out that having a dog is a lot more work than I ever imagined, but also a lot more fun.

Especially when I knew there were people around to take care of the store when I needed to be with Dozer.

Monday afternoon, I had my things all packed up and in the back of my SUV before Chelsea and Derek got home. I figured they would be exhausted and ready to relax, so I made sure the house was cleaned up, the sheets I'd used were washed and put away, and Dozer was fed and walked and all they would need to do was relax for the night.

Headlights shined on the front windows, sending Dozer into full alert. He went to the window, then barked and ran to the door.

A few seconds later, the door swung open and Chelsea backed a very excited Dozer up so she could greet him with a big hug and lots of laughs.

"Did you have a good weekend with Daisy? Are you

happy to see us? Oh, you're so good." Chelsea looked up at me. "Hi."

I waved. "Hi! How was your trip?"

Chelsea sighed as Derek walked in with their luggage. "It was wonderful. I didn't realize how busy we were until we had a few days without all the excitement of our lives. A part of me missed it—"

Derek snorted. "She couldn't sit still for the first day."

"I... No, I couldn't," Chelsea said with a laugh. "I was so used to working and walking Dozer and having Jude doing things and it was just so quiet without all of that."

"Well, I walked him today so you guys could just relax tonight. I know Jude's back tomorrow. And there's one thing you need to know."

Derek and Chelsea both froze and looked at me.

"Everything's fine now. I promise. But Dozer ate one of the toys I bought him. I took him to the vet, and Dr. Harris said he would be fine. The toy came out, and he's been totally fine since then. I'm sorry I didn't call you, but I wanted you to enjoy your weekend, and Dr. Harris said there would be nothing you could do anyway, but I don't want you to hate me for not calling you. Your mom said it would be fine, but I didn't tell her until after everything, either, so don't be mad at her."

Chelsea stepped forward and wrapped her arms around me, pulling me into a hug and shutting me up. "Thank you for being here for him."

I patted her back. "You're welcome?"

She chuckled and stepped back. "I mean it. Dogs eat weird things. He hasn't done a lot of that, but he's eaten pinecones and sticks. I don't think he's ever eaten a toy, but most of his toys are big, so maybe he just couldn't get the whole thing in his mouth. Either way, thank you for watching out for him."

"I'm just really sorry it happened. I picked up all the toys I brought him and put them in my car so he didn't eat another one. Dr. Harris said sometimes dogs confuse things that look like food."

"It's no big deal."

"He suggested a follow-up this week. I didn't want to schedule something that you guys couldn't do, but I'm happy to take him again, if you want me to. I just figured you'd want to hear from the doctor that everything is okay."

"Yeah, we'll call them in the morning. Dr. Harris is really good, though, so if he said there's nothing to worry about, I'm not worried."

"You know him?" I asked.

Chelsea chuckled. "Of course. He's Dozer's vet."

"Oh, you mean... The Dr. Harris I met is apparently his son. That's what your mom said. I keep forgetting they're both Dr. Harris because I've only met Kingsley, but obviously that makes sense."

"Kingsley? Wow. I haven't seen him in years. He's back?" Chelsea asked.

I nodded. "Yeah, for now, I guess. But I'm sure he's great. You should call tomorrow, just to make sure everything's fine."

"We will. Thank you, Daisy. Really. I would not have been able to enjoy the trip if you hadn't been here with Dozer. We really appreciate it." Chelsea hugged me tight.

"I was so happy to help. You guys enjoy your night. I'll see you soon."

"Did you already pack your stuff?" Derek asked.

I nodded. "I didn't want to hold you guys up."

"You wouldn't have. Thank you for doing this." Derek hugged me and kissed my cheek.

"I'd be happy to do it again if you decide to go on another honeymoon," I told them.

Derek laughed and hugged Chelsea to his side. "Don't tempt me."

I smiled and waved, leaving them to their privacy. I was so happy for them.

My house was quiet when I got home, and I assumed Natalie was staying with Omar again. She had been more and more lately. Another happy couple. I was surrounded by them.

And eager to be one of them.

Maybe I should give those other guys a chance. I wasn't going to meet someone if I wasn't open to it.

I opened Book Boyfriends Wanted and sent one of the guys a message asking what he would name a boat if he had one.

I put my phone away and fixed dinner, already tired and knowing morning was going to come before I knew it.

THE DELIVERY for the day was backed into the loading dock when I arrived at work the next morning. I was happy to see Penny was there and taking care of everything. It was a step in the right direction, especially after I didn't check in with her for a few days.

"Morning," Penny said when she saw me. "How was your weekend?"

"It was good. Thanks. How was yours?"

"So good. I spent it with my sister and her family."

"That's so nice."

"Do you have siblings?"

I nodded. "I do. I have twin brothers. Younger than me."

"Oh, wow. That had to be fun growing up. And a little crazy."

I chuckled. "Definitely both."

"Is that why you opened a toy store?"

"It's a big part of it," I said, knowing she would assume what everyone did. I loved kids so much that I wanted to play all day. The truth was that I missed out on so much in my own childhood that I wanted to make sure no other kid felt like they missed out because of their siblings.

"Very cool," Penny said. "I want to talk to you about some inventory stuff today, if you have time."

"Of course."

"Okay, sounds good. I noticed a few things that seem to be moving, and a few that aren't moving as much. And then you're going to show me how to put in orders right?"

"Yep. We'll take care of all of that today, and we'll talk about everything else. You're working all days this week and off the weekend, but working next Saturday for the delivery, right?"

"I am. All set."

"Excellent. Thank you."

"It'll be good."

The truck driver walked up and had a question, so Penny moved off to speak to him, and I started my day.

The morning went by quickly, and before I knew it, it was time for lunch. Natalie and I were supposed to meet, so I checked in with Penny and Wendy, then headed out to Just Tacos.

I was almost there when I felt my phone buzzing. I waved to a family who stopped by the Grand Opening of

Mountain View Retreat and answered the call from Natalie. "Hey. I'm almost there. Did you already order?"

"That's why I'm calling. I'm so sorry, but I can't make it."

"Is everything okay?" I stopped on the sidewalk.

"Yeah, it's just busy today. I feel like I should stay."

"Okay. How about dinner tonight then? I haven't seen you much."

"I know. I'm sorry. Um…"

"If you already have plans with Omar, it's okay. We'll catch up when you're free."

"Are you sure? He made reservations somewhere. I can cancel, though. He'll understand."

"You will not cancel. It's okay. You deserve to be happy, and you deserve to have a summer camp full of kids."

"I don't want you to hate me."

"I would never."

"This weekend, we need to have a day just the two of us."

"Aren't you guys going away this weekend?"

"Crap." Natalie sighed. "I'm a horrible friend."

"No, you're not. You're the best friend I could ask for. And your life is busier now than a year ago. We will find time to get lunch or dinner or something. But you need to be living your life."

"So do you. I don't want you to think I'm not around anymore."

"I don't, Natalie. We're all good."

"Okay. Have an extra taco for me. And I'll see you… sometime."

A shout in the background had me worried. "I'll see you soon. Go take care of whatever that's about."

"Thanks. Bye!"

She hung up before I could say anything else. I stared at my phone. I missed my bestie. I was thrilled for her, but I missed her. For years, it had been just the two of us. I always knew she could do anything, and I was so proud to watch her become stronger and more confident as she built and opened her camp. But I missed her.

I shook off the melancholy and continued to Just Tacos. I had to eat, and tacos still sounded good.

The restaurant was busy when I walked in, so I got into the line and waited for my turn to order. A woman and a little girl were in front of me, talking about choices.

"I don't like beans, grandma. Daddy says they make you toot."

I laughed before I could stop myself, and grandma turned to me and grinned.

"Her daddy's not wrong," I said.

"No, he's not."

"Can I get a taco with just cheese?" the girl asked.

"That's like a cheese sandwich. You need more than that. How about some chicken?" grandma suggested.

The girl wrinkled her nose. "Do I have to?"

"Chicken or ground beef."

"What's that?"

"Like burgers, but all mashed up."

"I like burgers."

"Let's try the ground beef then."

I nodded, deciding to get the same. "Good choice," I told the girl.

"Do you like burgers?"

"I do. Burgers are delicious."

"My daddy makes good burgers."

"That's very important."

Grandma snickered at us. "Her father loves to cook."

"So do I. I don't do it as often as I'd like since it's just me and my roommate, but I enjoy it."

"You should come over so my daddy can cook for you," the little girl said.

"You're very sweet. Thank you for the offer." I winked at grandma, knowing the little girl would forget quickly, and grandma wouldn't have to explain why inviting a stranger to dinner was not a great idea.

"Next!" the woman at the counter called.

The girl and grandma stepped forward and ordered their food. They grabbed drinks, then stepped to the side. I told the server I needed my food to go, deciding a little sunshine and fresh air sounded like a good plan.

I carried my tacos to Catherine Park and settled on a chair near the gazebo. Kids ran around and played, friends hugged and talked. It was a beautiful day. Perfect for the start of summer.

"Ms. Daisy!" I heard as I finished my last taco.

I searched for the voice and found one of the kids who'd been in the store a week ago. He was hurrying toward me, his dad following a little farther behind.

"Hi, Stevie! How are you?"

Stevie ran up and gave me a hug, giving his dad time to catch up. "Hi. Ms. Daisy! Daddy and I are playing with the frisbee we got last week. I'm really good at throwing it really far."

I looked up at Dad, who was clearly exhausted from chasing not only Stevie but also the frisbee. "I bet you are."

Dad nodded, dropping his hands to his knees while he sucked in a breath. "Yeah."

I laughed with Dad. "I think next time I see you, you need a toy that doesn't wear Dad out so much."

Stevie shook his head. "But that's not fun."

A laugh popped out of me. I shook my head. "You're right. But maybe it would be for Dad."

"Okay." Stevie took the frisbee from Dad. "Bye, Ms. Daisy! Come on, Dad!"

"Good luck," I told Dad.

"Thanks. Bye!" Dad waved as he took off after Stevie.

One day I'd have that.

# 8

## KINGSLEY

I knocked on the exam room door and let myself in. I was almost immediately bowled over by the overly excited dog on the other side. A very different dog with a very different woman than the last time.

"I see why everyone was so worried about Bulldozer now." I rubbed the dog behind his ears and reached to shake hands with the woman struggling to hold him back. "It's nice to meet you. I'm Kingsley Harris."

"We actually went to high school together. You graduated with my cousin, Elise." Her handshake and smile were both friendly. "I'm Chelsea Moss, now Bailey. This is my husband, Derek."

"Oh, wow. I'm so sorry. I didn't put it together when I saw your name. It's good to see you again. And I hear congratulations are in order." I shook Derek's hand, and he met my gaze with a question. "Daisy said you were on your honeymoon."

A smile lit Derek's face, and a blush stained Chelsea's cheeks.

"We were. And Daisy was a huge help for us. I know she felt horrible that he ended up here," Derek said.

"Happens to most pet owners at some point. But now that I see him at full health, I get why she was so worried. He's a very different animal."

Bulldozer stuck his nose in my crotch and tried to go through my legs. Sad to admit it was the most action I'd had in years, and not the first time, or likely the last, it would come from a dog.

"Dozer, stop!" Chelsea scolded.

The dog sank and loped back to his person, shamed and looking for sympathy.

"Hazard of the job," I told her with a grin. "Let's take a look at him, okay?"

Chelsea nodded and encouraged Bulldozer up onto the table.

"He seems to be feeling much better. He's active, isn't he?"

"My son is in love with him," Derek said. "As much as I hated this beast at first, he's the reason we ended up together."

"Oh, yeah? That's not something I hear every day."

"Dozer almost knocked down the fence between our houses, and Jude adored this lovable lump. We started spending time together so Jude and Dozer could play, and Derek reluctantly accepted that I'm not such a horrible neighbor."

"You're a much better wife," he told her.

I smiled and continued my examination of Bulldozer. He didn't whimper or cry out with any of my poking or prodding, and I had no reason to believe any additional tests were required. My biggest concern was if a piece of the toy was left behind in his body, or if his intestines were damaged as it moved through, but he seemed good.

"I think he's very healthy," I told them as I used hand sanitizer after my exam. "He was lucky, too."

"That's what we told Daisy. She was there for him. God, she felt so bad."

I smiled, hating that my heart skipped every time they said her name.

"She's a good friend," Derek told his wife. "You would have been the same if the situation was reversed."

Chelsea laughed. "True. I'd have been a wreck. Speaking of, how's your dad? I heard he was in the hospital."

I nodded. "Recovering well, thank you."

"Oh, good. Not that I don't want you here. I didn't mean that."

"It's fine. I understand."

"Do you have plans later?" Derek asked.

"Excuse me?"

"A bunch of local men get together every Thursday night. We're getting together tonight because of the July Fourth holiday, but I wondered if you had an interest in joining us."

"Oh, that's kind of you, but—"

"Before you say no, think about it," Derek said. "It's a good group of men. We meet at O'Kelley's at seven. If you don't make it this week, we'll be there next Thursday night, same time."

I nodded, knowing I wasn't going to go but strangely appreciative that he invited me. "Thank you."

"You're welcome. I hope we see you again. Although in different circumstances, Doc."

"You as well."

I led them to the front and said goodbye when I heard Karen say they were all set.

"We always pay for appointments," Chelsea insisted.

"Is there an issue?" I asked.

Karen shook her head. "Nope. It says the bill for today was already paid in advance by Daisy Lincoln."

Chelsea gasped. "She didn't have to do that."

"But that was very nice of her. We need to do something good for Daisy," Derek said. He waved and led Chelsea toward the door. "Something to thank her since she wouldn't take anything."

Their conversation faded as they walked away, and I found myself wishing I could follow them so I could hear more about the woman.

"Dr. Harris?" Karen asked. "Did you need something?"

I shook my head. "No. I'm good."

I walked back to the exam rooms and continued my day, absolutely not thinking about Daisy Lincoln. Not even a little.

Nope. It was definitely a lot.

THE LAST THING I needed when I got back to my mom's house from another long day was a lecture about my late nights and not spending enough time with Isla. I fully expected one, especially since I'd intended to spend more time with my kid this summer than I'd done yet.

What I didn't expect was my father to be sitting in his chair in the living room, Isla on his lap.

"What's this for?" Isla asked, touching the puckered scar on his dark skin.

"My heart wasn't working like it was supposed to, so the doctor had to get a closer look at it and make it better."

"And are you better now?" Isla asked.

"I am. I'm much better. And I'm always better with you here." My father hugged Isla tight, and she closed her eyes and returned the hug.

My gut twisted. I wanted to yank her out of his lap, to take her away and never come back. To keep her from him so he didn't poison my sweet girl.

"Kingsley," Dad said, finally seeing me at the door. Or finally acknowledging me.

I nodded at him. We hadn't spoken. I hadn't spoken to him. Not since the day he asked me to keep what I'd seen to myself, and I left and never came back.

"Daddy!" Isla shouted, climbing off my father's lap and rushing to me.

I scooped her up and hugged her close. I breathed in her baby powder scent and coconut shampoo and closed my eyes. She knew how a person should treat their partner because of me. She would always know. It didn't matter that she didn't remember her mother, she would always know to expect to be a priority to the person she ended up with. And to make them a priority in her life, too.

"Can we go swimming? Grandpa said he can't swim yet. Grandma never wants to swim. But you swim with me."

"Yes, we can go swimming."

"Yay!" Isla scrambled down and took off down the hall toward her room. She shouted for my mother, who answered from somewhere in the back of the house.

"Hello, Kingsley," my father said when it was just the two of us.

I grunted.

Dad sighed. "Won't even speak to me in my own home."

"Still needing me to keep your secrets?" I spat.

He shook his head like he was disappointed in me.

I wasn't the one who cheated on my wife! But I couldn't say that to him. Not with my mother in the house.

"Thank you for coming to help."

"I didn't do it for you."

He nodded. "I know."

"Oh, Kingsley. Isla said she was going swimming. I figured you were home."

"Yeah. I'm going to go change."

"Good. Isla is so excited to swim. She's a little fish."

I breathed a laugh and kissed Mom's cheek, then moved past her to go down the hall.

I wanted to take a shower, but I knew Isla would be ready to jump in the pool faster than I could shower and change. I grabbed my swim trunks and changed into them, making my way outside without stopping to speak to my father again.

Isla was already outside, and as soon as she saw me, she went to the edge of the pool and jumped in.

"Isla!"

"It's okay, Mom. She saw me."

"Oh, Kingsley. She gave me a fright. How was your day?"

"Daddy, come swim with me!" Isla called.

"My day was good. A local guy invited me to meet up with some others at O'Kelley's."

Mom nodded. "Hudson Grant owns that place."

I shook my head. "Don't think I know him. Is he my age?"

"No, ten years older than you, maybe? I'm not sure. Baseball player."

"How do you know him?"

"I've been to O'Kelley's before, Kingsley. Your mother does leave the house sometimes."

"I know you do. I'm just surprised."

"It is a small town, son. Everyone here pretty much knows everyone else. Who invited you out?"

"Derek? Chelsea Moss's new husband."

"Oh, Derek Bailey. He owns Stone Auto Repair now. Mr. Stone retired and Derek bought it. He's not from here, but he moved here with his son. Jude is a sweet kid."

"How do you know them?"

"I volunteer at the library some. Jude has been in a few times. But he's in the new summer camp now. And you remember I'm friends with Chelsea's mom, Cathy. Chelsea is sweet as can be. She is the co-owner of the salon in town. They changed the name to Serenity Salon, but it's still the only place in town anyone goes."

"Okay."

"Daddy!" Isla whined.

"You go get in. When are you going to O'Kelley's?"

I shook my head and moved toward the pool. "I'm not. It's tonight."

"You could have gone. We would have been happy to watch her."

I shook my head. "I've missed a lot already this summer. Besides, I need to find a place for us to stay now that Dad's home."

"You don't have to do that, Kingsley. You can both stay here. There is plenty of room."

"You're going to be busy enough taking care of Dad. You don't need Isla underfoot, too."

"She's not underfoot. I love having her here as much as I can get her. Besides, where else is she going to go when you're at the clinic?"

"There has to be a camp or something."

"The camps have been full for months, Kingsley. Please stay here. I know you weren't expecting your father to be here today, but when he called and said he could come home, I couldn't tell him no."

"I know, Mom. I get it. But I don't know if I can stay here with him."

"Oh, I wish I knew what happened between the two of you to make you leave. I always thought you'd run his practice when he was ready to retire. It was always his dream."

I grunted and avoided answering by jumping into the pool with Isla.

Isla squealed and swam over to me, climbing up onto my shoulders and asking me to walk her around.

"You're supposed to be swimming, little fish. Why are you on dry land?"

"I'm not on land, silly. I'm on your shoulders."

I laughed with her and continued the trek around the pool. I splashed water on her legs, and she kicked her feet with joy.

Life was simple for a four-year-old. Something I wished I could tap into more often. Instead, I was torn between thoughts of a woman I didn't want to want and the presence of my father I didn't want to be around.

Being four would have been so much easier.

I SPENT MORE and more time at work the rest of the week. Late nights doing paperwork, early mornings catching up on the schedule for the day. I worked through the holiday, too. Anything to avoid seeing my father and having to talk to him.

All that work meant less time with Isla, though. Less time with the one person I wanted to see. Which was why I suggested a daddy-daughter day on Saturday. Just the two of us, away from my father and any other distractions. And if we happened to find a place to stay for a few weeks, all the better.

We started our day at Cracked, the egg-centric diner where my mother worked when I was in high school. Isla loved eggs, so it was a great option for her, one I was sure would end with a too full four-year-old and lots of leftovers. It was perfect.

The server who saw us when we walked in waved and indicated to seat ourselves as she hurried to the back to put in an order.

Isla picked a table against the wall and climbed onto the booth side in the back. She opened her menu and studied it, pretending she could read the words.

"What's this one?" she asked, pointing to one of the items.

"Up here," I showed her the title of the section, "it says French Toast. They have a lot of different kinds with different toppings. The one you're pointing to says topped with strawberries and bananas."

"I don't like strawberries," Isla told me.

"I know. But there are ones that are covered in cereal. And they have omelettes and scrambled eggs and quiche."

"What's that?" she asked, looking up at me.

"Quiche is eggs in a pie crust with other stuff and baked. I think grandma made it for you last weekend."

Isla nodded, as though considering her options. All she needed was to rub her chin and she'd look like my mother.

I smothered my grin before she caught me and was relieved when the server arrived at that moment.

"Good morning. I'm Blake. Welcome to Cracked. Have you two been here before?"

"I have," I told her. "I don't think she has."

"My grandma used to work here," Isla told her proudly.

"She did? What's your grandma's name?"

Isla shrugged. "Grandma."

Blake snorted and nodded. "That's a good name." She winked at me.

"My mom is Tina Harris."

"Oh, I worked with Tina when I started here. You're Kingsley?"

I nodded. "I am. Good memory."

"I'm good friends with Chelsea and Derek, and Daisy. I heard about Dozer, and everyone is so relieved you were able to help him."

My heart jumped at Daisy's name, but I ignored it. "I didn't really do much."

"Still. Thank you. How is your dad? Home this week, right?"

"He is. That's why we're here."

Blake nodded as though she understood, but there was no way she did. Not really. She focused on Isla again and asked, "Would you like some coffee to start your day today?"

Isla giggled. "I don't drink coffee. Daddy said it's for adults."

Blake slapped her forehead. "Oh, jeez. I forgot. You're so grown up, I assumed you were an adult."

"I'm only four!" Isla shouted, full of giggles.

Blake's eyes bugged out. "What? I thought for sure you were twenty-four. How did you get so mature?"

"My daddy says I take after my mommy. But I don't remember her."

Blake gave me a sympathetic smile. "Mommies are always there for us, even when we don't remember them."

Isla nodded. I'd told her the same thing her entire life.

"Is the French Toast any good?" Isla asked.

Blake nodded, not missing a beat at the sudden subject change. "It's delicious. My son is two-and-a-half, and his favorite is the stuffed one. It has blueberries inside and is coated with sugar flakes cereal."

"I like blueberries."

"Me, too."

"I'll take it," Isla declared, closing her menu and handing it to Blake.

Blake nodded. "Would you like something to drink that is not coffee? We have hot chocolate, milk, juice, water?"

"Milk, please."

"You got it." She smiled at Isla, then turned to me. "And for you?"

"Definitely coffee for me. Keep it coming. And I'll take the mushroom and Swiss omelette with breakfast potatoes and bacon."

"Excellent. I'll bring your drinks right back."

"Thank you."

"Thank you."

Blake grinned and walked away, stopping at another table before she went to the back.

"What are we going to do after this?" Isla asked me.

"I don't know. What do you want to do?"

"Can we go to the zoo?"

I shook my head. "There's not a zoo around here."

"What about the aquarium?"

"Not one of those, either."

"What can we do?"

"We can go on a boat ride and see a castle," I suggested,

remembering the tours of the river and knowing a castle would probably grab her attention.

Isla's eyes got huge. "Really? There's a castle?"

Blake chuckled as she set my coffee and Isla's milk down. "My friend does the boat tours. It's a very cool trip."

"You have a friend who drives boats?" Isla asked.

"I do. And my husband builds boats. Do you like boats?" Blake asked.

Isla nodded. "I love boats. Daddy says I'm a water baby."

"This is a good place for a water baby to be. My sister-in-law has a pool at her house, and we spend a lot of time there in the summer."

"My grandma has a pool, too. We're living with them, but Daddy wants to find another place to stay." Isla sipped her milk.

"It can be hard to live with people you're not used to living with," Blake said diplomatically.

"I like living there. Grandma is really nice, and Grandpa tells me he loves me all the time. At home, it's just me and Daddy, so it's quieter. I like having other people to talk to."

And just like that, my heart broke. I was being selfish wanting to take Isla away from my parents. I believed it was for the best, but the best for who? She was my priority.

If she wanted to stay with my parents, I needed to get over it.

"Around here, there are lots of people to talk to. I have a big group of friends and a lot of us have kids. Maybe you can meet them sometime?" Blake suggested.

"Can I, Daddy? Grandma gets tired, and she doesn't like to swim, so it can be kind of boring." Isla wrinkled her nose.

"Isla!" I chastised.

Blake chuckled quietly. "I understand. There's a big event later today in Catherine Park. You guys should come after your castle tour. It's family friendly and you can meet a lot of other people. If you're available."

"Yay!" Isla shouted.

"Thank you," I told Blake. "We'll see what time we can get a tour and hopefully see you then."

"Looking forward to it." Blake walked away with a smile, and I felt a little better about spending the rest of summer in MacKellar Cove.

9

---

After breakfast, which Isla did not finish, we packed up her leftovers in the cooler I brought for that purpose alone, then headed toward the dock where Blake said we could catch a tour boat.

When we arrived, the woman behind the counter told me tickets had already been taken care of for us and we were on the next boat with a captain named Elise.

I chuckled and shook my head, knowing Blake had a hand in that.

At the boat, I was surprised to see I recognized the captain. Elise Webber graduated high school the same year as me.

"Kingsley Harris. Blake didn't tell me you were the one she was sending over," Elise said warmly. "How are you?" She opened her arms to hug me, and I smiled and wrapped her up.

Going to a small school like MacKellar Cove High School, it was almost impossible to not know everyone. Elise and I had classes together every year from sixth grade through graduation. She was funny and friendly and easy to like. "I'm good. It's good to see you. I didn't realize you were the captain."

She nodded. "I am. I love it." She pulled us to the side and focused on Isla. "And I hear this is your first trip on the boat. How would you like to ride with me?"

"I can do that?" Isla asked with awe.

Elise nodded. "If it's okay with your father."

"Can I stay with her?" I asked.

"Absolutely. I used to be a guide so I can tell you everything you will hear on the tour, and I can give you a little more behind the scenes stuff. The only thing you have to do is make sure you listen to me and your dad. Do you think you can do that?"

Isla nodded. "I can. I will."

Elise looked at me and grinned. "Follow me." She led us to the front of the boat where she had an unobstructed view of the water. She went through all the buttons and levers and explained every detail to Isla, keeping her enthralled until a radio said they were all loaded up and ready to push off.

Elise picked up the radio and replied, "All set here. Checks are done and ready to float."

The speaker outside was muffled, but I could hear the guide talking to the rest of the passengers.

Elise focused only on Isla. "Isla, tell me your favorite thing about the water?"

"I like everything about the water."

Elise chuckled. "Yeah, I understand that. I live on a maple farm. Have you ever been to one?"

Isla shook her head.

"Do you like maple syrup on your pancakes? Oh, nope, French Toast, right?"

Isla nodded. "I love maple syrup."

"My husband owns Jones Family Maple Farm, and he makes maple syrup. Maybe you and your dad can come out and see the farm sometime." Elise raised her brows at me in question.

I nodded, knowing I didn't really get a vote. Isla would be all over that.

"Can I taste the syrup?" Isla asked.

Elise laughed. "You can. And we have other treats we make that we don't give to just anyone. You're special so we will make you something special."

"You don't have to do that," I told her.

Elise shook her head. "It's fun for us. We don't have kids, so we spoil our friends' kids, and most of them have been over for different events. We don't get a lot of kids who haven't seen everything on the farm."

"How did you get into this?" I gestured around the boat.

"I'm like Isla. I love the water. Anything open and outdoors, really. I was a guide for a long time before I met Colin."

"So not a local?" I asked of her husband.

Elise shook her head. "He moved here when he inherited the farm. He was born here but didn't grow up here."

"This place tends to suck people in," I said, already feeling the small town pull.

Elise chuckled. "Too true. I left town for college, like you did, but I moved back right after. Wanted to be close to my family. Chelsea said she saw you at the clinic the other day."

I nodded. "Yep, she reminded me who she was. I didn't recognize her at first. I should have. She was a year or two behind us, right?"

"Yep, but high school was... ahem... a few years ago."

I laughed. "Yes, it was."

Elise winked, then continued her personal tour for Isla.

The boat moved through the water easily, Elise's skills making it seem like we were on glass-smooth water even though we weren't.

When we made it to the castle, Elise asked to trade numbers. "You guys can wander, but if you wait until we're heading back to pick up, you can ride back with me and I can give you the rest of the tour. No pressure, though."

"Can we, Daddy?" Isla begged.

I nodded and exchanged numbers with Elise. "Thank you. This was amazing. And it was so good to see you."

"You, too. Blake said you're coming to the event later?"

"We were thinking about it."

"You can meet everyone else. Derek and Chelsea will be there with Jude, too. It'll be a lot of fun."

"Thanks, Elise. This has been a great day."

"Good. I'll see you guys soon." Elise waved to Isla and me, letting her guide lead us to the dock.

"That was the coolest thing ever," Isla declared as we walked up the pathway from the dock to the castle. "Wow."

I grinned. My princess had never seen a real castle, and she was about to forget all about the boat.

We walked through the castle and toured the grounds that surrounded it. Boldt Castle was not new to me, but it still amazed me every time I toured it. Settled on one of the Thousand Islands, it was a landmark for the area that everyone wanted to see.

Isla couldn't get enough and asked me if we could move there. I had to tell her it wasn't for sale, but that we could come back before summer was over. That had to be enough for her.

Elise texted when she left shore letting me know she would be at the castle in about thirty minutes. We made our way through the grounds once more, then headed to the dock when Elise said she was five minutes out.

The ride back to shore was much faster, but no less informative. Isla hung on Elise's every word and declared she wanted to be a captain when she was older, just like Elise.

Elise's eyes welled up. "You are the sweetest thing ever. I am looking forward to seeing you at the farm. Your dad has my number, so he can let me know when you're available."

Isla nodded.

"Thank you. And we'll see you later tonight."

Elise grinned. "Good. I was hoping you'd say that. It's going to be fun."

"Thanks, Elise. Bye."

"Bye!" Isla called as we disembarked.

Elise waved, then turned her attention to the new group of passengers.

Isla was slow walking back to the car, so I decided to head back to my parents' house so she could take a nap before we went out again. She protested, but she was asleep by the time we made it there. I debated driving around instead of carrying her inside and drove right past my parents' house and kept going.

MacKellar Cove had built up since I'd left. It was still a small town, but there was a lot more than when I was in high school. I headed out of town and drove north, then went back toward town so we weren't late for the event.

I found parking a few blocks from Catherine Park and woke Isla gently. She blinked her eyes open and stretched with a big yawn.

"Where are we?"

"We're going to see if we can find some friends. Do you still want to go?"

She nodded, not reaching for her buckle. She was exhausted.

"We don't have to. If you're tired, we can go back to grandma's."

She shook her head. "I want to see Elise."

"Okay. Then let's go." I turned the SUV off and went around to her door, helping her unbuckle and offering her a hand to climb out.

The center of town was packed and loud when we made it. July Fourth was the night before, and we sat on Mom's back patio and watched fireworks, but this seemed to be a continuation of the celebration with people waving flags and families dressed in red, white, and blue.

Isla held my hand tightly, her grip squeezing when the crowd grew thicker.

"Want me to carry you?" I asked her.

She nodded and lifted her arms for me to pick her up. She immediately put her head on my shoulder and wrapped her arm around my neck.

I pressed a kiss to her forehead and hugged her tight. It wouldn't be long before I couldn't carry her, and before she didn't want me to, but for now, I was going to enjoy the little moments with her.

We made it to Catherine Park and looked around for anyone who was familiar. I wove through the families and friends who waited for food from food trucks, sat on blankets and chairs and listened to music, and shouted greetings across the park to each other.

We went from one side of Catherine Park to the other and found ourselves in front of Cracked. Where a massive mural of Mom's friend Ms. Georgia smiled down at us.

"Wow," I breathed. Ms. Georgia was kind and funny and welcoming to everyone. She and Mom worked together for years, forming a friendship that left Mom broken when Ms. Georgia died years ago.

"Who's that?" Isla asked me.

"That was grandma's friend, Ms. Georgia. She was a very nice woman."

"Yes, she was," a Black woman said, stopping next to me. "She was my mother."

"Karissa?" I asked.

The woman nodded. "I am. Do we know each other?"

I shook my head. "No, but my mom is Tina Harris."

Karissa grinned widely. "Oh, Kingsley. Good to see you. Mom loved Ms. Tina. They were so close. How is your mom? Oh, and your dad? He's home?"

I nodded. "Dad's home. Mom is doing well. She's taking care of him, and us. We're staying with them so I can run the clinic for him. This is my daughter, Isla."

Karissa's eyes narrowed, clearly knowing my history but not asking in front of Isla. "It's so nice to meet you, Isla. Tell your parents I said hello."

"I will. The mural is stunning. I didn't know MacKellar Cove had someone who could do something like that. It looks just like your mom."

"My friend, Blake, did it. She worked with your mom, too."

"I know Blake!" Isla said. "She gave me French Toast."

Karissa laughed. "She knows her French Toast."

"I had no idea she painted. We saw her this morning. She suggested we come here for this."

"Oh, good. I was heading back to them. Want to walk with me?"

I nodded, and Isla wiggled to climb down. She reached for Karissa's hand.

"Is that okay?" I asked Karissa.

"Of course."

Isla grabbed my hand, too, and the three of us moved through the crowd. Karissa waved to a dozen people, and said hello to more, but she didn't waver from her path.

When she stopped, we were met with a huge group of people, about half of whom I recognized.

"I found Kingsley and Isla," Karissa declared.

"Oh, good. We were wondering if you were going to make it," Blake said. She smiled at Isla. "Nice to see you."

"Hi, Blake!"

Blake took Isla's hand and looked at me with raised eyebrows. I followed her gaze to the kids in the center of their circle, free to be kids with adults surrounding them, and nodded.

"Do you want to meet the other kids?" Blake asked.

Isla nodded, following Blake without a second of hesitation.

"Hey," a woman said with her hand on my back.

I turned and saw Elise. "Hey. This place is busy."

She hugged me, then gripped my bicep. "It is. I'm glad Karissa found you two. Come meet everyone."

I followed her around the circle where she introduced me to her husband, Colin, then to a dozen more local men. I recognized many of them, but I knew they were older than me and not men I went to high school with. The women were the same, familiar but not classmates.

When Elise made it around to Derek and Chelsea, Chelsea hugged me. "Good to see you again. Out of the office this time."

I smiled. "You, too."

"Maybe you'll take Derek up on his offer to meet up with everyone since you're meeting them all today."

I grinned at Derek, who only smiled. "My wife's a little pushy."

"It's okay. It's good to have people you can count on."

"Very true."

"No Dozer today?" another woman said from right next to me.

I knew that voice, and my body responded instantly to it. Tingles erupted everywhere, my dick springing to life. In the middle of a park full of families.

Chelsea laughed, oblivious to my reaction. "We figured it would be too busy today. Too many distractions for him to listen well. But you need to come visit."

"I will. I already miss him. I'm just happy he was okay." Daisy smiled and looked up at me, then startled. "Oh. I didn't realize... How are you, Dr. Harris?"

"Fine," I said, half-grunt, half-grumble.

Daisy smiled, but I couldn't take it.

I moved away, going to the other side of the circle of friends so I was not near Daisy and her brightness. I would do something incredibly stupid if I was close to her for too long.

I took in the crowd and kept an eye on Isla, smiling as she played with the kids older and younger than her. She didn't have a lot of kids she spent time with at home. I was always working, and she didn't have a friend she was close to.

But here, she was one of many. She laughed and helped the little kids, and she looked up to the bigger kids. She was in her element, her earlier exhaustion gone.

"She's fitting right in with the rest of them," Blake's husband, Ian, said. "They're a great group of kids."

"They are. Isla doesn't have that at home."

"Where's home?" Ian asked.

"Near Philadelphia."

"But you're from here?"

I nodded.

"I can't imagine living anywhere else. Of course, this is where Blake is, so leaving wasn't ever an option for me."

"You two have been together a while?"

Ian snorted. "Not as long as I've been in love with her. I fell hard for Blake in high school, but she didn't give me the time of day until a few years ago. After Ms. Georgia died, actually. She pushed me to tell Blake how I felt about her."

"That doesn't surprise me. She was always one who wanted people to live every minute and share your love."

Ian nodded. "Yeah, she was. Still miss her."

"Yeah."

"Blake says Isla is a fan of water. I have a few boats I let friends take out if you're ever interested in cruising around the River."

"You don't even know me, though."

Ian chuckled. "You've been away too long. Everyone knows everyone. And Blake knows your mom, Elise knows you. We're all good. And I know how tough it is to keep kids busy. Especially without summer camp."

"I'm working constantly to keep my dad's practice alive, so my mom's watching Isla. I haven't spent nearly enough time with her as I'd planned to this summer," I confessed.

"That happens. And it sucks. Our parents take care of our kids when we're working. My schedule is pretty flexible, but I still need to work." Ian nodded to the two little ones Blake was talking to in the middle of the circle.

"With my dad home now, I think it's going to get harder on my mom to take care of Isla and my dad. I just don't know my options. My wife died before Isla turned one, so it's always been just the two of us, and I usually take all my vacation in the summer."

"I'm sorry. I didn't know," Ian said, his eyes glued to his wife. "I can't imagine it."

"I hope you never can."

Ian smiled.

"Hey, can you watch her for a minute? I'm going to grab something for us to eat."

"Of course. She's good here."

"Thanks." I told Isla I was going to get food and to listen to the other adults, then went in search of dinner that would be better for her than loaded French Toast.

I walked the line of all the food trucks and decided to get us grilled sandwiches and waters. As I was waiting for the line to move forward, I looked back at the crowd of people and tried to ignore the pang of loss in my chest.

This could have been my home. It could have been where I raised my daughter, where Faith and I built our lives together.

Instead, we were just visiting. Isla would have to go back to her school, and I would go back to my job. It would be just the two of us again.

I stumbled as someone ran right into me, nearly knocking me off my feet.

"I am so sorry. I wasn't paying attention. Are you okay?"

It was her. Again. I couldn't get away from her. And I couldn't stop thinking about her.

I opened my mouth to tell her I was fine, but that wasn't what came out.

"Go out with me."

## 10

DAISY

I grinned before I could stop myself. Yeah, he always seemed annoyed by something, and maybe giving him another chance was insane, but I was also so drawn to the man I literally couldn't avoid him.

"Yes," I said.

But he spoke at the same time. "No."

"No?"

"I mean... Yes? You said yes?"

I eyed him. "I did. But you said no."

"I..." He shook his head, as though shaking some sense into himself. "Are you sure?"

I chuckled. "Well, you're the one who asked me, and you're the one who ran out on our last date, so maybe I should ask you if you're sure."

He stared at me, gawked really. His brown eyes were intense, like he was seeing inside me instead of just the woman on the outside. It was... exciting.

I didn't want to hide from him because this man had already seen me terrified, and rejected, and he was trying again. It wasn't his fault his mother signed him up for online dating. But this time, it was up to him.

"Yeah, I'm sure," he said after a very long minute.

"Okay then."

He smiled. "Okay then."

"Next!"

"Um, it's your turn," I said, laughing that he was just staring at me instead of paying attention to the long line of customers behind him.

"Oh. Thanks. Um, do you want anything?"

"Is this our date?" I asked, smirking and secretly hoping he'd say no.

He shook his head. "No, but I am happy to get you something if you're hungry."

"I'm always hungry, but I'm going to the next truck. Thanks."

He nodded, then stepped up to the window. He ordered two sandwiches, and I wondered if he was buying me lunch anyway, but as I waited for my line to move, he turned and walked away with his two sandwiches and two waters.

I ordered my lunch, then carried it back to the group, a little surprised to find Kingsley talking to Ian when I walked up.

I moved to the other side of the circle where Chelsea and Derek were talking to Haley and Knox and cooing over Haley's latest ultrasound pictures and looking at each other like they were going to be next to get pregnant.

"How are you feeling?" I asked Haley. She was my hair stylist and one of the sweetest people I'd ever met. She and Knox were adorable together, and I was so happy she ended up staying in town.

"I'm tired all the time, and it's getting harder and harder

to stand all day, but I've been really lucky. It's been a pretty easy pregnancy," Haley said.

Knox rubbed her lower back. "She's amazing. There's a reason women have babies and men don't. I'd have been on the floor and ready to give up months ago, but she just keeps going. She's stronger than me, that's for sure."

"You're helping more than you know." Haley turned to me. "He rubs my feet every morning and every night. He rubs my back when I get home from work. And he hasn't let me do anything at home in months. He cooks and cleans and is there for every appointment. He's already an amazing dad."

Knox kissed the side of her head and whispered something in her ear. Haley looked up at him and puckered her lips for a kiss.

Love was such an amazing thing. It gave Haley a home, and it gave Chelsea a family, and it gave Natalie a new level of confidence. It gave all my friends something they never knew they were missing.

But I knew I was missing it. I'd never been someone's priority. I never had a man who would do everything for me the way Knox was for Haley, or a man who encouraged my dreams the way Omar did for Natalie. I loved their men because I loved my friends, and I was ready to find my own.

Maybe I had, I thought as I caught Kingsley watching me. He looked away quickly, like he was embarrassed to be caught, but it just made me smile.

Because life was full of chances.

How do you go on a date with someone who doesn't have your phone number and doesn't know much of anything about you? I wondered about that for a few days, until I got a message on Book Boyfriends Wanted.

DRGRUMPY

So, I never got your number. And I never set a time to meet. Are you still interested?

I grinned to myself. He was definitely not used to dating. That was okay with me. It meant I'd see the real man instead of the person he thought to show to others.

FOREVERPLAYING

Yes, I'm interested. Are you available tonight?

DRGRUMPY

I work until 6.

FOREVERPLAYING

Do you want to meet after?

DRGRUMPY

As long as you don't mind me coming straight from work.

FOREVERPLAYING

I don't mind at all.

I smiled to myself. Definitely not getting something less than all him.

DRGRUMPY

Do you want to meet at the same place as last time?

FOREVERPLAYING

Works for me. See you then.

DRGRUMPY

I locked my phone and went back to work. I had a date. With the sexy, grumpy doctor.

Wait. It was with him, right? Not his mother?

I opened the conversation and went through it again. There wasn't much to it, but when I read what we'd written before, what his mother had written, it felt different.

Did she know we were planning to meet up? That he asked me out? Or was it really him?

I shrugged and put my phone down again. The only way to find out was to show up. I had a feeling his mother wouldn't set us up again after last time, but how did he get access to the conversation?

I couldn't worry about that. It was going to work out or it wasn't. Stressing never changed things, so I had to choose to be open to the possibility of meeting a man I was attracted to.

It was all going to be fine.

I SAT at a table and sipped my drink. Hudson wasn't there, so I was fairly anonymous as I waited for Kingsley to show up for our date. I recognized a fair number of people, but none I knew well enough to speak to without a reason. And I wasn't looking for a reason when I was waiting for my date.

I watched the door, hoping Kingsley walked in. If it wasn't him, or if this was another setup by his mother, I would be disappointed, but he asked me out in person, so I was hopeful he was going to show up.

My drink was almost gone. It was six-thirty. I was starting to lose hope that he was coming. But the door opened, and there he was.

He looked around, and when his gaze landed on me, the corner of his mouth quirked up.

He took the seat opposite mine. "Hi."

I grinned. "Hi."

"Can I get you something to drink?" the server asked, appearing next to us.

Kingsley gestured to my drink. "Refill?"

I nodded. "Peach margarita."

She nodded, then turned to Kingsley. "Club soda with lime, please."

"Be right back," she said, walking away without writing anything down. I was always impressed by that, especially when I saw her stop by two more tables before going back to the bar.

"I would ask if you've been waiting long, but if you've finished a drink, obviously you were. I apologize for that."

I shook my head. "It's okay. I didn't have anything going on this afternoon, so I came early. I wasn't sure what time you'd get here."

"Before I forget, can I get your number?" He offered me his phone, letting me choose if I wanted to take it.

I took it, seeing he had already unlocked it, and added my contact information. "I was wondering how you reached out."

He chuckled. "That was not a fun conversation with my mother. She was thrilled, though. Said this was only proving she was right. I'm never going to live that down."

I laughed.

"I just sent you a text so you have my number, too."

"Thanks," I said.

The server brought our drinks back and asked if we needed anything else. We both shook our heads.

"So..." he started.

"So?"

He shrugged. "I haven't been on a first date in more than a decade. What am I supposed to ask you?"

"Whatever you want. I'm not really a serial dater, but I'm also interested in finding someone to settle down with one day."

His brows shot up.

"Yeah, I know. Saying that on the first date is rushing things. I'm not saying that's what I expect. We've only had a few conversations, and mostly not by choice. But I don't think hiding the truth is the right thing to do."

"I'm not... I don't live here. When summer is over, I'm going to back to Philadelphia."

I nodded. "I know." I sipped my drink, knowing it was giving me a little extra courage. "But I find you attractive."

His eyes heated at my admission. "I feel the same."

"Good. That's step one."

"Step one?"

"If there's no attraction, this is a waste of our time."

"True. Are you always this direct?"

"No. But something tells me you appreciate it."

"I do. I'm just not used to it."

"Did you read the messages on the app?"

"Messages? Oh, from my mother?"

I nodded.

"I did. Is that okay?"

"Of course. It makes it easier to know you have seen them, even though you didn't write them."

"Some of it was me."

"Excuse me?" I tilted my head, entirely confused.

"Not that I was messaging you, but she asked me questions."

"Okay..."

He laughed. "I know. She asked what my last supper would be when we were cooking one night. Said it was something online."

"Not a lie. Interesting way of concealing the truth."

"Yeah," he said with a chuckle. "That's one way to put it."

"What about the turtle cheesecake?"

He nodded, his throat working hard. "My wife used to make it all the time for me." His voice was soft, like talking about her was hard.

I wasn't sure if I was supposed to know anything about her or not. What was the protocol for something like that? "Um, so I know she was in an accident. I'm so sorry."

He pressed his lips together. "I figured you knew. And thank you."

"I also heard you two were perfect together."

He breathed what might have been a laugh. "We were. She made me a better man in every way."

"Have you dated a lot since?"

He held my gaze and shook his head. "No."

"Does... Does that mean not much or not at all?"

"Not at all."

"Oh."

"Look, I know after four years I should be ready, but I have been busy with my kid."

"I'm not judging you. I promise. It had to be hard to lose her. To believe your whole life was planned out, and then it all changes. I... I would never presume to understand what that would be like."

He held my gaze for a long moment, then nodded. "Thank you. Most people ask why I'm not dating. Why I'm not remarried. It's all... I never considered it before I—"

"Before you what?" I hung on every word, desperate to know what he was thinking. What changed? When?

His gaze burned mine, sending heat through my entire body. "Before I met you."

I gasped. "Is that a line?"

He puffed a laugh. "No. I'm not staying here. I'm not building a life here. But I seem to keep running into you. I... I like running into you."

"I am not complaining."

"It's not really fair of me to get involved with you, though."

"Why not?"

"Because you're looking for forever, and I'm not there yet."

"Isn't that how all relationships go? One person is ready for more, and the other one either catches up or things end?"

"Yeah, but if we're going into this knowing things are going to end, is it worth it?"

I grinned. "Every experience is worth it. Even the ones that don't work out have the opportunity to teach us something. Something about ourselves, about others, about what we want or need or like. If I said no to everything because it wasn't going to last forever, I'd never do anything."

He stared at me for a long moment, then shook his head. "I don't know if I have the same ability."

"Would you have dated and married your wife if you knew her life was going to end when it did?"

He jerked back and sucked in a breath. "Wow."

"We don't usually get to know the ending. We hold on to hope, praying what we want is ours forever, but it's not always the case. There are so many things in my life I wanted to last forever but didn't. But if I never experienced those things, I wouldn't be the same person I am now."

He nodded. "That's true."

"With this, with us, we know it's going to end. There's a deadline. You're leaving…"

"End of summer. End of August."

"So we have six or seven weeks until then?"

"Yeah."

"We can enjoy that time and know it'll be bittersweet because it will end, or we can stay away from each other and wonder if we could have had a great summer."

"You're…"

"I know," I said, my cheeks warming. Most people didn't understand me. I was an eternal optimist who believed in the good of the world. I was always looking for the bright side of things. It would be hard to end a relationship, but it would be easier knowing the end was coming. Knowing we were just going to spend time together and have fun. There would be no deep feelings. No attachments. No pain. Because we knew the end would come.

"Amazing," he finally said.

My head jerked up. "What?"

"I feel like I'm taking advantage of you. Asking you to… I don't even know what I'm asking. This makes no sense to me."

"It doesn't have to make sense. Honestly, it doesn't make sense to me either. I know you're leaving. That's not what I want. That's not what I'm looking for. I know my screen name makes it seem like it, but—"

"That didn't even occur to me." He smirked.

"That's not what it's about. I want a future. I want a partner. But I want to stay in MacKellar Cove."

He nodded. "And I can't."

I nodded with him. We were in complete agreement, and completely confused.

"So, is that a yes?" he asked.

I offered him my hand. He looked down at it, smirked, then shook my hand. "To a temporary future that is whatever we decide to make it."

"Does this mean I have to tell my mother she was right?"

I snorted. "I'd rather not have your mother involved in this, but it's up to you what you tell her."

"Would you feel better if no one knew about us?"

I considered the question. I wasn't leaving at the end of summer. I would be the one facing rumors. But that didn't mean I wanted to hide. "I think it should be based on what feels right. I will tell some of my friends, probably, but I'm not going to show up at your clinic and demand to see you because we're... something."

"Dating?" he offered.

"Dating." I rolled the word around and liked it. I couldn't think of a word that worked better.

"So now what?"

"Now?"

He leaned closer. "Do I get to kiss you?"

I grinned. "I think that could be arranged."

One eyebrow quirked up. "Good to know."

"Good to know."

He tossed cash on the table and stood, offering me his hand. He helped me to stand, not yanking me against him like I half-expected. He allowed me to go ahead of him, one hand resting on my lower back and sending tingles all through my body.

We got outside, and he turned to the right. "Can I give you a ride home?"

"You don't have to do that."

"You had two drinks, and I'd rather not have you drive, if that's okay."

I nodded. "Thank you. I walked here, though. I wouldn't drive after I had something to drink."

"Are you trying to get rid of me?"

I shook my head. "No. Not at all. I just…"

"Don't like counting on others?" he suggested, hitting far closer to the mark than I liked.

"Maybe."

He nodded. "I know the feeling. What if I told you I'm being selfish, too, and hoping I can kiss you when I drop you off?"

"Well, that's a whole different thing. You should have led with that."

He laughed loudly and shook his head. He jerked his head to a dark SUV that blinked at us. "That's me."

I walked with him, smiling when he opened the passenger door for me. I took a second to look around the vehicle when he walked around to the driver's side. The booster seat in the back reminded me he was a father. A single father.

I'd never dated a single dad before.

Was I making the right decision?

I chewed my lip until he got in next to me. The interior lights went out, plunging us into darkness, and Kingsley leaned across the console.

"Can I kiss you now?"

I nibbled my lip and nodded.

He moved cautiously, like he wasn't sure I meant it. His hand went to my cheek, smoothing over my skin. His gaze dropped to my lips. He leaned closer, the whisper of his breath across my cheeks growing stronger as he approached.

It felt like high school. My first kiss with a boy who

didn't know what he was doing. I didn't then either, and we fumbled through it together.

But I wasn't that innocent teenager anymore. I was a grown woman who knew exactly what I wanted. And this man was it.

I hooked my hand behind his neck and brought my lips to his, meeting him closer to his side. A surprised grunt escaped him, but I didn't stop.

His lips were warm, soft, and insistent against mine. He didn't wait for permission to slick his tongue over my lips and seek entry.

I welcomed him in, teasing him with my tongue and letting myself get lost in the kiss.

He groaned softly, his fingers tightening next to my jaw, tilting my head to suit his needs. His thick tongue filled my mouth, turning me on in ways I hadn't been in far too long.

He pulled back after a minute, panting and gripping his steering wheel like it was the only thing keeping him from stripping me right then and there.

"Definitely a good idea to spend the summer together," I whispered.

He turned to look at me and laughed. "You're not going to get any complaints from me."

I grinned, and he pulled away from the curb, following my directions until he made it to my house. We kissed in the driveway until all his windows fogged up and his phone rang and we agreed to get together again soon.

Very soon.

# 11

I woke up in a tangle of sheets with Kingsley's kisses on my mind. I smiled to myself and enjoyed the feeling of being wanted. It had been a while since I'd felt that. Longer than I realized. Building Lincoln Toys and running it the first year meant a lot more time alone than I'd expected.

But things were improving. I had a staff that was helping keep the place running on a day-to-day basis, and things were working well with Penny handling the inventory. Dating shouldn't have been an indulgence, but it was.

A sexy, fun, sweaty indulgence. One I couldn't wait to explore more of.

I jumped in the shower, taking an extra few minutes to enjoy the sensations of desire running through me, and got dressed. Natalie was not a morning person, so I attempted to tamp down my AM energy, but I was really excited to tell her about my date.

"Morning," she said when I walked into the kitchen.

"Hi!"

She cringed at my exuberance.

"Sorry. I know it's too early for you."

"I don't know how you do it."

I grinned. "I had a really good night."

"You did? What happened?"

I had her full attention. She stared at me with wonder in her eyes and a smile on her lips. "You know, don't you?"

She shook her head. Her smile faded. "Know what?"

"That I was on a date last night. How did you know?"

"You had a date?"

"Don't sound so shocked," I said, fighting my smile. "I've been in a dry spell, I know."

"You know I'm not going to judge that. But I really didn't know you had a date. Who was it with?"

"Kingsley Harris."

"Dr. Harris?" Natalie shouted.

I nodded.

"I thought he was married."

"He was, but his wife died in a car accident."

"Seriously? How did I not know that? When?"

I shrugged. "I don't know. Four years ago, I think. I didn't know you knew them."

"Not well, of course, but there's only one vet in town. Everyone knows him, I think. I thought he was just in the hospital or something? You didn't give him a heart attack, did you?"

"What? He's..." I realized what Natalie thought and burst out laughing. I laughed so hard I had to put my coffee mug down and sit in a chair before I fell over.

Natalie gawked at me. "It wasn't that funny of a question."

"No, it was. Oh my God. I'm dying. And I'm not seeing him. His son."

"You said Dr. Harris!"

"I know. He's a vet, too. I didn't expect you to think I was dating a married guy who's twenty years older than me. Maybe more. I've never even met the older Dr. Harris."

"Okay, that makes a lot more sense. I was starting to worry about you!"

"I was wondering what you were thinking."

I snorted and shook my head. "Well, thank you for setting me straight."

"Okay, so the son. I didn't know there was a son around."

"He's not. Not really. He lives in Philadelphia. He's just helping out for the summer."

"For the summer?"

I nodded and sipped my coffee.

"So, he's going back to Philadelphia?"

"Yeah. At the end of summer."

"But... So... What am I missing, Daisy? I thought you wanted a family. To settle down."

"I do. But I like him. He's interesting and really cute and he intrigues me."

"But he's leaving."

"I know."

"And you're okay with that?"

"Yeah. It's fine. We know the score. It's not something that's going to be a problem."

"I'm not so sure about that, Daisy. It's really easy to fall for someone who feels right, even when you know you shouldn't."

"I'll be fine, Natalie. I'm not worried."

"I just don't want you to get hurt."

"I won't. It's fine. We're good."

She pursed her lips and studied me carefully.

I was hurt. She was my best friend. The one person who'd always been there for me and always made me feel like I could do anything. And instead of supporting me, she was questioning me. She was making me feel like I was wrong for choosing to spend time with Kingsley.

I encouraged her with Omar. Every step of the way. I always supported her.

"I love you, Daisy."

"I love you, Natalie."

"Just... be careful, okay?"

"I will. It's fine. I should get to work. I'll see you later."

She nodded, not stopping me as I headed for the door.

I got in my car and realized I ran out before I had breakfast. I was running away from my best friend. It was not how I wanted to start my day.

I spent my drive to work changing my mind about my day. I wasn't going to let Natalie convince me I was making the wrong decision. It might be the wrong decision, but I was okay with that. I knew if I didn't take chances once in a while, I would never experience anything. And after more than a year of concentrating on work and not dating at all, I was ready to have some new experiences.

Doing that with someone who was not going to be a forever person worked for me.

It didn't matter that Natalie didn't get it. She didn't have to. It was going to be hard to keep it from her, but it would be okay. I was okay with a summer fling.

I stopped by Cracked and picked up breakfast to go, then headed to work.

My earlier excitement came back when I got to work. It wasn't about Kingsley, but I was at my happiest place. Things were going well, deliveries were coming in as planned, and I was finding a way to have a life.

It was a busy day with parents shopping with kids, adults shopping for friends' kids, and kids running around and enjoying their day. I couldn't have asked for anything better.

By the time I was leaving work for the day, I regained my good mood. I understood where Natalie was coming from, but I didn't share her concerns. It was all going to be fine. Kingsley and I were good. We were getting to know each other, having fun together, and when he left, it was all going to be fine.

Natalie wasn't home when I got there, and I had to admit I wasn't entirely disappointed. I loved my bestie, but I wasn't ready for another argument. Nothing had changed, and rehashing the same thing would not make either of us feel better.

I changed out of my clothes from the day and looked through the fridge for something to eat, smiling when I found a container with leftovers from two nights ago. "Jackpot."

I heated up my food, then carried it to the couch, curling up on the end and turning on a baking competition show. I was constantly amazed by the talent of the bakers and daydreamed about being able to produce something half as stunning without actually wanting to put in the time to learn how.

One episode turned to two, and I covered up with a blanket, settling in for another hour or two of the show. Just as the judging started, there was a knock on my door.

I stared at the TV as I walked to the door, remote in hand so I could pause the show. I hit the pause button and opened the door at the same time.

"Kingsley."

"Hi," he said, stepping into my home.

I backed up to let him in, smiling when he kicked the door closed.

"I wanted to see you."

"Well, you can see me."

His gaze scanned my body. His eyes lit up. "Are you busy?"

I pointed to the TV. "Very. I'm about to find out who made the best cake."

He followed my gaze to the TV and smirked. "Important stuff."

I nodded. "It is. Their whole futures depend on me watching the show and finding out how it ends."

"You are a very important person."

I smiled. "I am. You should remember that."

"I will." He moved closer to me. "Do you live alone?"

I shook my head. "Roommate."

He sighed.

"But she's not home."

He smirked. "Is that so?"

I nodded. "It is."

He reached for my hand and plucked the remote from it. He tossed the remote onto the couch and stepped into my personal space, slowly, so I had plenty of opportunity to move away from him.

Silly man. That was the opposite of what I wanted.

I stood still and allowed him to draw closer and closer until there was no space between us. I looked up at him, the four or five inches of height between us more pronounced when he was so close.

"I haven't been able to stop thinking about kissing you," he rasped.

"I haven't been able to stop thinking about it either."

"I couldn't wait another day to see you."

"I'm happy to hear that."

"I'm going to kiss you again, Daisy."

"Are you? Because there seems to be a lot of talking—"

His lips claimed mine, stealing the words from me and showing me he was serious.

I returned the kiss with a moan, wrapping my arms around his neck and pulling him impossibly closer.

His hands went to my hips, dragging our bodies into full contact. Hard met soft, fingers met flesh, and I backpedaled toward my bedroom, wanting him all to myself.

We bounced off the walls, but kept moving, finding the hallway in between kisses that had me grinning and eager for more. More of him, more fun, more of all of it.

His hand found my bare skin just as we moved into my bedroom. I paused, moaning at the contact. He felt so good. How could I resist this? How could I say no to a few weeks of him?

"You're thinking very hard," he whispered against my lips.

"Then maybe you should make me stop."

He slid his hand up and cupped my bare breast, groaning when he found my exposed skin. "No bra?"

"I wasn't planning on company tonight. Are you complaining?"

"Hell no," he growled, tugging my shirt up and lifting it away from my body. His gaze dropped to my breasts seconds before his lips followed.

He pressed me against the wall next to my door, devouring my nipples and leaving wet kisses on my breasts as he teased and tortured me with his tongue.

I held his head, running my fingers through his hair and closing my eyes to enjoy the sensations. I couldn't think of the last time I had someone worship my breasts the way he did. It was transcendent. Like going to another plane of existence. I was a sucker for a man who spent his time on my breasts instead of jumping down my pants, and this one was definitely taking his time.

His teeth bit into my skin, making me gasp with pleasure. "You like that?"

"Yeah," I breathed, trying not to be too eager for more of him. God, was this what it was like to be with a man who was in no hurry? Who wanted to draw every last ounce of pleasure from me?

He turned to my other breast and flicked the tip of his tongue over my nipple, pinching the first one at the same time.

My hips rocked with his movements, an orgasm building. He hadn't gotten my pants off, and I was panting and halfway to heaven.

"Damn, you're stunning," he said. "Are you gonna come like this?"

"I might," I admitted.

"That sounds like a challenge to me."

"Please," I breathed.

He cupped both breasts and brought my nipples to his mouth. The sharp tug of lifting them up made his bite more potent, more torturous.

I pressed my breasts into his mouth, loving that he didn't fight me on it. He sucked them in, his tongue flicking both together, then circling each before he bit down and tugged, sending a spark through me that lit me up.

"Kingsley," I groaned.

He didn't reply, didn't look up, didn't change a thing.

I loved it.

His licks and nibbles cranked up my blood pressure and desire. My hips continued to rock, my release building with each tug on my body, each swipe of his tongue across my primed skin. Then he changed the game and pulled back, blowing on my wet flesh, then sucking them back into his mouth with a deep pull that sent an answering tug between my thighs, one that tipped me over the edge.

"Oh, yes," I breathed, letting go and falling as he deep-throated my breasts, rolling my nipples against the roof of his mouth.

"That was amazing," he said, releasing me with a pop. He breathed on my soaked skin, sending goosebumps all over my body. "Tell me you're not done."

I shook my head, eyes closed to half-mast and watching him from the edge of my lashes. "Tell me you're not done either."

"Not even close. But I'm hoping our clothes might be."

I nodded and reached for his shirt. He helped me tug it over his head and toss it with mine, then we both fumbled to remove our bottoms and underwear, finding each other naked at the same time.

"Fucking hell, you're stunning," he whispered, reaching out to touch me.

"You're beautiful," I said, letting my eyes roam his body. Dark hair curved around his pecs and narrowed to a line on his abdomen, pointing to a very hard, very thick erection nestled in more dark hair. His legs were thick and strong, his abs not at all defined and soft. I felt just a tiny bit less self-conscious about my body when faced with a man who clearly cared about more than hitting the gym every day. He wouldn't judge me for skipping... every workout.

I hoped.

"I... Shit. I don't have any condoms," he said, his hands dropping to his sides.

"I do," I told him, remembering the box Natalie picked up a month ago. I hoped there were still some left. Or that she'd bought a new box.

I hurried across the hall to her room, opening her sink cabinet. There in front was a box, opened, but still mostly full. I'd have to buy her a new box, but it would be worth it to not delay my night with Kingsley.

I raced back to him, a strip of condoms in my hand.

He smiled when he saw how many I brought back. "Feeling ambitious?"

I laughed. "I figured it would be better to have a few in here. Just in case we need more than one."

"I like the way you think."

"Good."

He took the condoms from me and tore one off. He tossed the others toward the bed and ripped into the package he kept.

I stared as he squeezed himself, stroked once, then positioned the condom at his tip. He paused and looked up at me, smiling when he saw me watching him, then rolled the condom down his length.

He jerked his head toward the bed and held out a hand for me to join him. He waited for me to climb on the bed first, then stretched out over me, lowering his body onto mine.

I loved feeling the weight of him on me, pressing me into the mattress. He kissed me, taking his time again instead of pushing into me and pumping away. It wasn't what I expected, but I was not going to complain about a man who wanted to kiss me and play with my body and get me all revved up before sex.

He held himself up on one arm, using his other hand to toy with my nipple again. His kisses were sweet, gentle and teasing and in total contrast to the way he twisted and pinched my nipple. I found myself writhing against him one second and sighing in pleasure the next, my body and brain fighting to figure out which it wanted to lean into.

Both.

When his hand skimmed down my belly, abandoning my breast, and settled between my thighs, I finally made a choice. That one. That was the one I wanted to focus on. His fingers pressed into me, his cock twitching against my hip as a groan escaped him. He pumped his fingers into me, withdrawing completely and spreading my wetness up to my clit.

He pinched my clit between his fingers and tugged, pulling on the tight bundle of nerves and nearly ending up with a black eye when I jerked forward and almost headbutted him.

"I'm sorry," I breathed. "Oh, shit."

"Would have been worth it," he gritted out.

He kissed me again, stealing my breath as an orgasm rushed up on me out of nowhere. My hips bounced on the bed, fucking his hand as he tugged and rubbed my clit, sending me up and over the edge and into a blissful warmth.

He kissed me back to reality, brushing the hair back from my face as he lined himself up between my legs. I gasped at the fullness of him when he surged inside me.

A moan fell from one of us, maybe both of us, and I wondered why in the hell I waited so long to have sex again.

"Waited for what?" he asked, pulling back just enough to get the words out.

"It's been a while," I admitted.

"Same," he said, avoiding my gaze.

Shit. Shit, shit, shit. Was he telling me? No. I couldn't be the first woman he'd slept with since his wife died. No, there was—

"Oh, fuck," I cried when he retreated, then slammed deep into me again.

He did it again and again, his strokes deep enough to steal my thoughts and send them scattered to the far edges of my consciousness.

I lifted my knees, spreading myself wide to take more of him in. He grunted and pumped harder, his gaze landing on me. He looked at my breasts, bouncing with his rhythm, and went faster.

The two orgasms he gave me had me more than ready, and when he shifted just slightly, I soared without warning. "Oh, shit. Kingsley. Yes."

My whispered words were met with excess grunts and a soul-deep thrust that left him still inside me, a twist of pleasure on his face as he let go.

I watched him, loving the look of pure bliss on his face, and trusting that I was making the right choice. Sex had never been so good for me before. Not even once. And this man, this gorgeous, absent, wounded man, he was not going to break me. Because he was safe. I knew the score with him, and when our time was up, I'd let him go back to his life and I'd find someone else who made me feel the way he did but wanted to stick around MacKellar Cove forever.

It was all good.

## 12

KINGSLEY

I HADN'T PLANNED TO GO SEE HER. I DEFINITELY HADN'T planned to end up in her bed. But as I walked to the bathroom to get rid of the condom, I couldn't stop smiling.

She was a surprise. Being around her was easy. All I really wanted was to get rid of my bad mood from work before I had to spend the evening with my father. I was going to go for a drive, but my car ended up in her driveway.

She was still spread out on her bed when I walked back into her room, looking thoroughly ravished and very content. I leaned over to kiss her, smiling when she returned my kiss with an eagerness that said she enjoyed herself as much as I did.

"I hope you didn't mind me stopping over," I whispered against her lips.

"You are welcome to stop over any time you want," she said, the implication heavy in her voice.

I chuckled. "Good to know."

She let go of me and sat up, rushing to take her turn in the bathroom.

I didn't know the protocol for casual flings, but I was

pretty sure hanging around after sex was not part of the plan. Plus, I needed to get home to Isla.

No. I wanted to. I resented my dad for keeping me away from her. For having a heart attack and requiring me to be there instead of having time off to spend with my kid.

Add it to the list of reasons I didn't like him.

I pulled on my underwear and pants as the toilet flushed. By the time Daisy turned off the water, my shirt was on and I was ready to go.

She walked out and saw me, grinning before she grabbed her clothes. Guess she was in agreement with my thought. She pulled her shirt over her head and stepped into her shorts.

"I'll buy some condoms so you don't have to get them from your roommate," I said. Wow, I sucked at sexy talk.

She snickered. "Sounds good. Not that she minds, but..." The look on Daisy's face said her roommate might mind.

I considered asking, but I didn't think it was my place. Was it my place? What was I supposed to do here?

I hadn't been involved with a woman since Faith died. I hadn't even considered it. I hadn't wanted to. With Faith, I would have asked what she was thinking.

But Daisy wasn't Faith.

Shit. Daisy wasn't Faith.

"Um, I should go," I said quickly, making a move toward the door.

*Daisy wasn't Faith.*

"Thanks for stopping by," she said, opening the door and smiling as I stepped outside.

"Yeah. Thank you. Um, wow, that sounds weird."

She snorted. "I know what you mean. Hopefully you can stop by again soon."

I stopped. Did she expect to see me every day? "Um, tomorrow I have a thing."

"Okay," she said.

"I was invited to O'Kelley's."

"Oh, guys' night. Have fun."

"Is it a big thing around here? Derek made it sound like no big deal." I wasn't anxious before.

Daisy shook her head. "No, it's local men about our age. The women get together on Sunday nights, the men on Thursday. It's the same people who were together on Saturday at the event."

"Oh, okay. I wasn't sure…"

"From what I hear, it's very relaxed. It'll be good to meet some other locals. Or see them again. I forgot you probably know everyone."

I shook my head. "Not really. It's been a while since I've lived here. I don't know that many people anymore."

"Well, I hope you have fun anyway."

"Even though it means I won't be able to see you?" I blurted. Was she trying to trick me? Trap me? Make me feel bad for doing something else?

She shrugged. "I wouldn't expect to see you every day. We both work, you have a kid. We're not living together, and we're not heading that way. Have fun tomorrow."

I wasn't sure what to expect. She sounded sincere, and I wasn't into games or tricks. I could either choose to believe her or walk away. "Thanks."

She smiled and waved, then stepped back into her house. I waited until she closed the door, then went to my car and left.

Dating was never my strength. Faith found me, and even then she had to drag me out of the library to get me to do anything. It took me far too long to realize I was missing out on life by not spending more time with her, and after she died, I knew I would have done anything to have those days back.

But Faith was gone. I knew that. I accepted it. But dating wasn't something I thought about until Daisy.

But Daisy wasn't Faith.

Faith would have told me exactly what she was thinking. She would have ripped into me if I was being obtuse. Was Daisy the same? Did I want her to be?

It didn't matter because it was temporary. We were only going to last a few weeks, and when Isla and I went home, I'd never see Daisy again. She didn't have to be Faith because we weren't going to end up together. It was all good.

I parked in the driveway and sat there for a minute. My day was forgotten, the frustrations of working with my father's mistress gone. Because of Daisy. Because of a woman I'd known a few days and had no intention of staying involved with for long.

I warred with myself over the idea. Was it fair of me to do that? To sleep with her for a few weeks, then leave?

I'd never been that man. High school meant experimenting with girls and I wasn't a virgin when I started college, but once I met Faith, there was no one else.

Guilt swamped me, and I felt like I was going to be sick. Faith was no longer the last woman I slept with. The last one I kissed or held or let go with. On our wedding day, I thought she would be. Until a few weeks ago, I thought she would be.

Going from that to Daisy...

"Daddy!" Isla called, knocking on the door of my SUV.

My mom was on the porch, Isla at my door. Mom had a worried look on her face. Isla was trying to get to me.

I opened my door and scooped her up. "What are you doing out here?"

"You didn't come inside. Grandma said we should come get you."

I tickled Isla's side, making her squirm. Her little arms wrapped around my neck.

"I love you, Daddy."

"I love you, too, Isla."

I hugged her tight for a minute, then carried her inside, leaving all my worries about Daisy behind.

THE NEXT NIGHT, I forced myself to O'Kelley's instead of showing up at Daisy's house again. After pointed looks from my mother and questions about why I was so late, I made sure to tell Isla and my mother I was meeting Elise's husband and a few other local men for a drink. Once she heard who was going to be there, she encouraged me to have fun.

Fun. I was doing too much of that. I needed to get focused again. Work, Isla, home.

O'Kelley's was busy when I walked in, and I looked around for a group of men I recognized. My gaze strayed to the booths where I met Daisy for our date, but they were packed with couples and groups of friends. Daisy said guys' night, so I was expecting a bigger crowd.

A cheer went up from the bar, and I rolled my eyes before following the sound and realizing the cheer came from the group I was supposed to be meeting.

What did I get myself into?

I made my way over slowly, debating sticking around when I heard the animated conversation taking place.

"This one pulled his gun," one guy said, hooking his thumb toward a man I didn't know. Both appeared to be cops. "He was so freaked out, he was going to shoot her!"

The others laughed heartily, which gave me pause. Cops waving guns around and almost shooting people was not something I took lightly.

"Hey! Kingsley! You came," Derek said, waving me over to an empty seat next to him.

I nodded and moved past the cops to where Derek sat with a beer and a smirk. "What's going on?" I asked him.

"James and Rowan are local police. They sometimes partner up and it's always a disaster."

"Cops waving guns around usually is."

Derek nodded, his look telling me he understood exactly what I wasn't saying. As a Black man, I knew he got it. With a Black father and a white mother, I passed as white half the time, but racism was something I was well aware of and had witnessed my fair share of times. Especially with a Black wife and a daughter who looked more like her mother.

"Agreed," Derek said. "They're talking about tasers. It's rare they pull an actual gun around here. They've considered not having the cops carry them at all, but because they cover some areas closer to the mountains, they still have loaded weapons. Usually the weapons stay in the vehicle, though."

"That's good. What happened?"

"Raccoon," Derek said. "They got a call about a disturbance behind a property. Raccoons got into recycling and apparently someone dumped a mostly full bottle of booze without realizing it. Raccoons were drunk."

"Really?"

Derek nodded. "Yeah. Small town life. It's why I stuck around."

"Stuck around?" I asked, realizing I didn't know much about Derek.

He sipped his beer as another man came over behind the bar. He offered me his hand. "Kingsley Harris, right?"

"Yep. Forgive me, I can't place your name." I shook his hand, searching my memory.

"Hudson Grant. I'm a decade older than you, but Derek and Colin mentioned you were going to stop by. I think I saw you here with Daisy Lincoln a week or so ago."

"Baseball player," I said, remembering what my mother said and ignoring the question about Daisy.

"That's me. Now bar owner. And widower. I didn't have kids, though."

"Sorry to hear that. It's not something I want to have in common with anyone."

"Same. Welcome back to town."

"Thanks. It's temporary, but thanks."

"This place has a tendency to grow on you," Derek said. "I moved here with my ex. She left, I stayed."

"And then you met Chelsea?"

Derek nodded. "She bought the house next door to me, where Dozer almost knocked down the fence. I wasn't a very good neighbor."

"No, you weren't." Hudson chuckled, then turned to me. "Can I get you a drink?"

"Yeah, something on tap. Local?"

"Got it," Hudson said, grabbing a glass and walking to the other end of the bar to fill it.

"He'll get something you like," Derek said. "None of us know how he does it, but he has a sixth sense about what people like."

"Really?"

Derek nodded. "Craziest thing, but yeah."

"Interesting."

"Yeah."

Hudson set the beer in front of me and jerked his head to the side. "It's on James. He buys first beer for newcomers."

"Hey! What the heck?" the cop who was talking when I walked in shouted back.

"I can buy my own beer," I argued with Hudson.

Hudson shook his head. "All good. I like to mess with him. Beer's on the house."

"You don't have to do that either."

"Tradition around here. First time here for guys' night, and I buy the beer."

"How come I didn't get that deal?" James asked.

"Because I can barely get you to pay anytime you come," Hudson shouted back.

"Whatever." James got off his stool and walked over to me. He offered me his hand. "Kingsley, right? How's your dad?"

I bristled at the question, but I tried to cover the reaction. Not fast enough for a cop, though.

James's eyes narrowed, but he didn't ask me about my reaction.

"My dad's recovering. Driving my mom a little crazy."

"And you, I imagine."

I nodded. "Yeah, a bit. It's not how I hoped my summer would go."

"I imagine it never is when something like that happens. My wife's grandmother has had a few medical issues, and whenever something happens, we're gone, ready to be there. But they're only a couple hours away. We can be back home at night. You're here for the summer?"

"Yeah. I was planning to take some time off for the

summer, spend time with my daughter. Long days weren't part of my plan."

"How old?"

"Isla's four. Five in September."

"Is she into crafts and stuff? My wife makes jewelry and runs a program at the community center during the school year doing crafts with the kids. Because of summer camp, she doesn't do it this time of year, but she's gotten a few of the kids together if Isla ever wants to join." James looked down the line of men, encompassing the others in his conversation.

I was surprised by his willingness to include my kid, a stranger's kid. "She would love that. She's not getting a lot of interaction with other kids right now."

He pulled out his phone and tapped the screen a few times. "Oh, cool. She's got a thing tomorrow at four. Every Friday actually. Want me to send you the information?"

I nodded, surprised by James. "That would be great. Thank you."

"You bet." He handed me his phone to add my number. "And if you or your mom ever need an extra hand, let us know. Trinity works from home, but she's pretty flexible with her schedule. She's offered for a few of the others and sometimes will take some of the kids to Catherine Park or she'll get together with one or two stay-at-home moms and they'll watch a few extra kids for the day."

"Wow. That's..."

James grinned. "She's amazing. I don't know how I got so damn lucky, but she's one a kind, man." He turned his phone to show me a picture of him and a Black woman. "So you know what she looks like when you see her tomorrow. The thing is at Trent's house." James pointed to a Black man at the other end. "He's got the space."

I nodded, wondering what that meant but assuming I'd learn the next day. "Sounds good. Thanks for the invite. And you're sure she won't mind?"

He chuckled. "No. It's fun for her. We don't have kids, but she loves spoiling everyone else's kids."

"That's very cool of her."

"Yeah, like I said, I'm a lucky man."

I nodded, thinking I judged him all wrong, and was happy to be corrected.

"This group can get pretty big, so I'm glad I had a chance to say hello. I'm not sure if I'll be there tomorrow, but I hope to be. If not, I think Ian's going to be there." James looked at Derek. "You're at work?"

"I am, and Jude's at camp. We're going to catch one of Trinity's weekend events. Jude liked her projects when he was in afterschool care." Derek looked at me. "Jude's going into seventh grade and thinks he's an adult. But he's in summer camp for one last summer since Chelsea and I are both working full time. Her parents offered to keep him, but we didn't want to put that on them."

"I hate leaving Isla with my mom all day. She was signed up for a few weeks of camp in Philadelphia, but I canceled all that when we came here and realized we'd be staying all summer. It's a huge change for all of us."

James clapped both of us on the shoulder. "You're both amazing fathers."

"Thanks," we said together.

"You don't usually get too emotional," Derek said, raising one eyebrow at James.

James chuckled. "Yeah, well, maybe it's age. Trinity just turned thirty-nine in May, and I hit forty-four last month. We've been talking about kids a lot lately, and we're at that point where we feel like we're too old and missed out. We didn't really want kids, or were mostly undecided about having them, but now we feel like we're out of time, and it's a little different. Even if we adopted, I'd be in my sixties before a kid was out of high school, and Trinity would be late fifties."

"I'd never trade Jude, but the younger years were a lot. I'll be forty-four in October, but Chelsea's only thirty-two, so she's leaning toward more kids for us." Derek shrugged.

"One and done for you?" James asked me.

"My wife died in a car accident before Isla turned one, so kind of necessary," I told him.

"Fuck. I'm sorry, man. I didn't realize." James shook his head. "Hudson lost his first wife."

"First wife?" I asked. "He mentioned he was a widower, but he got remarried?"

James nodded. "Yeah, he's married now. It's been a couple of years. Anna has two boys, and they both call Hudson *dad*."

"Wow, that's..."

"It was a long time before he was willing to date. Anna came out of nowhere for him, but they're great together." James laughed at a memory. "He was a bit grumpy before her, but she challenged him. Pushed him in ways he needed to be pushed. And I think he did the same for her. She was a neighbor of mine, but we hadn't been in touch much before she and Hudson got together."

"You talking about me?" Hudson asked, pausing on the other side of the bar.

"Just telling Kingsley about you and Anna," James said.

Hudson's smile was pure and honest. "One of the best things to ever happen to me."

"One of?" I asked.

"I'd never trade the time I had with Hillary. Or discount

it. They're different, but both made me a better person. Anna's sons are another gift I didn't expect, but I love them like they were my own."

"I was telling them Trinity and I feel like we missed the boat on kids and are adjusting to that," James continued.

"I thought you guys didn't want kids," Hudson said.

James shook his head. "We didn't, but it was always nice to know the chance was there. I think it's okay, but something Trinity's been talking about. She just turned thirty-nine, so she's lamenting she's almost forty."

Hudson laughed. "Tell her to call Anna. That'll put her mind at ease. On both things."

James snorted. "I might do that. Hey, is Anna bringing Matty tomorrow?"

James followed Hudson down the bar and sat in his seat again, leaving Derek and me.

"Watch out for these guys," Derek said. "They'll try to set you up on the dating app everyone's used. Crazy accurate matches."

"Dating app?" I asked, my neck tingling.

"Yeah. But if you're happily single there's nothing to worry about. Just make sure they know that or they'll have you signed up and married off before you know it."

Derek laughed, but mine got stuck in my throat. There had to be more than one dating app. I was fine.

And I was not sticking around anyway.

It was fine.

## 13

---

THE LOOK ON ISLA'S FACE WAS WORTH EVERYTHING I'D
suffered through this summer. Worth the awkward days
with Sheila, worth the conversations my father tried to have
with me, worth the questions my mother asked that I
dodged.

It was all worth it for my daughter. Seeing the joy in her
eyes and the smile on her face, and the frustration, as she
worked hard to create the bracelet Trinity showed her, was
everything.

"How are we doing over here?" Trinity asked, joining Isla
and me at the table.

We were outside on MacKellar Cove, overlooking the
cove and Saint Lawrence River, on the most stunning piece
of property I'd ever been to. When James invited us, he
failed to mention *Trent* was Trent MacKellar. Trent
MacKellar whose family founded the entire damn town. To
say I was starstruck and felt way out of my element was an
understatement.

But Trent and his wife, Finley, were welcoming and kind

and generous in ways I never expected but should have from people opening their home to others.

"This won't work," Isla said, the frustration in her voice telling me it wouldn't be long before I needed to step it.

"Can I look?" Trinity asked. It seemed small for her to ask, but I appreciated the hell out of Trinity for it. Most adults wanted to jump in and tell Isla, and all kids, how to do something, but giving Isla the opportunity to choose if she wanted help was invaluable.

Isla nodded, showing Trinity the bracelet and what she was struggling with.

Instead of taking it, Trinity examined it closely, then pointed. "I don't think this is going to fit. It isn't the right size."

"But that's how I want it," Isla said.

I hid my snicker since I told her the same thing ten minutes ago. She chose a string for her bracelet that was thicker than the opening in the bead she was trying to put on it.

"Then let's see what we can do. Sometimes, we can encourage it a little bit..." Trinity looked around the table before her gaze landed on something. Her eyes lit up. "Do you mind if I try since this is sharp?" She held up a needle.

Isla handed over her bracelet.

"These are beautiful colors you have together," Trinity said as she threaded the string into the thick needle. "Are these your favorite colors?"

Isla nodded, her eyes locked on Trinity's hands. "Yep. My daddy said my mommy always liked purple, but I like pink, so I like both. Daddy likes green."

"They work very well together," Trinity said, pushing the needle through the bead slowly, the strain on her face not coming through in her voice. "I like all colors." She shook her wrist. "See my bracelet? It has lots of colors because they're all pretty to me."

"Wow. That's pretty. Daddy, can I get one like that?" Isla lifted big eyes to me.

I nodded. "Of course. We just have to ask Ms. Trinity where she got it."

"Ms. Trinity, where did you get your bracelet?" Isla asked.

Trinity smiled, pursing her lips together to stop her laugh at Isla's proper manners. "I actually made this bracelet. I make jewelry." The needle pushed through the bead, and she laughed. "There we go." She pulled the needle from the string and handed it back to Isla, then slid her bracelet off. "You can have this one if you want it."

"Oh, no—" I said, but Isla interrupted with a shout.

"Yes!"

Isla stopped and looked up at me. I shook my head. "Sweetie, we can't take Ms. Trinity's bracelet."

"But she said I could have it."

Trinity stood and focused on me. "It will be a little big for her, but I'm happy to give it to her. I love what I do, making jewelry, and I wear a lot of my pieces because I'm proud of my work, but I promise you, I've given things I'm wearing to a lot of the kids I work with. It wouldn't be safe to show her how to do that at her age, but it's a joy for me to know she'll enjoy it."

"That's your hard work, though. At least let me pay you for it."

Trinity shook her head. "That's kind of you, but I'd love for it to be a gift."

"Thank you!" Isla shouted, her focus back on the bracelet she was making while the new one from Trinity bounced on her arm, way too big but a proud gift for her.

"You're welcome, sweetheart," Trinity said. She looked up at me, raising her brows in hopeful question.

"Thank you. That's really generous of you."

Trinity shook her head again. "I'm lucky to have a job I absolutely love. Something that affords me the opportunity to be creative and have fun with what I do. I know James told you we've been talking about missing the boat on kids, and it's given me a perspective I didn't have before. I love kids, and I love being able to do things for kids we know. But I also love not having my own kids and being able to pick up and do whatever we want when we want."

"You definitely can't do that with kids," I agreed.

Isla finished her new bracelet and added it to the one Trinity gave her, then took off to chase after the other kids running around.

"Yeah. And that's okay. I have enough friends with kids to where I can shower them with love and gifts and know I'm in a good position to be okay doing that."

"Thank you. This is amazing, and the bracelet is a true gift."

"Isla said she's spending a lot of time with your mom. It's nice for her, and maybe for you, to be here this summer."

I grunted. "Yeah, it's been great for her."

Trinity was far too astute to miss what I didn't say, but she didn't comment. "I know there are a lot of people in town who know you and your life story, or think they do, but I hope you are enjoying your summer. I'm really happy James invited you two here today."

"I am, too. Isla loves this. And being around other kids is great for her. My mom has been stuck at home with my dad since he got back from the hospital, so Isla's been stuck there, too."

"Like James mentioned, my schedule is flexible, and if

you ever want her to get out, please let me know. I am happy to play babysitter. And Finley has a bunch of kids out here every Friday for a fun day, if Isla wants to join us."

"Talking about me?" Finley asked, wrapping an arm around Trinity.

"I was telling Kingsley Isla can join us here on Fridays if he wants," Trinity explained.

"Absolutely. I was going to say the same. We're so happy you joined us today." Finley smiled in a way that made me feel like I was truly welcome, and that Isla was as well.

"Thank you both. I was telling James and Derek this has been a significantly different summer than I'd planned. I was not looking forward to leaving Isla with my mom all day every day, and having a break for both of them might be a great idea."

"Please, bring her. I'm up early with George, and Blake is usually here with her kids by seven. What time does the clinic open?" Finley asked.

"We open at eight on Fridays."

"Oh, yeah, drop her off on your way in. We're up and moving by then," Finley said.

"That's a long day for you to have my kid."

Finley chuckled. "It's really very selfish of me to offer. With all the kids together, they entertain each other. We have an elementary teacher who nannies for us in the summer so my parents aren't always having to take George, and she's here all day on Friday, too." Finley turned to the yard and pointed to a brunette woman near the pool. "That's Reegan. She's great. CPR certified and a licensed teacher and very good with the kids. None of us drink when the kids are here. Trinity comes most Friday afternoons, and we have space where the kids who want, or need, to nap can do that. We have time in the pool, and time running around, and we make it a fun day. But I promise you, Isla will be very welcome."

Isla was running around after two girls a few years older than her, laughing and playing with them. They waited for Isla, making sure she was still part of their game, and my chest swelled with gratitude for these kids. "She's never had this. She goes to school, but it's not easy as the single dad to call up other parents and invite someone's kids over."

Finley sighed. "I never would have thought of that." She looked at Trinity. "I'm even more grateful James said something to you. Ian said he spoke to you last weekend, too."

"Yeah. Blake's husband, right? Ian Jameson?"

Finley nodded. "And my brother."

"Oh, I didn't realize. Sorry."

Finley shook her head. "No, you're good. We're a few years older than you, so I'd be surprised if you knew all of us. I don't remember you."

"That makes me feel better. I graduated with Elise, and Chelsea was a little younger than me. But it's been a long time since I've been here."

"We're happy you and Isla are here for the summer," Finley said.

"Thank you."

A cry from across the yard took Finley's attention, and another kid asked Trinity for help, leaving me to look out over the space and wonder if this would have been my life if we'd stayed in MacKellar Cove.

Hanging out at Trent MacKellar's house? Getting to know people who were a decade older than me but felt like people I'd like to know? A group of kids for Isla to spend time with?

And what about Faith? If we'd stayed, I always told

myself she would still be alive. What would she have thought about all of the things we were doing?

My throat tightened with that thought. Faith was gone, but I vowed to love her for the rest of my life. How did I balance that with spending time with Daisy?

I didn't know the answer to that, and didn't think I'd ever get one. What did that make me?

"Daddy, can I swim with Amber and Alexis?" Isla asked, tugging me out of my thoughts.

"Of course, honey. Be careful."

She hugged me around the middle, then took off, racing to the pool and tossing her clothes until she was down to her swimsuit just before she jumped in.

Laughter and excitement rang out all around me, and I told myself there was no way I would give up this time with Isla. The rest was something I'd figure out later. When I wasn't surrounded by people and could think about my wife without feeling guilty.

As if that could happen.

ISLA WAS EXHAUSTED when we made it back to my parents' house. She fell asleep on the drive there, all five minutes of it. I carried her inside and laid her in her bed, knowing she'd be up at some point for dinner.

I was tempted to lie down with her, but my mom called out to me before I could decide. I brushed the hair back from Isla's face and kissed her forehead. I closed her door and went back to the living room.

"Yeah, Mom?" I asked.

"How was your day?"

"Um, exhausting."

"Did Isla have fun?"

I nodded. "Of course she did. She played with other kids, made some crafts, and swam for hours."

"Did you two eat?"

"Yeah, they had food for everyone."

"Whose house was it?"

"Trent MacKellar's. His wife is Finley Jameson."

Dad's brows shot up. "I know the family. They're patients. Trent's dog, Kenny, is an older dog, but he's very calm."

I didn't want to talk to my father, about work or anything else, so I kept my mouth shut.

"Finley owns a bookstore in town. Next to O'Kelleys," Mom said.

I shook my head. I hadn't noticed a bookstore, but I also hadn't been looking. "Isla loves books. Maybe I'll take her there sometime."

Dad chuckled, and Mom shook her head. "It's a romance only store. No kids books."

"Oh."

"But Lincoln Toys has books."

My heart squeezed at the name. I'd heard it a few times, and knowing it was also Daisy's last name made me wonder, but I couldn't exactly ask if she worked there.

"There are a lot of things to do in town. Isla and I will have to do some more. Maybe we can get to Lincoln Toys next week."

"Finley invited Isla to spend Fridays with her and some other kids she knows," I said.

"Isla doesn't know them," Mom argued, sitting up straight. Her brows tugged together.

"Isla met them all today."

"Am I not taking care of her?"

"Mom, I didn't say that. I just—"

"He wants her to have a chance to be a kid, Tina. It's a good thing. Lets her run around and have friends in town," Dad said, surprising me with his defense.

"Yeah," I said.

"Oh, well, I do want her to have fun and enjoy her time here. But I don't want you to worry that I'm not taking care of her."

"I don't worry about that, Mom. Isla loves being with you. Something different is nice for her, too."

Mom nodded, looking slightly less hurt. "Okay. If you think it'll be good for her."

"I do."

The door down the hall opened, and footsteps dragged toward us. Isla held Sabie in her arms. She made a beeline for me, not saying a word, and lifting her arms for me to pick her up.

I lifted her, then sat with her on my lap, holding her close. I missed those moments where she wanted to snuggle, where she was sleepy and a little out of it and just needed me.

She rested her head on my shoulder and toyed with the side of my shirt, holding onto her stuffed animal and not speaking.

"Are you tired, sweetie?" Mom asked, brushing her hair back.

Isla shook Mom off.

"She doesn't like to be touched when she's like this. Give her a few minutes," I explained, not wanting Mom to be hurt but knowing it was more important to protect Isla and make sure she felt safe.

"I didn't realize. Should I make her a snack?"

I nodded. "Probably a good idea. She ate, but she did a lot of running around, too."

"I'll go fix something," Mom said, rushing out of the room. The fridge and cabinets opened and closed before the sounds stilled to background noise.

I rocked with Isla, letting her wake up slowly and feel better. She didn't nap much anymore, but when she did, it was hard on her. She was usually crabby after a nap, still exhausted and unsure of how to function.

"So you're hanging out with the in-crowd these days?" Dad asked.

I ignored his question, knowing he didn't really want an answer. He was only looking to rile me up. And unfortunately, it worked.

"Too good for your family?"

"Really?" I growled.

Isla nuzzled against me, not liking the conversation anymore than I did.

"You weren't friends with them before. Now that you're back, you're going to spend all your time there?"

"Can you just not?" I hissed.

"Daddy," Isla whined.

"I know, honey. I'll stop talking." I shot my father a glare, hoping he got the message.

Isla didn't like a lot of noise when she first woke up. Faith had been the same way. Mornings were quiet for us, and after a nap was even worse.

My father didn't get the message. "Your mother missed you today. She was looking forward to time with Isla."

"Yeah, well, so was I this summer. And instead of spending time with her, I'm making sure your business doesn't go under. So maybe you could back off and say thank you or something."

I didn't wait for him to respond, just stood with Isla in my arms and walked away. We went to the kitchen and sat at the table where my mother was quietly slicing cheese. She turned and saw us come in, a smile lighting up her face.

Mom grabbed some of the cheese from the cutting board and put it on a plate, added some crackers, and brought it to us. "Isla told me she likes cheese and crackers sometimes, so I got it today."

"Thank you," I whispered.

Mom got the hint and smiled, going back to the cutting board as Isla reached for a slice of cheese and a cracker.

Isla nibbled on the first one, then turned to face the table and took a second. She stayed on my lap, enjoying her snack and slowly waking up.

When the cheese and crackers were gone, Isla looked up at me. "Daddy? What's the in-crowd?"

I tried to figure out an answer that would explain it to her and not make it sound like we shouldn't be friends with people. "It means a group of people who others want to be friends with."

"Everyone wanted to be friends with me today. Does that mean I'm the in-crowd?"

I nodded. "Yes, you are. Because you are a sweet girl who is smart and kind and fun to be around."

"Why did grandpa sound mad?"

I shook my head. "I don't know, sweetie, but it doesn't matter. We should be nice to everyone, and if they're not nice to us, we should still be nice, but we don't have to be friends with them."

"Is that why you're not friends with grandpa?" Isla asked.

I sucked in a breath. My mouth opened and closed. Mom stopped what she was doing to face us. "I'm friends with grandpa."

"But you don't talk to him. Is he mean to you?" Her lip wobbled.

"No. Your grandpa is not mean."

"Are you sure?"

I nodded. "Yes. I would not have you here if I was worried about you not being safe. There's nothing to worry about."

"Okay. Can I go play now?"

I released her so she could climb off my lap. "Tell grandma thank you for the snack."

"Thank you, grandma," Isla said, throwing her arms around Mom's legs.

Mom patted her head. "You're so welcome, my love."

Isla ran off, and Mom looked closely at me. "Did you mean what you said?"

I sighed and stood. "I really don't want to talk about this."

Mom watched me leave the room, but she didn't fight me on it.

I went to my room, leaving the door open so I could hear Isla, and put my head in my hands. It was a good day. Why couldn't it be a good night, too?

**14**

---

DAISY

Sunday night was my favorite time of the week. I knew I was lucky to not fear going to work Monday morning since I'd opened Lincoln Toys, and I got to spend Sunday night with some of my favorite people. What was not to enjoy?

Natalie had been coming to book club more often in the last few months, with less encouragement from me, which was a great thing, but we were still in a weird place. We'd talked, we'd hung out, we'd been fine, but I didn't mention Kingsley coming over and she didn't say anything about me dating him. So, weird. For us.

Which was only made worse when I took a piece of cake from Trinity and shoved a bite in my mouth right as she said, "Who can we set Kingsley Harris up with?"

I choked. Inhaled my cake. Coughed up my lung.

I set my cake down and raced to the bathroom, hoping everyone thought I just forgot how to eat a slice of cake.

Thankfully, I managed to keep the cake in, because it was really damn good, and my lung in, because it was really damn necessary, and breathe like a normal human again.

"Are you okay?" Finley asked from right behind me.

I jumped, not expecting her. "I didn't see you."

"I followed you. Are you okay?"

I coughed and laughed and washed my hands, rinsing my mouth, then dried myself off with a paper towel. "I'm good. Went down wrong."

"Your face turned bright red. I thought you were dying."

I shook my head. "All good. Cake tried to kill me."

"I had that happen with salad once. I breathed in a piece of lettuce and it got stuck on my windpipe. I couldn't suck in a breath to cough it out. I was honestly scared. Haven't eaten salad since."

"I don't blame you. But I'm not giving up cake."

"Oh, of course not. It wasn't the cake's fault."

"No. Definitely not. But it was totally the salad's fault," I told her with a wink.

"See. You get me."

I laughed and followed her back to the group, where they were still talking about Kingsley.

"His daughter is precious," Trinity said. "And he's a nice guy. Cute, too. Daisy? You're single."

"I'm good," I told her.

"Are you sure? He's going to bring his daughter to my house every Friday. You could just happen to be there this week," Finley said.

I shook my head. "I don't need to meet him."

"Daisy already met him. She took Dozer to him," Chelsea said. "If she wanted to date him, she'd already know."

Trinity wrinkled her nose. "Oh. Well, who else do we know that's single?" She looked around the room at the others.

"Casey is single," Melody said.

I didn't know who Casey was, but I didn't like the idea of

them setting Kingsley up with someone else. We agreed what we had was temporary and that if either of us met someone else we were more interested in, especially someone who had long-term potential, we would walk away with no hurt feelings.

But I didn't want him to meet someone else. I didn't want him to look at someone else. I wanted him all to myself for a few weeks. We only had a few weeks.

"Do you think Casey is ready to date again?" Natalie asked.

How did she know Casey? How did I not know Casey? Who was Casey?

Melody scrunched up her nose. "Probably not. She's only been divorced a little while, and she's just getting her feet under her at the paper. I don't want her to feel like I'm only telling her about Kingsley because she has to have a significant other."

Oh, Casey! Melody's friend who did the story on Omar. Right. Casey. Cute, funny, newly divorced, single mom, Casey. Dammit.

"He's leaving at the end of summer, anyway," Chelsea said. "He told Derek he's only here until his dad is back to work, then he's going back to Philadelphia with his daughter."

"Unless he meets someone," Trinity said, wiggling her eyebrows. "Are you sure you're not interested, Daisy?"

"Daisy barely has time to relax, let alone date," Natalie said, cutting off any chance I had at saying anything. "Plus, a single dad who's working full time, living with his parents, and has a young kid? That doesn't sound like a really good idea for anyone. He's probably not all that interested in dating for... what? A month?"

Natalie shot me a look. Was she helping me? Deflecting?

Or was she just trying to talk me out of seeing Kingsley without talking to me about it?

Trinity grimaced. "Okay, fine. You're probably right. I was just hoping they'd stick around. He's a nice guy."

"I wonder why he didn't," Elise said. "He planned to when we were in high school. Said he was going to become a vet, then take over his dad's clinic. I didn't think about it before, but now that he's back, I wonder what happened."

"Maybe his wife didn't want to live here," Trinity speculated.

"That's possible. She wasn't from here. He met her in college," Elise continued.

"What matters is we make sure he's welcome, and if he decides to stick around, we know he's a nice guy with a great kid," Finley said.

"True," the others agreed.

I kept my mouth shut. I took another bite of my cake, thankful when I didn't choke on it.

Natalie caught my eye and gave me a small smile. Trying to help.

Good. I didn't want to tell them all I was involved with Kingsley. I didn't want the judgement I got from Natalie. They all stopped pushing once they realized he wouldn't be around long. It was just like Natalie.

But I wasn't giving him up. I was going to keep seeing him. Because I enjoyed seeing him. There was nothing wrong with that.

ON MY WAY TO work on Tuesday, I decided to reach out to Kingsley. We hadn't seen each other since he showed up the week before. We traded a few texts, but nothing about setting up plans again. I was letting other people and their opinions get in my head and steal the little bit of time I had with Kingsley.

No more.

As soon as I got to work, I sent him a text asking if we could get together that night. He could say no, but he wouldn't say yes unless I asked. And yes was always possible.

I got out of my SUV just as a truck was pulling around the end of the building. I waved to the driver and headed inside to give Penny a hand unloading the truck.

But Penny wasn't there. Wendy was.

"Hey. What are you doing here?" I asked Wendy.

"Penny asked if I could handle the delivery this morning. She said she had something to take care of and wouldn't be able to get here until later," Wendy explained.

"It's her job. She shouldn't be passing it off onto you."

Wendy shrugged and hit the button to roll up the equipment door to the loading dock. The truck was locked in place, ready to be unloaded. "I don't mind."

"Is this the first time she's asked you to do this?" I asked, sensing something in the way Wendy avoided my gaze.

"It's no big deal."

"It is for me. This is her job. She shouldn't be pawning it off onto others."

"It's fine. I don't mind. I was going to be here around the same time anyway to open the store. It just means I was here first and am handling the delivery."

The personnel door opened and Dick strolled in. "Good morning, ladies. How are we doing today?"

"Hi, Dick," Wendy and I both said.

"We're good," Wendy continued. "How was your trip?"

"Always better when I'm home," Dick said. "Got a full truck for you today."

"You do?" I asked, taking the clipboard from him. We never ordered enough for a full truck because space was limited. That much was going to end up causing other issues.

"I was surprised, too. You don't usually order this much at once. Not that I see. Figured you have a big promotion coming up or something."

I shook my head and reviewed the order. I approved it when it came through the week before, but I didn't realize Penny put all of it to arrive together. I was expecting the order to last us weeks.

"Not that I know of. Penny's taken over the ordering. I'll have to talk to her later about this," I said.

"I didn't mean to cause any trouble," Dick said.

I shook my head. "Not any trouble at all. And not on you. Wendy is helping out this morning. We'll get you unloaded and headed home."

"Thanks. You know that's my favorite part of the day."

"Of the week, I think."

Dick chuckled. "Yes, ma'am."

Wendy got on the forklift and grabbed the first pallet of toys. She stacked it near the shelves so we could organize and store everything once Dick was on his way. We liked to get trucks unloaded quickly, then verify each pallet before we stacked them on the shelves.

I marked off each pallet as Wendy unloaded it, marking everything against the shipping manifest. When Wendy was done, we waved goodbye to Dick.

And I wondered how in the hell we were going to store all the toys Penny ordered.

"Where do you want these to go?" Wendy asked, staring

at the load. She pushed everything as far to the walls as possible, but we didn't have enough shelf space to put all the pallets up. We were going to be dealing with things on the floor for weeks.

"We will do the best we can. I'll go look at the floor and see if we can add to some of the displays we have and get some of these unboxed."

"I'll come with you," Wendy said.

We walked the aisles and found a few places we could add things, but not nearly enough to manage the mountain of merchandise we had in the back.

I had no idea what Penny was thinking ordering that much stuff. But I was going to find out when she arrived.

Wendy and I worked until the store opened, stashing things everywhere we could in an attempt to prioritize safety. It was not easy, but with some creative storage, thanks to Wendy, we made it work.

I worked the floor with Wendy and the associates, needing to be around the kids to let go of my concern. I was starting to wonder if I made the wrong decision by promoting Penny. I thought she would be a good fit, but she was skipping out on her responsibilities, letting others handle the job, and not showing up when she was supposed to be there.

That was not management material.

She never did those things when she was a store manager. What was the difference?

"Can you help us with this?" a woman said, catching my attention as I walked through the store.

"Of course," I said, walking toward them. I realized when I got closer that I recognized them. "Oh, hello again. I saw you two at Just Tacos last week. No beans."

The girl giggled. "They make you toot."

"That's what I hear." I winked at her. "What can I help you two with?"

"Mrs. Harris!" Penny called, coming from the other end of the aisle. "How are you?"

"Oh, Penny! Hello, dear. How are you?"

"I'm good. How are you? I haven't seen you in forever." Penny hugged the woman warmly, holding her at arm's length and grinning.

"It's been a while. How's your mom?"

"She's good. She missed working with everyone at Cracked, though. She's trying to enjoy retirement, but she keeps saying Florida isn't home."

"Your dad always wanted to move south."

"I know. I think she's working on him to come back. Especially with a grandson around."

"You?" Mrs. Harris asked.

Penny laughed. "Oh, heck no. My sister. I'm not looking to have kids any time soon, if ever."

"Oh, kids are a wonderful blessing."

"That's what my sister says, when she's not complaining. Who is this?" Penny asked.

"This is my granddaughter, Isla. Kingsley's little girl."

My heart stopped. Kingsley. Mrs. Harris. Oh, shit. The adorable little girl was Kingsley's daughter. He was the daddy who made good burgers and didn't like beans because they made you toot.

"You look like your daddy," Penny said, crouching to get eye-to-eye with Isla. "You're very pretty."

"Thank you," Isla said, hugging grandma's leg and half hiding from Penny.

Penny stood and focused on Mrs. Harris again. "How is Dr. Harris? Home, I hear?"

Mrs. Harris nodded. "He is. Ready to get back to it. He

can't stand to sit still. I keep telling him Kingsley has a handle on everything, but Gregory wants to be working."

"I imagine everyone who's used to working all the time is like that. Especially since he knows he'll be back to work at some point."

"You're probably right. When I retired, I was ready to not be on my feet all the time, but Gregory isn't quite done yet."

"He'll decide when it's the right time." Penny smiled. "I didn't mean to interrupt what you were looking at, though. Daisy knows everything there is to know about toys." Penny cupped her hand and stage-whispered, "She's my boss."

Mrs. Harris chuckled. "Well, I think we found the right person then. Isla was looking at this for the pool, but I wasn't sure if it was going to be the right size for her."

Penny snuck past us while I opened the box with the pool float inside. "Let's see what you think." I held the float up next to Isla. The bottom nearly touched the floor, and the top was a foot above her head. "Well, I think the question is, are you going to grow a lot over the next few weeks? Because if you're going to grow this much before summer ends, then you might need something bigger."

Isla giggled. "I don't think I can grow that much."

"Then you might be okay. But only if you're sure you're not going to grow more than that."

Isla laughed and shook her head. "No. I don't grow that fast."

"Well, that sounds perfect, then. Is there anything else you're looking for?"

"Isla is going to meet up with some new friends on Friday and we wanted to have something for her to take over there. Maybe something all the kids can do together?" Mrs. Harris suggested.

"Sure, let's go look at the outdoor games. How does that sound?"

"Yeah!" Isla said.

We talked while we walked and I was careful to pretend I had no idea where they were going, because it would be weird if I did, even though I did, but it was weird. Isla picked out three games I was fairly sure Finley didn't have, and grandma helped her narrow it down to just one.

"We can come back and get another one if you guys get tired of this one," Mrs. Harris said.

"Okay. Thank you, grandma."

"You're so welcome. And thank you for your help, Daisy," Mrs. Harris said.

"It was my pleasure. It was so good to see you both again. Stay away from those beans."

Isla laughed fully, her little head tipping back with her laughter. She held her grandma's hand and followed her to the register.

I smiled, then went to find Penny. I was not looking forward to the conversation we had to have, but we had to have it.

"Hey," Penny said when I found her in the back.

"Hi. Why weren't you here this morning for the delivery?"

"Wendy was supposed to be. Didn't she come in?"

"She did, but it's your job to be here to manage deliveries."

"I thought as long as it was handled, it was fine."

I shook my head slowly. "That's not what we discussed. You were supposed to evaluate what products are moving, place new orders, and be here to unload trucks and verify deliveries."

"Okay, I'm sorry. I didn't think it was a big deal. I had to help my sister this morning, and Wendy said she could help out."

"If this job isn't a good fit—"

"It's fine. I just misunderstood. I'll make it work."

"Good. Thank you. Now what about this order? This is a lot more than we usually bring in at any one time."

She pointed to a pallet. "These have been selling a lot lately. I looked and in the last six months, we've sold twice this amount. And those," she pointed to another pallet, "have been selling twice that fast, so I ordered double the amount. The sales for these have been climbing, too."

"How long are you projecting all of this inventory to last us?"

"A few months?"

"Months? Okay. That was my thought, too. But we don't really have good space for a few months of storage."

"But the shipping was a lot cheaper when we ordered this much."

"I know. It always is. But if it means we have to move things three times, it's a waste of a different kind. The storage area is borderline hazardous right now with the pallets stacked up the way they are."

"I thought you would be happy that I saved some money," Penny said, crossing her arms.

"I am happy, but I also had planned for the extra shipping costs, and carrying this much inventory will hit my books for the end of the month. There are reasons I've been doing things the way I was."

"Okay, but you said you wanted me to try new things. You wanted new ideas. You were willing to let me do things my way. And now you're telling me it was all wrong?"

"No, I'm not. And you're right. I will back off. But we can't have any more deliveries until we get all these pallets off the floor. We need to make sure this space is safe, especially because we use the forklift back here and it can be dangerous if we can't see."

"Fine."

I rolled my lips in, resisting the urge to pacify her. She was an employee, and she needed to learn to see the full picture. "I want this to work, Penny. We have to be willing to hear each other."

"I'm good."

"Okay. Thank you for listening to me."

"Uh huh."

I drew a breath and walked away, still wondering if I made the wrong decision.

## 15

I NEEDED A DRINK. I COULDN'T REMEMBER THE LAST TIME I had that thought, but it was the only one running through my head when I walked out of work.

Penny was passive-aggressive all day. Answering me with one-word replies and avoiding me when possible. That was not a good sign, and not a good attitude.

Things would get better, and I knew that, but it was a struggle. It was a struggle to not pull her aside to talk about it, but that didn't work with everyone. I liked to resolve things as quickly as possible, but Natalie always reminded me not everyone was like me. A lot of people needed time to think through things and process their feelings, especially when they felt attacked.

Penny had no reason to feel attacked, but just in case, I let it go and promised myself I'd speak to her in a day or two.

I pushed her from my mind on my drive home and realized I never got a reply from Kingsley. After meeting his daughter and mother, I wasn't sure getting together was a good thing, but I didn't regret reaching out. Or seeing him at all. It just reinforced for me that temporary was the right decision for us. His daughter had to be his priority, and I understood that, but if it was serious, that would bother me.

I'd never been someone's priority. Not in my memory. The curse of having twin brothers. My parents had to put them first because they demanded the attention, and even as they got older, it was second nature to spoil them.

I didn't resent my brothers, but I wanted someone to treat me the way they were treated. I wanted someone who looked at me and their face lit up, who made me feel like I was the most important person in their world.

Kingsley would never be that person, and I knew it before, but meeting his kid was a good reminder.

So him not returning my text was fine. It wasn't a big deal. He was busy, and I was busy, and what we had was temporary. He was leaving in a few weeks, and he was...

On my front porch.

I breathed a laugh and put my SUV into park, getting out with a smile on my face. "What are you doing here?"

"You asked if we could get together today. I had a short day at the clinic and thought I'd stop by and surprise you."

"I was at work."

"I figured. I was going to wait another little while, just so your neighbors didn't get worried and call the cops on some strange guy lurking outside your house."

I shook my head. "Then I guess you better come inside so they don't see the strange guy."

He stepped to the side for me to unlock the front door, then followed me into the house. "I'm glad you texted me. I was thinking about you today."

"Oh, yeah?"

He nodded as I set my handbag on the table by the door.

"Yeah. It's been a really long time since I got my hands on you."

I raised one eyebrow. "That hasn't changed yet."

He surged forward, cupping my jaw and bringing my lips up to his. All the air rushed from me when he backed me against the wall and kissed me like a man starved.

I was not going to complain. I wrapped my arms around his waist and pulled him closer, loving the feel of his body against mine. I slid my hands down and grabbed his butt, getting a groan from him.

"Bedroom?" He asked the question like I was going to deny him.

I nodded, pulling him back in for a kiss as we made our way to my room. I closed the door, locking it just in case, and tugged him back to me. His skin was warm from being outside, and the ridge in his pants was hard. My reaction to him was immediate, my body ready for him with all our clothes on. Again.

He lifted my shirt and spread his hand wide on my side, sliding it around to pull me closer. His tongue pressed deep into my mouth, tasting every inch of me and making me crave more from him.

I tugged at his shirt, lifting it between us so I could feel his body pressed to mine. He was warm and the short hairs on his belly bristled on my skin, adding to the intensity of my reaction to him.

Kingsley stepped back and yanked his shirt off, his hands going to my shirt the next second and dropping both to the floor. He dragged me back in with one hand on my jaw and the other on my breast, plucking my nipple through my bra.

I writhed against him, breathing heavily and wanting to feel him on my skin. I tried to push the cup to the side, but he fought me, breaking our kiss and ducking his head to suck my nipple into his mouth, bra and all.

The friction of the cotton added to the pleasure, and I moaned. He tugged my other breast, tweaking my nipple before kissing his way to it and soaking that cup with his torturous mouth.

"So good," I breathed.

He grunted in reply, pushing at my shorts to get his hand inside. I shoved them down, spreading my thighs wide to allow him access. God, this man. He was not afraid to tease and tempt me before taking his own pleasure. It was an intoxicating combination, one that negated my earlier need for alcohol. Kingsley was so much better.

His fingers slid into my wet channel easily, pressing that spot deep inside that made my knees weak. I rocked against his palm. He drug the heel of his hand against my clit with each pump of his fingers inside me, sending me into a frenzy.

He stood up straight and claimed my lips as my orgasm raced down my spine. I came with a shout that he swallowed and groaned his way through, his erection hard against my hip.

"Again," he breathed, nipping at my lips before he licked them and plunged his tongue into my mouth again.

He withdrew his fingers from me and brought the soaked digits to my clit, spreading them around and pinching the bundle of nerves between two fingers before tugging on it and splintering reality for me.

I hung on him, wholly unable to support my body weight as my orgasm tore through me. My hips bucked against his hand, my legs turned to mush, and my belly flipped over.

Sex was not going to make me fall in love with a man, but if it could, this would be the man.

His wife taught him well.

Which I absolutely did not want to think about when I was riding his hand and whimpering my way through aftershocks that had my brain scrambled and my body begging for more from him.

"Condom?" he asked, and my body sang for joy.

"Nightstand," I was able to breathe. Then he removed his hand, and I shuddered a breath.

His cocky grin said he knew exactly what he'd done to me. Not that I was hiding it or fighting the orgasms he gave me.

"Yeah, yeah," I teased. "You try to stand after something like that."

"I'm already struggling," he whispered against my lips before kissing me hard, his breath whistling past my cheek. "I can't resist you."

"Same," I admitted, grabbing his arm for support.

He helped me to the bed, then shoved his pants down, letting his cock spring free. I had the sudden urge to taste him, but that felt more personal, more intimate than sex for some reason, so I laid back and watched him roll a condom down his length.

He crawled onto the bed and positioned himself between my thighs. I let my eyes stray over his body, loving the way he didn't hide himself from me. He stroked his erection once, then lined himself up and pressed inside.

I didn't resist him at all, and he sank all the way into me in only a handful of strokes. I shivered at the feel of him, and he groaned.

"How do you feel so good?" he whispered.

"I've been wondering the same. Right place, right time."

He grinned. "Definitely that."

He pulled out, then slid back in, figuring out the right rhythm. I clenched my walls around him, loving the way it made his nostrils flare and his breath pop out of him. I lifted one leg, wrapping it around his hip, and he sank deeper.

"Fuck," he hissed, his tempo increasing. He cupped my ass and tilted my hips, and I squeezed around him.

"Oh, yeah," I breathed.

He sped up again, our bodies slapping together in the otherwise quiet house. He shifted, supporting my hips on his thighs, then brought a finger to my clit.

"Fuck," I gasped at the first swipe. I was close, already on the edge from my earlier orgasms and teetering with one touch.

He pounded into me, his finger rubbing a fast pace that had me frantic for a release.

He grunted, his jaw tightened, and he slammed hard into me, swelling before he came with a moan and a long exhale.

I was there, so close, hanging on the edge, but left to suffer, and more than a little disappointed. I ached to reach down and finish what he started, but I came twice. I could finish myself off later.

Then he started to move again. His cock was softening, but it was still there. And so was his finger.

"Sorry. You felt so good around me. I tried to hold it off."

"It's okay," I breathed, the words coming out in a choppy breath.

"I like watching you," he whispered, almost too low for me to hear. "That sounds creepy."

I gasped and shook my head. "I liked watching you, too."

He pinched my clit and tugged it with each stroke inside me.

"Oh, yes," I breathed.

He cupped my breast and tugged the cup of my bra down, finally getting his hand on my bare nipple. He pulled it, nearly to the point of pain, and rocked my breast with the same rhythm, setting a pace for my body to follow.

It felt like a full body orgasm, where everything was building from my toes to the ends of my hair. It had never felt like that before, like every cell in my body was coming.

"Oh, God. Kingsley. Yes. Oh, yes. Oh!"

"Fuck, you're beautiful," he whispered, the words barely making it through the fog of my orgasm.

He kept pumping his hips, even though I could tell it wasn't doing anything for him. He rode out my orgasm with me, staying inside, hands on my flesh until I shivered and finally relaxed.

I pried my eyes open a minute later and found him watching me with a satisfied grin on his face. "What can I say? You're very good at that."

His chest rose with pride. "I'll take that compliment, but I definitely wasn't alone in making that happen. You're stunning when you come."

"So are you."

He leaned forward to kiss me, his softening cock sliding from my body. He didn't rush through the kiss, taking his time to hold himself above me and kiss me like I was someone who mattered.

Maybe sex was going to make me fall for him.

No. No. It wasn't. It couldn't. He was unavailable. He was leaving, and he had a daughter and a dead wife, and I wasn't signing up for that.

He was just showing me what I deserved. What I wanted. I was going to take this experience and use it to find the man who was truly and totally right for me.

"Thank you."

I grinned, remembering his embarrassment at thanking me last time. "Thank you."

He kissed me again, breathing a laugh as he did, then pushed himself off the bed. He went to the bathroom, the water running when I heard the front door close.

"Daisy?" Natalie called.

"Shit. Shit, shit, shit," I hissed. I jumped out of bed and grabbed for my clothes. Natalie wouldn't just walk in, but she obviously saw Kingsley's car, and she would definitely know why he was there.

The bathroom door opened, and I was so ridiculously grateful we had our own bathrooms so Kingsley wasn't walking around the house naked, although the sight was a damn good one.

"My roommate's home," I whispered, dragging my shirt over my head.

"Oh, um, okay?" He grabbed for his pants and stepped into them. "I'm guessing you don't want me here. This really is a roommate thing, right? Not you telling me it's a roommate but you're really dating?"

Natalie knocked on my door. "Daisy? You in there?"

"Yeah, Nat. We'll be right out."

"We? Oh. Um, okay. Sorry! Don't rush... I mean, shit. I'm walking away now!"

Kingsley looked at me, still waiting for an answer.

"No, it's not a dating or cheating thing. She's my best friend, and she's very much in love with her boyfriend, who is great."

"But you don't want her to know about us?"

"She knows. She just..." I stepped into my panties and shorts.

"Doesn't want us together. Do I know her?" He grabbed his shirt and pulled it on.

I shook my head. "I don't think so. And it's nothing personal. She's protective of me and worried because you're only here for a few weeks."

"You don't do this kind of thing."

I shook my head again. "Nope."

He walked over to me and cupped my jaw. "I don't want to hurt you."

"I know, and you're not going to. I know the deal, I agreed to it. Hell, I think I proposed it. We're fine. She's just in the honeymoon phase of her relationship and doesn't understand why I would be interested in something that has no long-term potential."

He nodded, the move a little jerky. "It's good to have friends who care. Even when we don't agree with what they're trying to protect us from."

"It is."

"Do you want to distract her while I sneak out? Or..." He glanced around the room. "I don't think I've ever climbed out a window, but I can try it. Thankfully this is the first floor."

I laughed as he went to the window and peeked out. "You don't have to do either. She knows you're here. She saw your car. You're not my dirty secret. Not from her, at least."

His brows shot up. "But from others?"

I nibbled my lip. "I'm friends with Finley and Trinity and the others you met Friday. They were singing your praises on Sunday and suggested setting us up."

He grinned. "It sounds like your friends have a good eye."

I snorted. "Yes, but I didn't tell them we were already sort of seeing each other."

"You don't want them to know?"

I shook my head. "It's not you. I..." I looked at my door. "After the way Natalie reacted, I didn't want to hear it from everyone else."

"Ah." He nodded, rubbing his jaw. "I understand that. I haven't told anyone about us, either."

"Speaking of, I met your mom and daughter today."

"What? Where? How?"

"They came into my store. I didn't know who they were. We met last week, too. I was in line for lunch behind them, but I didn't know... Is that okay? I didn't tell them I knew you."

"Yeah." He ran a hand through his hair. He shoved his feet in his shoes and straightened. "Lincoln Toys is you, isn't it?"

I nodded. "It is."

"It was inevitable that they would end up there. I never told my mom who you were when we met. She asked, but I refused to tell her in case she tried to convince you to convince me to stay."

"You think she would do that?"

"Yes. She'll do anything to get her way. But it's not happening. I'm not staying here."

I flinched at the anger in his voice.

"Sorry. I... I should go. Get home to see my daughter."

"Okay." Avoidance seemed to be my best friend today.

"Do you... What..."

I wasn't going to help him, so I waited for him to figure out what he was going to say. He surprised me when he got it out.

"Are you free this weekend?"

I nodded. "I am."

"Can I see you again?"

"I'd like that."

"So would I."

He reached for the doorknob, then stopped and reached for me instead. He pulled me in and kissed me until I was panting and he was hard again.

"I would really like that," he whispered.

"Good."

He kissed me quickly, then released me and adjusted himself. He unlocked the door and opened it for me to go first.

Natalie was in the kitchen, trying to act like she wasn't watching for us.

Kingsley went right to her and offered her his hand. "I know you aren't sure about this, but I promise you, I have no intention of hurting Daisy. She's a very special person."

Natalie shook his hand and examined him. "She is. That's what I worry about. People take advantage of her because she's so kind."

"We have an agreement," I told Natalie. "Neither of us is going to get hurt."

Natalie looked between us and nodded once, not agreeing but not arguing either.

"Nice to meet you," Kingsley said.

"You, too," Natalie agreed.

I walked Kingsley to the door and smiled when he kissed me before he left. I closed the door and prepared myself for disappointment from my friend, but when I turned around, she had a carton of ice cream and two spoons.

"Friends?"

I smiled. "The best."

Natalie grinned and met me on the couch for a night of movies and ice cream. Just the two of us.

# 16

## KINGSLEY

I HURRIED THROUGH THE LAST PATIENTS OF THE DAY ON Friday, anxious to get out of there. I had important things to do, and I was ready to go.

I was almost there when Sheila stopped me and said I had one more patient. I'd checked and knew I didn't, so I growled at her. "I was supposed to be done at four."

"It's a walk-in, Dr. Harris. New patient and the owner wanted to see you now."

"And you approved this?"

Sheila shook her head. "No."

I sighed. If the patient was already in a room, I had no choice. "Please don't accept more patients today."

Sheila nodded.

I grumbled my way to the exam room, hating that my plans would have to wait. I knocked once, then opened the door and heard a tiny meow.

My gaze scanned the room, taking in a man holding a tiny kitten that had seen better days. "Andre Davidson?" Andre was two years ahead of me in school, but we had a few classes together.

He looked up. "Kingsley Harris. How the hell are you? Or should I call you doctor?"

"You can call me Kingsley, Andre."

"You sure? Real adults are called by their titles."

"You're two years older than me. Aren't you a real adult? Should I call you Mr. Davidson?"

He snorted. "Please don't."

"Then Kingsley, please. I didn't realize you were in the area. How are you?"

"I'm good, man. Good. Moved back a few years ago. My dad had a stroke, and I came back to help out, found it hard to leave again. What about you? Helping out while your dad's recovering? Sorry to hear about his heart attack."

I nodded. "I am. He's getting better, though. Hopefully back here soon."

"That's great news."

I nodded again. "Who's this little one?"

"Molly," Andre said, rubbing the kitten's head. "That's what I've been calling her. I think she's a stray, but she's the sweetest thing. She's been hanging around at Mountain View Retreat. I'm out there every weekend to take care of the landscaping, but had to check on a few things today and this little one finally let me pick her up."

"Let's take a look at her." Andre handed over the tiny cat, who let loose a growl that told me just how happy she was to be handed off. "Sounds like she's gotten attached to you."

"Feeling's mutual. I was hoping to adopt her, if you tell me she's not someone else's."

I nodded, giving Molly a quick exam before setting her on the table. She made a beeline for Andre, burrowing against his belly and doing her best to hide from me. "Let's check." I grabbed the scanner and waved it over Molly's back, watching for any indication there was a microchip. I shook my head. "Doesn't appear to have a chip. Most pets do these days. How long has she been hanging around Mountain View Retreat?"

"Couple months, best guess. I thought I saw her when I was first cleaning up the place, but she always hid. I started leaving food there, and she came around more often. I'm usually out there alone, so I try to talk to her and get close to her when I'm there, but she's skittish."

"Doesn't appear to be right now."

Andre chuckled. "Yeah. She's coming around. Screamed the whole way here, but once we got in the room, she just snuggled right up to me and refused to move away."

"She's feels safe with you."

"She is."

"That's a good thing." I scrubbed a hand down my face. "So we can do a few things. I can keep her here for a few days, do some bloodwork and tests and give her some shots, make sure all is good, then schedule to have her spayed and chipped, assuming you're okay with that."

Andre nodded without interrupting.

"The other option is you can take her home and come back next week for all of that."

"I'd rather she's with me, if you think that's okay. I don't have any other pets."

"That's good. Here's the thing. She has fleas, likely ear mites, and who knows what else. I would highly recommend she not sleep in your bed, and I would suggest letting her stay here for the weekend. Let the flea treatment work for a few days, let us check the results for ear mites, and get her surgery scheduled for first thing Monday morning. Then you can take her home after the surgery and be good to go."

"Do you think she's going to freak out?" Andre asked. He

rubbed the cat's back, protecting it in a way the little kitten had likely never known.

Molly purred and nestled against Andre like he was her personal hero. It was always tough to take pets away from their person.

"She probably will. She's definitely attached to you. Changing her environment is going to be a tough transition, then all this will make it harder."

"I don't want her to think I've abandoned her. Is there another option?"

I shrugged. "The fleas would be the biggest worry for me because your place can get infested quick. You can give her a bath. There is flea shampoo you can use, but cats don't like water."

Andre chuckled. "This one's weird. She plays in puddles."

"No."

Andre nodded. "She does. I actually think she'll like a bath."

"If you want to try it, we can get you everything you need and schedule her surgery for next week."

Andre nodded again. "Yeah, that's the best option. Thanks, Kingsley."

"You're welcome. Do you have a carrier for her? Litter box? Anything? Food?"

Andre shook his head. "Didn't really plan this one out. I was going to stop by somewhere and try to grab some stuff on the way home."

"We have some trial items you can take home with you, if you're interested. Get you through the weekend. Then maybe you can get everything you need when she's here for surgery. We will need to keep her overnight, but as long as everything goes well, it'll only be one night."

Andre sighed heavily. "Okay. Let's do it. Thanks. Man, this is so much better than I feared."

"It's a great thing you're doing for Molly." I clapped him on the back and opened the door for him and Molly to go out ahead of me.

Andre followed me to the storage room where all the samples were kept. I grabbed a litter box first, then added litter that would last a week, a small bag of kitten food, a brush, and a few packs of toys. We went to the medicine room next for the flea bath and flea treatment for him to use. I carried it all up front for him while he held on to Molly.

"Thanks again, Kingsley," Andre said as I walked him out.

"Any time. We'll see you Monday morning. Give me a call if you need anything over the weekend."

"Thanks. Hopefully I don't, but thanks."

I shook hands with Andre, then waited for him to get settled with Molly in the truck before I headed back inside.

It was a lot later than I'd planned, and later than I told Finley I'd be back to her house to pick up Isla. Dammit.

I rushed through my notes and got out of there, making sure everyone else was leaving or gone before I headed out. I pulled into Finley and Trent's driveway forty-five minutes later than I intended.

Andrew, the caretaker of the MacKellar household, opened the door and directed me to the backyard, where the kids were playing and the adults were sitting around a table overlooking the water.

"Kingsley! Welcome!" Trent said when he saw me. "Are you sticking around for dinner?" Trent was at a massive grill wearing an apron that proudly declared him World's Best Dad.

I shook my head. "We've already overstayed our welcome. I wouldn't want to intrude."

"No intrusion," Trent said. "I've got plenty on the grill, and the others are staying. You and Isla are always welcome."

Finley approached me and pulled me in for a kind hug. "Isla has been great today. She did nap for about thirty minutes when the other kids were resting, too, but she's been great. We had fruit for a snack, some animal crackers, and peanut butter and jelly for lunch."

"Thank you so much. This is so good for her." It was the second week Isla had been with Finley for the day, but the week before I made it there on time. Finley and Blake were there with the kids, along with the nanny Reegan, but this week, there was a bigger crowd.

"She's a delight. Very sweet kid. She's been really great with the little ones, making sure they're all okay."

"Thank you."

"As for sticking around for dinner, Trent always cooks enough food for about three times as many people as we have here, so there is more than enough for you two to join us, and we would love to have you stay." She grabbed my arm and squeezed, smiling as she did it, but not entirely tugging me toward the table surrounded by others.

I glanced at the table and saw Ian and Blake, Trinity and James, Karissa Thomas with a man who appeared to be hers, and another couple I didn't recognize.

"Reegan is sticking around for dinner, too. Not that I'm trying to pair you up! Just letting you know. Come meet the others." Now she was tugging me toward the table.

I shook my head and stopped resisting, letting her lead me to where everyone was seated.

"That's Laura and Nico Allison. Nico owns MacKellar

Cove Cancer Care and Margaret Allison Memorial Clinic. Laura is one of his best nurses," Finley said as we got to the table.

I shook hands with Nico and Laura. "The work you do is so important."

Nico nodded. "We believe so, too. You're Kingsley Harris?"

"I am."

"Nice to meet you."

"You, too."

"Kingsley's mom worked with my mom," Karissa said. "I adore Ms. Tina."

"She adores you. She said to say hello if I saw you again."

"Please tell her the same. Is your dad improving?" Karissa asked.

"He is. Every day. He's planning to start back to work next week. One day only," I told them, knowing everyone in town loved my father. They didn't know the same man I knew.

"Wow. That's great news," Trent said. "He's been so good for Kenny." Trent nodded to a dog sleeping on the edge of the yard. "He's getting pretty old."

"We all are," Ian said.

Trent chuckled. "All too true."

I offered my hand to the man with his arm around Karissa. "I don't believe we've met. Kingsley Harris."

"Xavier Hogan. Nice to meet you. Saw you a few weeks ago but didn't get a chance to say hello. Good to see you again."

"You, too."

I took a seat next to Ian, feeling out of place but happy for the familiar face.

"Long day?" Ian asked.

I nodded. "Yeah, and a last-minute patient when I was heading out."

"Everything okay?" Blake asked.

"Yeah, someone looking to adopt a stray and finally caught her. Brought her in for a checkup," I told them.

"How do you not have a dozen pets? The only thing Maddox wants is a dog or a cat or a hamster or a fish. He swears he'll do everything to take care of the pets, but we keep saying not until he's a little older," Blake said.

I chuckled. "I have been telling Isla since she was basically born that animals take a lot of work. Plus, I live in an apartment that doesn't allow pets."

"Smart!" Blake said. "Ian, we're moving."

Ian chuckled and kissed the side of her head. "Okay, babe."

"I don't know what we're going to do when Kenny dies. We know it's coming, but George is so attached," Finley said.

"Don't get a new pet too soon. I see it a lot, and it ends up being worse. You can't replace one pet with another. You can consider getting one now so you have two for a little while, but if you wait, make sure your family has time to grieve your loss. Then get a dog that's different. Don't get one that looks exactly like him or it'll be even harder," I told her.

"I never thought about any of that. We have considered another dog, but we were worried it would be a problem for Kenny," Finley said.

"It can be a struggle to introduce a new dog, but if you're careful about it and get the right dog, which is a bit of chance, then it's a good thing," I explained.

Trent came over with a tray full of steaks that looked perfect. "Everyone hungry?"

"Kingsley said we should get another dog," Finley said.

Trent gave me a look that made me wonder if my invitation to dinner was revoked.

I held my hands up. "I was talking about options."

"And my wife has been trying to convince me we should get another dog and probably heard what she wanted," Trent said, turning a glare on Finley.

"I'm just listening to someone who knows a lot more than I do about pets," Finley said, tilting her head back.

Trent leaned down and kissed her hard. "You're trouble."

"You love it."

"I love you. And we'll talk about it. First, let's eat." Trent turned to the yard and whistled. "Food, children!"

The kids squealed with delight and rushed over, all stopping before they got to the massive dinner table.

My brows shot up, and Finley just winked.

"Who was the most kind today?" Trent asked.

They each pointed to someone else.

"I think since Isla is our dinner guest for the first time, she should go first," Trent declared.

Three of the kids were pointing at Isla, and with his declaration, the rest of them pointed at her. My throat tightened with love for my girl, who looked like she couldn't believe she was honored.

"Come on, Isla. You get food first. What do you want, honey?" Trent asked her. He helped her load up a plate with food, then set it down at the seat next to me.

Isla threw her arms around my neck. "Hi, Daddy!"

"Hi, sweetheart. Did you have a fun day?"

"The best. And we get food. Mr. Trent is a really good cook. And he told us that the nicest people are the ones who are the best people. He said we should all try to make the world better," Isla bounced in her seat, picking up her fork and stabbing at the vegetable medley on her plate.

"He's right," I said.

Isla nodded. "I know."

My appreciation for the MacKellars grew instantly, telling me they were the kind of people I'd always wanted my kid around. Isla was learning things from others that I tried to teach her. Sometimes coming from another source was the best.

The other kids got their food and settled near their parents to eat. When they were quiet, the adults passed food around the table, everyone getting a steak, plenty of vegetables, baked potatoes, and salads. Water cups were filled and handed out, and someone said dessert was on the counter inside.

We ate and talked and I felt like I'd always been there. Like I'd known them my entire life. I hadn't felt like that with anyone in a very long time. Not with my coworkers in Philadelphia or friends or anyone since Faith.

Except Daisy.

But Daisy wasn't there. And Daisy and I were temporary. We were enjoying each other, and I was having fun with her, but that was it.

After dinner, the kids asked to jump in the pool, and all the parents agreed. We sat around the table talking about kids and life. The easy friendship and camaraderie among them was something I'd always missed in my life. People who knew you so well you didn't have to tell your own stories because they could tell them for you. People who were there for you and treated your kids like their own. People who supported you and cared for you and wanted the best for you.

I hadn't realized how alone I'd felt until I was surrounded by people who made me feel like I wasn't. It was a blessing and a curse because this place was not my future. It was not my home. Not anymore. Not ever again.

The kids dragged themselves out of the pool and started to fade, breaking up the night. Isla changed reluctantly, but I knew she would be out by the time we got to my parents' house. I thanked Finley and Trent and headed out.

I carried Isla inside and tucked her into bed before getting all her things from the SUV. The house was quiet, but when I was tossing a load of laundry into the wash, my mom appeared.

"Did she have a good time again?" Mom asked.

I smiled. "She did. They're pretty amazing people. Invited us to stay for dinner. I was late getting there, and they were about to eat."

"That was nice of them."

"It was."

"You seem to be building a little bit of a community here. And Isla is loving it."

"She is. It's been good for her to have other kids to spend time with. I know you want her here with you, but we don't have this in Philadelphia."

"Maybe you should think about moving back," Mom said.

The world stopped with those words. I couldn't. She didn't know why, but I couldn't. I couldn't be around my father every day. I couldn't stand to see him, and Sheila. I couldn't do it.

"No," I said.

"But—"

"I'm sorry, Mom, but it's never going to happen. We're not moving back here. Not now, not ever."

## 17

DAISY

I could not stop smiling. It was bad. I was always a happy person, but this was so much more.

It was all Kingsley.

Almost all. It was also Natalie because we were back to normal after our talk last week. She even asked how things were going with Kingsley as I was getting ready for our date.

"I'm really happy for you, Daisy," she said, sitting on my bed and watching me decide what dress to wear.

"Thanks. I'm having fun. I know it's going to end, and it's going to be sad, but I'm okay. He's helping me see what I want in a relationship."

"What do you mean?"

I pulled the latest option over my head. A soft blue dress with an empire waist that hugged my curves but made me feel sexy instead of like I looked pregnant. I turned to face Natalie, and she grinned, nodding. "Thanks. And I mean, before Kingsley, I dated, but I was always trying to be who the guy wanted me to be. I'd tone down my happy, I'd ask about his life, I'd accept whatever I got. There's a freedom in being with someone who's not sticking around. I don't need to pretend."

Natalie's brow wrinkled. "You shouldn't have to pretend. I didn't... I'm sorry you always felt that way."

I shrugged. "It's okay. I think it's part of dating, but with Kingsley, I'm seeing another side of things. Another option."

"I always did that, too," Natalie confessed. "Pretended I was different. I always pretended I was more like you."

I breathed a laugh. "And now I'm bursting your bubble, telling you I was always insecure."

"Yeah," she laughed. "You really are."

I chuckled. "Sorry."

"That's why you were so upset when I questioned you. Because you were being yourself with him and felt like it was a good relationship, and I was shitting all over it."

I nodded. "Yeah, a little. I know you're worried about me, but I promise, I am okay with this. If I fall for him, that's okay, too."

Her brows winged up. "You're falling for him?"

"No, but I could. He's a good person. Kind and thoughtful. He's..." I paused, then continued because it was my bestie. "He's really good in bed."

Natalie laughed. "Well, that's good."

"Yeah. I mean, like, I never knew sex could be so good. It's addictive."

"That's how I feel with Omar. It was a whole new experience."

"It really is. But that's another thing that's good. Because it's proving to me there is better out there for me than I've known so far. I've thrown so much of myself into Lincoln Toys over the last few years, between the idea for it, then making it happen and getting it up and running. I've barely dated, and I was starting to worry there was something wrong with me, or that I missed my chance at finding someone."

Natalie shook her head. "I don't think you have. Everyone is different."

I nodded. "I know. And I'm believing that again. I was coming to terms with not getting married or having kids, but now I'm enjoying things with Kingsley and open to meeting whoever I'm supposed to be with."

"Well, that's good. I'm happy to hear that."

"Thanks, Nat." I spun to face her, jewelry and lipgloss done, my hair in a loose knot to keep it off my neck on the warm summer night. "How do I look?"

"Like you're going to have a great night. Speaking of which, I'm staying at Omar's tonight."

"You don't have to do that."

She nodded. "I know, but going back to Kingsley's place isn't an option, and I wanted to make sure you two were comfortable being here."

"You're the best friend ever."

"No, you are," she said.

I chuckled and hugged her. Life was much easier when we were in a good place. Natalie was family, and being at odds with her was so hard. I was happy we were back to okay.

"Can I ask you a question?" she asked as she walked me to the door.

"Sure."

"Why didn't you tell the others you and Kingsley are seeing each other?"

I slipped into my sandals and slung my handbag over my shoulder. "I didn't want everyone telling me I was making a bad choice."

"Because of me."

I shrugged. "I know you meant well, I really do, but it was hard to hear it."

"I'm sorry. I think you should tell them."

"I'll think about it." A knock on the door put the smile back on my face. "He's here."

"Open the door. Have fun tonight. I'm going to pack a bag." Natalie hugged me quickly, then hurried to her room before I opened the door.

Kingsley was on my porch, looking hot in a pair of black shorts, a green collared shirt, and black sandals. His gaze slid down my body before he wiped a hand over his face. "Wow," he breathed.

"Wow yourself," I said.

He stepped inside and kissed me with a sweetness that had my head spinning and my heart pounding. My fingers curled against his shirt, wanting to hold him in place.

"You're beautiful."

"Thank you."

"Are you ready to go?"

I nodded. "I am."

He stepped back and let me walk outside ahead of him, then waited for me to lock the front door. He opened my door to his car, then put his hand on my thigh when he sat next to me. He looked over at me with a grin before he put the car in reverse and backed out of the driveway.

"What's Natalie doing tonight?"

"She's going to Omar's."

"All night?"

"All night. She wanted to clear out so we could have the place to ourselves. If we wanted. I'm not trying to pressure you."

He chuckled. "Trust me, you're not. I'm more than willing to come back to your place."

I grinned. It was going to be a good night.

We talked about our week on the drive to the restaurant. He told me about some weird things the dogs he treated ate, making me feel better about Dozer's rubber hot dog digestion. I told him about some of the new toys we'd gotten in, including a new line of toys from Timeless Timber Toys.

I also mentioned my struggles with Penny, which weren't getting better.

As he parked outside the restaurant, he asked, "Do you want my advice or just for me to listen?"

I waited until we got out of the car to look at him. "You'd do either?"

He nodded. "Sometimes we need to get things off our chests, so to speak. Sometimes we need an outside perspective. Before I choose which to do, I wondered what you need right now."

"Wow. I've never had someone ask me that."

"Okay, well, I am now. Think about it for a minute." He opened the door to the restaurant and let me go ahead.

The host asked if we had a reservation, then led us to the table Kingsley obviously reserved. It overlooked the water, giving us a stunning view of the Saint Lawrence River and the boats passing by.

He picked up his menu, not pushing me to answer his question.

I picked mine up, but I stared at the menu without seeing anything on it. Advice or listen? That was new to me. I liked it. He was right. There were times I wasn't looking for someone else to solve my problems. But I realized this wasn't one of them. I wasn't sure how to proceed with Penny, and I was curious about what he thought.

"I'd like your advice, please," I told him.

He folded his menu and rested his hands on it. "Okay.

First, I'd document everything. Even though you are the owner and don't have an HR department, it's still good to have documentation in case she ends up suing you."

I sucked in a breath. I hadn't even considered that she would, or could, do that. "Do you think she would? No. She wouldn't. Right?"

He shrugged. "I don't know her, so I can't say, but when people feel wronged, even if they aren't, they do crazy things. Our vet clinic was sued by a family after their dog died. They came in and the dog was very sick. One of my colleagues, one of the owners, saw the dog. The dog was clearly in distress, and he wanted to do X-rays and tests to see what was going on. The family refused. Said something similar had happened in the past and the dog needed medicine. My colleague refused, saying there were other possible causes. The dog's stomach was tender to the touch, and he growled at everyone. The family refused any tests and took the dog home. The dog died that night. They sued the clinic for refusing treatment."

"What happened?"

"Unfortunately, it went to trial, and what came out was the father was abusive toward the dog. Had kicked it and caused internal bleeding. If scans had been done, surgery would have been required, but the family thought the dog ate something that made him sick. They had no idea the father was hurting the dog."

"Oh, no."

Kingsley nodded. "It was pretty traumatic for everyone, and it was painful for us as a practice because we all swore to care for animals. Seeing one hurt and not being able to do anything is hard."

"Especially when you could have."

"Yeah."

The server approached with water and a basket of bread. "Can I start you with appetizers while you look over the menu?"

Kingsley looked at me. "I had my eye on a few things, but I'll let you go first."

I smiled at the server. "I haven't even looked at it yet. Do you mind giving us a minute?"

"Of course. Take your time. I'll be right back."

"Thank you."

He smiled and left us to our conversation and menus.

"Sorry," I told Kingsley.

"Nothing to be sorry for. Want to know what I was looking at? In case you want to share?"

"Sure."

He opened the menu again. "Stuffed mushrooms sounded good, and I was thinking about shrimp cocktail. Maybe the bruschetta."

"That all sounds good to me," I said, scanning the appetizers and finding those would be my top three, too.

"Good. And all of this is on me. I don't tell you that so you'll pick something affordable. I am telling you because I don't want you to debate if you should try for the check or not. It's my treat."

"You really don't have to do that."

"I know, but I'd like to. If you'll let me."

I smiled, nodding once, and ignoring the warm feeling spreading through me. I could definitely fall for this man.

But I wouldn't.

We studied our menus and were ready when the server came back over. After he was gone, Kingsley reached for my hand.

"We never know when someone is going to call a lawyer. There are plenty of times it's well justified. When my wife died, I had a lawyer handle her wrongful death lawsuit. No one calls a lawyer believing they're in the wrong, so it's smart to have documentation, if possible something she's signed, so you don't go bankrupt if the worst happens."

"I feel so over my head with this," I admitted. "I think I'm a good boss, and when I gave her the job, I did it because she had good ideas and saw things differently than I do, but after a few weeks, it's feeling like I was just wrong."

"Maybe you were. Sometimes we have to be willing to accept that and let it go, move on and make a change."

"Yeah, maybe."

"Only you know if it's time to make a change or not. I don't give people a lot of chances. Especially when we're talking about something important. Isla gets unlimited chances because she's still learning, but adults know better. Your employee knows the expectations and has chosen not to fulfill them. If you want to give her a second chance, make sure things are clear."

"I've given her a few second chances," I admitted.

Kingsley cringed. "Sorry. You have to run things your way."

"Yeah, but if I'm being too nice, she's going to walk all over me."

"She might, yeah."

The appetizers arrived, and the conversation moved away from my work troubles and toward getting to know each other.

"What's your biggest pet peeve?" I asked him over stuffed mushrooms.

"Dishonesty," he said without hesitation.

"I can get behind that one."

"What about you?"

"Meanness."

He nodded. "Similar lines."

"Yeah. What do you do when you're feeling happy?"

"Happy? Hmm. Doing you makes me happy."

My cheeks heated at his comment. "Well, that makes me happy, too."

He breathed a laugh. "What do I do when I'm happy? I don't know. I've never really thought about it. I think I spend more time not happy."

"Is that why your screen name was DrGrumpy?"

He chuckled. "Obviously, you know I didn't come up with that, but probably. I can be a little grumpy."

"So what do you do when you're not happy? Do you have a way of getting yourself out of that?"

He leaned back and shook his head. "I don't know. Isla changes my mood. She's always making me feel like everything will be okay. She's such a happy kid, even though she has every reason not to be."

"Why is that?"

"Without her mom. She could be angry."

"I'd say that's a credit to you. She could be angry, but she's a happy kid because she knows she's loved. She told me she likes purple because her mom did, so even though she probably doesn't remember her, her mom is still a part of Isla's life."

"She told you that?" he whispered.

I nodded. "She did. She's a very lucky girl to have you as a dad."

He reached for my hand and brought it to his lips. "Thank you, Daisy."

I smiled. "You're welcome."

"Dessert?" the server asked, interrupting the moment.

Kingsley raised his eyebrows at me, a mischievous look in his dark eyes.

"I think we're good," I said, more than hungry for whatever was on the other end of that look in Kingsley's eyes.

The server picked up our empty plates. "To go?"

Kingsley raised his brows at me in question.

"I could be talked into that," I said.

"We have tuxedo cheesecake, chocolate cream pie, a blondie with vanilla ice cream, key lime pie, and red velvet cake."

"She'll have the red velvet," Kingsley said before I could order it.

"How did you know I wanted that?" I asked.

"It's your favorite."

"I don't remember telling you that."

He smiled. "I told you I read all the messages you sent."

I pressed my lips together to keep from... I don't know what. Crying? Telling him I loved him? What?

I'd never told him, but he read the messages I sent to his mom. And just like I knew his favorite dessert was turtle cheesecake, he knew mine was red velvet cake.

He remembered that.

No one except Natalie knew it was my favorite. Not even my parents. They thought I liked vanilla because it was what my brothers liked.

I swallowed the tears back and told myself I absolutely was not falling for Kingsley. I couldn't.

But if he was a local, I would.

But he wasn't.

Kingsley ordered key lime pie for himself and thanked the server. He reached for my hand again. "Are you mad I ordered for you?"

I shook my head and squeezed his hand. "No. I... Not many people know I love red velvet. I was surprised."

"A good surprise?"

I nodded. "Definitely."

"Well, good."

Kingsley paid the bill, then grabbed our dessert and my hand and led the way to the door. He held my hand the entire drive back to my place, a decision made without having to talk about it or think about it.

"You asked me before if I read the messages. Was it okay I read them?" he asked when I put the desserts in the fridge at home.

I nodded and turned to him. "Of course. I mean, I thought they were for you anyway. Why would I be upset that you read them?"

He shrugged. "I wasn't sure where the line was. When I found out what my mom did, I was angry. I'm only here for two months. It was deceitful and wrong. I felt like she was trying to push me into something I wasn't ready for."

"Because you haven't dated much since your wife...?"

He shook his head. "My mother doesn't know. I don't talk to her about any of that. And that was only part of it. I was dealing with a lot when we got here."

"I can imagine. Your dad being sick, moving your daughter up here, jumping into his practice. It's a lot."

He nodded. "Yeah."

There was something in that one word I was missing, but I didn't know what it was.

"My mother wants us to stay here. She asked me last night when we got home from Finley and Trent's."

My heart jumped. Dammit, I wanted him to stay. I couldn't tell him that, but I hoped—

"I told her it's never going to happen. It's just... I don't want to be in MacKellar Cove anymore. She doesn't... understand that."

"Families are complicated," I said instead of asking why

not. I wanted to know why he couldn't be in MacKellar Cove. Why he couldn't stay with me.

But I couldn't ask.

"Yeah." He exhaled slowly. "But all that to say, I'm sorry if I invaded your privacy."

I quirked one eyebrow at him, pushing down the emotions threatening to come out. We were casual. We were having fun. We were not getting emotionally attached.

Okay, fine, I was, but I wasn't allowed to, so I shoved it aside and sauntered over to him.

"I think we're pretty far past the point of privacy."

He chuckled. "You've shared all your secrets with me?"

I shook my head and wrapped my arms around his neck. "Hardly. I have to keep some mystery alive."

He grinned and pulled me close. "I like figuring out your mysteries."

I moaned when he licked my throat.

"Like how much you like that."

"Oh, yes," I whispered.

"Let's see if I can find some more places that make you moan."

**18**

---

Shit. Shit. Shit. I was falling for him. Hard and fast. And it was going to be bad when he left.

But he wasn't leaving yet. He was guiding me to my bedroom with his lips against mine, his tongue plundering my mouth, and his cock pressed tight to my belly.

He flipped the light on when we made it to my room, and he stepped back. "I want to look at you tonight."

My breath hitched. I never had sex with the lights on. Not that I was fighting a lot of men on it, but the lights were always off. The other times Kingsley was in my bedroom, it was frantic and hurried and I didn't think about lights or no lights.

Not this time.

"Um, are you sure?" I asked.

He nodded, his gaze sliding down my body before returning to my face. "Yeah."

Every inch of me tingled. He was turning me on with the look in his eyes. A look he was directing at me. God, what was happening?

No. No panicking. No freaking out. I was going to enjoy

the night with the man I might, probably, kind of, maybe loved, and I was going to hold on to those memories when he went back to his life and I never saw him again. It was fine. It was all fine.

Kingsley moved closer to me again, his hands dipping low on my hips. He bunched up my dress, lifting the fabric of the skirt one inch at a time, the slow retreat of the fabric a tantalizing tease against my thighs.

His fingertips brushed my bare skin, and I gasped. He smiled, letting go of my skirt so he could cup my legs with both hands. He yanked me tight to his body, his mouth descending on mine at the same time.

Devoured from head to toe, his hands massaging my thighs and butt while his tongue worked my mouth, tasting me like I was the best thing he'd had all night.

Maybe all month.

My panties were soaked when one of his hands dipped between my thighs and rubbed over them. He groaned and pushed them to the side, pressing a finger inside me.

"Fuck, Daisy," he whispered against my lips.

"Yeah."

He added a second finger and brushed his thumb over my clit.

I gasped, my hips rocking with his movements.

He kissed me hard, his tongue pulsing into my mouth at the same pace as his fingers fucked me, dragging pleasure from all of me. My nipples were tight, my core soaked, my body tingling and ready to let go.

He rubbed the pad of his thumb against my clit, and I let go, gasping for breath and hanging on him, trusting he wouldn't let me fall.

But I did fall. My back hit the mattress, and before I could figure out what was going on, Kingsley was on his knees with my dress over his head, my panties sliding down my thighs.

"Kingsley," I breathed.

"Please say yes, Daisy."

"Yes," I gasped, his breath fanning over my heated skin and making me whimper.

He pressed gentle kisses to the inside of one thigh, then the other. He traced my tender flesh with his fingertip, or his tongue, I wasn't sure which. The touch was featherlight and sent a shiver through me.

His hands pressed my thighs wider, giving space for his shoulders. He leaned in, his breath growing stronger against my body before his tongue delved inside me.

"Oh, God," I breathed. I was already primed and ready, and there was a sexy, grumpy man on his knees trying to make me come more? How was this my life? And how could I have more of it?

Kingsley kissed his way up from my entrance to my clit, taking his time exploring the folds of my flesh. His tongue ran all over me, tasting every stretch of skin before he licked my clit, just once, and I thrust against him.

He chuckled, gripping my ankles. "In such a hurry."

"You feel so good," I breathed.

"You taste good. I don't know why I ordered dessert. If I'd known how sweet you were, I wouldn't have."

I shivered again, his words making me want to ask him to stay.

I couldn't.

He breathed against my overheated flesh, then covered my skin with his mouth, his tongue licking a path to my clit before he licked away.

I grumbled.

He chuckled again, his tongue still exploring me. He

stopped for a taste inside, then went back to my clit, teasing me all over.

"Kingsley," I breathed.

"Are you ready to come?"

"I've been ready for days."

"Days? You haven't taken care of yourself?"

I shook my head, but he was still under my dress and couldn't see me, so I said, "No."

"Were you waiting for me to help you out?"

"Yeah."

"Then I guess I should do that, huh?"

"Please."

He didn't rush, even though I was practically begging. He still took his time, his hands on my ankles drifting up my legs while his tongue continued his discovery. He cupped behind my knees, spreading my thighs wider before he hooked my legs over his shoulders and pulled me forward, leaving my bare ass hanging off the edge of the bed.

Then, and only then, did Kingsley focus all his attention on my clit. And when the man was focused, holy fuck, he was amazing.

Fingers pressed deep inside me, sending a jolt through me that I felt in my toes. His mouth came down on my clit, sucking hard until all the teasing he did before came together in one massive orgasm that I hadn't realized was building the entire time I was getting frustrated with him.

It couldn't have been more than a few seconds before I was panting and gasping and begging him to finish me off.

His fingers pumped harder, the curl of them rubbing deep inside me. I lost all sense of control, all sense of sanity. He was still hidden from me, but I needed to see him. I needed to watch his head between my thighs, to have the memory in me so when he was gone, I could replay it.

I lifted my skirt, flipping the fabric onto my belly.

Kingsley looked up at me, his dark gaze colliding with mine. The look in his eyes, the way he moved, the feel of his hands and tongue on my body, all of it came together and sent me flying on a high I'd never known.

My toes tingled, my throat tightened. I screamed, or moaned, or something, sounds coming from me that I'd never made before.

And the whole time, Kingsley held my gaze. His eyes stuck on mine, watching me lose complete control of everything as he dismantled me.

Holy fuck, I loved it.

"Don't move," he growled as he retreated. His fingers still played inside me, my body loose and fully pleasured and ready for everything else he could give me.

He held a condom in his teeth, tearing the wrapper with one hand still between my legs. He rolled the condom on, one-handed, then removed his hand from my body, making me shiver.

"You're so fucking beautiful." He lined up at my entrance, holding himself still as he pressed inside, inch-by-inch.

"You feel so good."

"You tasted good," he said. "I want to do that again."

"You do?" I squeaked.

"Fuck, yeah. Before I leave tonight I'm getting my mouth on you again."

"Tonight?"

He slammed in deep, sending those tingles back to my toes. "Yes, tonight."

"Okay." He'd never stayed after sex. I hadn't asked him to, but he always rushed out, needing to get back to Isla.

I didn't blame him, but I still hated that he ran right after sex.

Until tonight.

"You're thinking very loudly right now," he said.

"Sorry." I realized he wasn't moving. "Are you okay?"

"I was going to ask you. I wanted to make sure you're with me."

I sucked in a breath. This man. He was so dangerous for me. But so good. I didn't think men were like him. I'd just always chosen the wrong ones.

"I'm with you," I whispered.

"Good." He eased out, taking his time, then pressed back in at the same slow pace. "I love watching myself disappear inside you."

"I love feeling it."

"That, too. You're wrapped so tight around me, like you don't want to let me go."

"I don't," I blurted before I could think about what I was saying.

He grinned. "You still with me?"

I nodded.

"Good." He stroked in fully, pausing when his body met mine. The brush of his pubic hair against my clit made me shiver. "You like that?"

I nodded. "You were brushing against my clit."

"You can come more?"

"I think so. It felt like it."

"Are you going to squeeze my cock deep inside you?" He asked the question with a thrust, one that sent my head spinning.

"Yes."

He leaned over me, rubbing my clit with each stroke. "You feel so good."

"Same."

He chuckled at my stilted response.

"Sorry. Too good... to talk."

"Best compliment I could get."

I moaned in response.

"Maybe that was," he said.

I squeezed my channel in response that time, and he moaned. "Yeah, good answer."

He snickered and set his hands on the mattress next to my sides. The leverage of him over me had him rubbing me with every stroke, and my orgasm built even faster.

"You're getting close," he grunted. "I can see it in your eyes. Fuck, Daisy. Let go for me. Let me feel you."

I held his gaze, his growled words sending me over the edge as I stared at him. My mouth opened, breath rushing from me, everything tightening, then letting go as I clenched around him.

"Fuck, yes. Oh, fuck, Daisy." He stilled inside me, the swell of his cock matching my aftershocks as he came hard, his eyes rolling back in his head just before he collapsed on top of me.

His breath puffed against my shoulder, pushing my hair away with every exhale. The knot I'd put it up in was more like a puddle after that, and I couldn't have been happier.

"Wow," he whispered, still on top of me.

"Agreed."

He slid off me, kissing my neck, cleavage, belly, then thighs before he crawled to the bathroom, his bare ass the only thing I could see.

I laughed. "Wore you out?"

"You know you did."

I couldn't move either, the burn of his five o'clock

shadow between my thighs making me smile as much as the way the rest of my body felt.

Water ran in the bathroom, then a soft laugh met my ear. "Not the only one worn out."

"No, you are not."

"Dress on or off?"

"I think it needs a wash."

He laughed again. "I really like that dress."

"So do I." I smiled up at him, knowing I'd never wear the dress again without thinking of him.

"Let's get this off, then we can rest for a minute while I recover. Then I get another taste of you."

"Do I get a taste of you?" I asked.

He stilled his movements, waiting until I met his gaze. "That's up to you."

"I'd like that. If you're okay with it."

His cock bounced in response for him.

"I'll take that as a yes."

He chuckled, then helped me out of my dress and bra. He shut off the lights, then laid down next to me, pulling me into his arms and kissed the side of my head. "Just for a minute."

A MINUTE BECAME TWO HOURS, and when I woke up again, his fingers were between my thighs and I was halfway to another orgasm. As soon as Kingsley knew I was awake, he slid beneath the covers and licked me until I came on his tongue. He crawled up the bed to kiss me, then let me return the favor for a minute.

"I need to feel you again," he breathed as he rolled a condom on. He positioned himself between my thighs and took us both back to heaven, sending us into sleepy orgasms with our eyes still half-closed.

After, he rolled out of bed and went to the bathroom. I was vaguely aware of him picking up clothes and getting dressed in the dark. When he kissed me and said he had to go, I got up.

"Stay in bed."

"I need to lock the door."

"Oh, right. I'm sorry."

"It's okay." I grabbed a pair of shorts and a tank top, pulling both on and knowing I'd be back to sleep in minutes.

He groaned. "You're not even trying to tempt me into staying and I'm dying."

I chuckled. "I wouldn't know how to tempt you if I tried."

"Which is what I like about you." He kissed me softly, lingering just long enough for me to debate pulling him back to bed. Maybe he would stay.

He pulled away.

I let him.

I followed him to the door, turning on the outside lights for him. He kissed me once more, then said good night and went to his SUV. I watched until his headlights turned to face the road, then disappeared before I carried myself back to bed.

I really didn't like being wrong, but I was. I was falling for Kingsley, and I was going to be crushed when he left.

Dammit.

NATALIE SPENT most of Sunday at Omar's, which was good

for me. I had lots of time to figure out how I really felt about Kingsley.

Unfortunately, it meant I had lots of time to obsess over every little thing.

I wasn't going to be one of those people who twisted reality and saw things that weren't there. Kingsley had been honest with me from the beginning. He told me about his mother as soon as he found out about the app. He said he didn't like when people weren't honest. He said he was going back home and didn't want to stay in MacKellar Cove.

Falling for him was my problem, not his. He did nothing wrong. I would get over him eventually. And until I did, I was going to enjoy our time. It might hurt worse, but I couldn't let him go. Not now. I would when it was time, but until he left, I was going to love him and never, ever, tell him.

And I was definitely not going to be sad about it. I found love. Just because it was going to end didn't mean I shouldn't enjoy it. So I would.

But listening to my friends talk about setting Kingsley up with someone else, again, was my limit. And that was exactly what happened at book club Sunday night.

Natalie made it home just before I was getting ready to go. She wanted to go with me, so I drove, and she asked how my night was.

"It was a lot of fun. Thank you for that, but I feel bad we chased you out of your own home."

Natalie shook her head. "No chasing. And not a hardship for me to stay at Omar's."

I chuckled. "That's good."

"When are you getting together again?"

"I don't know," I told her. "He left really late, and we didn't talk about it."

"If you need me to give you space again, let me know."

"Thanks."

"Of course."

My light and happy mood stayed until Finley brought up how much fun they all had with Kingsley Friday night. "His daughter is so cute. Absolutely adorable. She kept hugging me all day."

"Aw," the other women said.

Natalie gave me a secret smile.

"He would fit in so well with our group. Trent said he's been going to guys' night and gets along with everyone. If we set him up, maybe he'll stick around," Finley continued.

"Don't even look at me," Casey said. "I just barely got divorced, and I can feel your eyes on me. The answer is no."

"Melody said the same thing," Elise said. "Only you know when you're ready."

"Thank you," Casey said. "And thanks, Mel. I would love to feel ready to date again, but I'm just not there yet."

"We understand," Melody said.

"I said we should set him up with Daisy, but she said no," Finley said.

Natalie looked at me, brows raised.

I smiled and leaned forward. "Actually, we're kind of already seeing each other."

The room went silent.

Elise leaned forward and held her hand up, then opened it. "Mic. Drop. Damn, girl. Good for you."

The questions came in all at once.

"How long have you been dating?"

"When did you meet?"

"Is he sticking around?"

I shook my head and held up my hand. "It's crazy, but..." I chuckled. "It's been a few weeks. I like him. A lot. But I know he's leaving, and I'm not going to ask him to stay or try to convince him. He doesn't like it here."

"Are you going to move there to be with him?" Haley asked.

I shook my head. "No. We're not that serious."

"He's not or you're not?" Elise asked. "Because I'm seeing all kinds of emotions on your face."

I smiled and shrugged. "I might be falling for him, but he's not feeling the same. And that's okay," I rushed to add. "We both knew that going into it. He's a good man, and I'll get over him. He's showing me what I want in a relationship, and that's a really good thing."

"So you want that with him or not?" Haley asked.

"I do, but it's not an option. I know that. I would never ask him to stay. Not when I know he doesn't want to be here. And when I meet someone else, I know it'll be right."

"Will it, though? Will it ever be right if he's not Kingsley?" Finley asked.

"It will have to be, because Kingsley and I are not meant to be forever. And I'm okay with that."

"Are you?" Natalie asked.

I nodded. "I am. I love him enough to want him to be happy, and he's not happy here, so I'll love him and I'll let him go when it's time, and I'll remember this time and know it was the right guy at the wrong time and that's good enough."

"Oh, Daisy," Finley said.

Tears filled my eyes, but I brushed them away. "It's okay. I promise."

I was surrounded in seconds, hugs and comfort and another piece of cake. And if I had any doubt before, I knew I would be okay, because I had the most amazing family of friends in the world, and they would make sure I was okay.

That would be enough until I met the man I was truly meant to be with.

# 19

## KINGSLEY

It was not a good day. Not at all. It should have been a good day, but dammit.

My father was back to work.

Everyone was so fucking happy to see him, so excited he'd returned. He was the hero, back from the dead, almost, and they were thrilled.

It should have been good news. It was good news. It meant I was closer to getting the hell out of MacKellar Cove, going back home. Getting away from him.

So why was I an asshole to everyone who dared look at me?

First patient of the day? I snarled at a little girl who was trying to protect her new puppy from a shot and got too close.

Second patient of the day? I snapped at Megan when she opened the door into me when I was standing too close.

Third patient? The dog bit me because she sensed my mood and reacted with fear. Not the dog's fault. My fault. But didn't help me.

I was washing my hands and bandaging my finger where

the dog cut through my skin when my phone rang. I typically ignored it when I was working, but I checked to make sure it wasn't my mom and saw Daisy's name on the screen.

"Hey," I said, answering before I thought twice about it.

"Hi," she said, the sigh in her voice one of relief.

"Are you okay?" I ducked into a storage room for a little privacy.

"Yeah. I needed to hear a friendly voice. I know you're in the middle of your day. I thought I'd get your voicemail."

"I'm... between patients. What's going on?"

"You know the employee I was telling you about?"

"The new inventory manager?"

"Yeah. She didn't come in this morning. Again. She has one of my store managers doing her job and hiding it from me."

"Ooh, that's not good."

She huffed. "No. It's not."

"What are you going to do?"

She was silent for a long moment. "I don't know," she whined.

I chuckled. "Yes, you do. You know what you want to do, and you know what you think is right, but you don't want to do it."

"I know." She exhaled roughly. "I don't like being the bad guy."

"Few people do, but it's part of being the boss. You have to do it."

"What if she sues me?"

"You have your documentation. You have proof. If she was a good employee in her other position, maybe you just need to shuffle things around again."

"You mean demote her?"

I shrugged. "I don't know what would be the best option,

but maybe it's something to consider. Something that would mean she's still employed, but she's doing something that was more within her skillset."

"I never thought about that."

"You said the store manager is doing the work. Maybe they swap places."

"Then I don't have to fire her."

"It's an option. If she needs to be fired, you have to do that, but if there's another reason why it's not working out, maybe going back to the old position would be better. Not everyone is meant to advance, and I don't say that to be mean. Not everyone wants more responsibility or advancement. Some people are content to do their job and have the freedom and flexibility to enjoy their non-work time without having to think about work."

"Say it ain't so," she breathed, a laugh in her voice.

I chuckled at her response. "I know, right?"

"She does talk about her sister a lot and helping out with her nephew. Maybe that's part of it."

"Then maybe you found your answer. Something that'll work out for everyone. If the other employee is willing to do the job."

Daisy sucked in a breath. "She's already doing it, but yeah, I think I need to do a little more thinking about that. And have a few conversations with her about it."

A noise in the background had me pausing before I heard a man's voice calling out to Daisy.

"Coming, Jeff!" she replied.

I should not be angry she was talking to an employee. Or a customer. Or whoever the hell Jeff was. I was leaving soon. My father was back to work. My bosses had been in touch asking when I was coming back. Summer was rushing to a close.

Daisy would stay in MacKellar Cove and live her life with Jeff and whoever else was around when I wasn't, and I would go back to my lonely existence hundreds of miles away.

"Sorry," she said. "I need to get back to work, but thank you. I feel better after talking to you."

"Happy to help," I said, hoping my voice sounded normal.

She didn't call me on it, so mission accomplished. "Thanks. I'll talk to you later. Bye!"

"Bye," I said, but she already hung up. Rushing back to Jeff.

I squeezed my phone tight, wanting nothing more than to smash it and let out my anger. Nope. I couldn't do it.

I slid my phone back into my pocket and stepped out of the storage room.

Only to see Sheila and my father at the other end of the hall. They were huddled close, whispering.

Her hand was on his arm. A smile on her face. The look in her eyes...

What the fuck?

And him! He was looking at her like she was the best thing that'd ever happened to him. Leaning toward her as they spoke. Not a care in the fucking world that they were in plain view of anyone who walked by.

I turned the corner and walked away, fighting back the vomit rising up in my throat. He promised me. He fucking promised me.

Fucking liar.

I squeezed my eyes shut and shoved the tears back. One day back to work and he was screwing around on my mother again.

And he wondered why I never wanted to talk to him.

"Dr. Harris?"

"Yeah, Megan?" The words came out more like a growl, and I regretted them immediately. "I apologize."

"It's fine," she said, sounding like it was definitely not fine. "Room six is ready for you."

I nodded and pulled my head out of my ass and went back to work. I had a fucking job to do, and the sooner I did it, the sooner I could get the hell out of there and get away from my father and Sheila.

I WAS SO DAMN ready to leave. So ready. But as I got in my SUV and pulled out of the parking lot, I knew going to my parents' house was not where I needed to go. If I did, I would blurt out something that would hurt my mother, damaging my relationship with her forever, and ruining any chance Isla had at staying in touch with her grandmother.

That and I might scare my kid. I was not going to unleash my anger with her around. I'd worked hard to isolate her from it, to let her only see the sides of me that she should know. I never wanted my daughter afraid of me, and I would not go back on that now.

Not because of him.

So when I ended up in front of Daisy's house, I wasn't entirely surprised. I sat in the driveway, staring at the house, and her car parked next to me, and knew I wasn't being fair to her either.

I was there because I was in a mood. I was there because she made me feel better. I was there because she went running when fucking Jeff called her.

I was an asshole, and I needed to just leave before she saw me. This wasn't our agreement. I wasn't supposed to get jealous of other men in her life. We said if either of us wanted someone else, we would end it.

But she didn't tell me she wanted to end it. She just hung up when another man called her name.

Fuck.

I reached to turn my SUV back on the same second her front door opened and she appeared on the porch. She smiled at me in that way of hers, the way that made me think everything was going to be okay because nothing bad could happen when she smiled at me.

Her brows went up, a question in them.

She didn't approach, standing on her porch and letting me decide if I wanted to join her.

I should leave. I should put the car in reverse and spare her my mood and my jealousy and my frustration. I should go for a drive and get rid of all of it another way.

But I opened the door.

The edge of her mouth kicked up with her smile. She stepped backward into the house as I approached, holding the door for me as I stalked her like she was my prey and I was a hungry animal desperate for a taste of her.

I didn't stop until she was in my arms, the door was kicked closed behind me, and my lips were on hers.

She squeaked in reply, then moaned when I pressed past her lips and took a taste of her. Her arms went around my neck, holding on like she was just as desperate for me as I was for her. She walked back with me, our rhythms out of sync as we fought to get closer to each other and closer to her bed at the same time.

Teeth clashed. Hands groped. We never stopped.

Her bedroom door was kicked closed the same as the front door, but she paused to flip the lock on this one. The sound was the first since I got out of my SUV and forced my way into her house.

"Who's Jeff?" I asked, hating myself as soon as the words were out.

"Jeff?" The look of confusion on her face was replaced with a dawning. "My new store manager?"

"You hung up when he called your name," I confessed, letting her understand my frustration.

"I was at work, and he had a question. If it helps, he's six years younger than me, my employee, and married to his high school sweetheart."

"You should have led with that last one."

She chuckled. "What fun would that have been?"

I growled and claimed her lips again, loving the way she responded to me with a matching eagerness. My hands went to her shirt, lifting it up so I could get my fingers on her flesh. I wasn't gentle with her as I shoved at her shorts and pressed a finger inside her warm center.

She fucking moaned and rocked against me. "Kingsley."

"Fuck," I grunted, dragging my soaked finger out of her to spread her wetness on her clit. "Already?"

"I guess the angry look works for me. Maybe the jealousy thing, too."

"Should I tell you about the busboy at dinner I wanted to strangle when he checked out your boobs? Or the men at O'Kelley's I thought about punching when they got too close to you? Or the woman I overheard telling her friend how she wished you were into girls so she could hit on you?"

She laughed, moaning when I pressed down on her clit. "The only one I see is you."

"The only one I see is you, too, Daisy. You've made being here bearable. You've made it fun."

"Oh," she gasped. Her fingers dug into my arms, her hips rocking faster.

"Are you going to come for me?"

"Yes."

"Fuck," I growled, doubling my efforts to bring her to the edge. I needed to feel it, to know she was right there with me, to leave my mark on her. I was leaving, and when I was gone, she'd find someone else and move on with her life. That was the deal.

But until then, I was going to make sure she didn't think about another person making her come.

"Kingsley," she whispered.

"Come for me, Daisy. Come on my fingers."

She bucked against my hand, rocking with my fingers.

I spread them around her nub and pinched them together, holding the bundle of nerves tight as I dragged my fingers up and down. I couldn't move far since we hadn't managed to shed our clothes yet, but I could tell by the way she hung on me that it was good enough.

"Oh, yes. Kingsley. Yes. So good. Fuck." She came with a whimper and a few teeth on my shoulder and a gush against my fingertips.

"Fuck," I breathed, barely catching my own orgasm before she carried me with her. Just feeling her come had me halfway there.

"Yeah," she said, shivering when she moved and my fingers rubbed her clit again. "Fuck."

"Clothes," I said, using my other hand to shove at her shorts without removing the hand inside her panties.

She helped, shimmying to get her shorts down her hips, her panties following a second later.

I swiped my fingers through her folds, but she dropped to her knees before I could work her up again.

She looked up at me, her shirt still on, a glazed look in her eyes, and unbuttoned my pants. She gave them a shove and let them fall before she hooked her fingers in my boxers and dropped them.

Before I could step out of either, she wrapped her lips around my cock, taking me in deep and moaning when I hit the back of her throat.

"Fucking hell," I groaned, my clean hand going to her hair. I cupped her jaw with my other hand, and she looked up at me.

The look in her eyes was one of pure lust, and my dick swelled.

She took me in again, breaking the connection between us and pumping me in and out of her wet mouth. My balls tightened, and I thrust into her mouth once, then stepped back, nearly tripping on my pants.

Her mouth was wet from licking my cock, still an O. She finally looked up at me, her gaze drifting to my dick before she rose to her feet.

She tossed her shirt, then unclasped her bra without a word, getting a condom from her nightstand before I caught up and got my shirt off.

She dropped to her knees again, and I stepped back. "I won't last."

She held up the condom, one brow raised in question.

I closed my eyes and drew a slow breath, needing to get a hold of myself before she did.

Too late.

She wrapped her hand around me and pumped me, making me growl. She smiled, then rolled the condom down my overeager length.

"You're a temptation I never saw coming."

"Same," she said. "But I'm not regretting it. Are you?"

"No," I said instantly, without a second of hesitation. I crawled onto the bed over her, kissing her hard, then pulled away from her, kissing my way down her body. I licked her nipples, nibbled her hip, then settled between her thighs for my treat. "So good."

"Yes," she whispered back.

I dove in, not pausing to ease her in, just feasting on her sweet pussy. She answered with a lift of her hips and a moan that filled the room. Her clit was already sensitive from my fingers, and I focused on that with my tongue, licking it in quick flicks before closing my mouth over it and sucking hard.

She gasped and grunted, the sounds coming from her like the ones animals made when they were mating. It was fucking amazing. To know I took her out of her head and gave her a few minutes of pure pleasure. To know she could let go completely and come hard against my face.

I licked her again, teasing her a little before sucking on her clit once more, thrusting two fingers inside her just as she started to come. She screamed, the good kind of scream, and rode my face through the whole thing, panting and gasping and begging me not to stop.

As if I would.

When she collapsed back against the pillows, I lined up with her entrance. Her eyes flipped open when she felt me and watched my face as I sank into her warmth.

All the way in until she took every inch of me. I groaned as she tightened around me, wondering how in the hell it was so fucking good with her.

I leaned over her, knowing she liked that best when I rubbed her clit as I fucked her.

She smiled, a lazy smile full of pleasure, and her entire body shook.

I grabbed her hand and brought it to my lips, then lifted it above her head, not letting go. Her breast lifted with the move, and I took the other hand, offering her breasts to myself.

I leaned down and captured one nipple between my teeth. She squeezed my dick hard and moaned loudly.

I bit the other one, and she did the same thing.

"I love learning what makes you feel good," I whispered against her breast. "Knowing that your nipples are so sensitive, that you like to come with me rubbing your clit. Fuck, Daisy."

"I like when you talk to me," she whispered.

"You do?"

She nodded.

"You like knowing how good you feel wrapped around me? How hard it is for me to hold back when all I want to do is lose my mind and fuck you hard?"

"Please," she whimpered.

"You want me to fuck you, Daisy?"

"Yes. Kingsley, yes."

I leveraged myself up, not releasing her hands, and got onto my knees. I slammed into her, knowing she liked it when her eyes bulged and her whole body shivered.

"Good?"

"Ye-es."

"You're so tight around my cock, gripping it and squeezing it. Your boobs bouncing around with each stroke. You can't even look at me because you're so close to coming on my cock. Are you going to come for me again?"

"Yes," she moaned, dragging the word out as her orgasm hit her. "Oh, fuck, yes."

The flood of come rushed out with her words, adding to

the slipperiness of her channel, letting me fuck her faster and harder.

She grunted and shook her way through it, meeting my strokes with her frantic pace and dragging me over the edge with her, our bodies erupting together as we both let go.

"Daisy," I breathed, burying my face in her neck as I came so hard I thought I was going to pass out or throw up or maybe just never leave her bed.

Fuck.

I collapsed onto her and immediately rolled to the side, dragging her with me. I couldn't let go of her yet. I knew I needed to. I needed to release her from everything I was, but not yet.

Not yet.

Not yet.

## 20

THE LAST TIME I COULDN'T BRING MYSELF TO LEAVE A woman's bed, I married her. I made her bed my bed and never left.

But I couldn't stay in Daisy's bed. Because I couldn't stay in her town. I had to leave. I had no choice.

The memory of my father and Sheila tried to drift in, but I pushed it away. I was not going to think about them when I was wrapped around Daisy, our bodies still sweaty from sex.

I closed my eyes and admitted the truth to myself. That wasn't sex. It wasn't fucking. It was loving her. It was showing her who I was. And she took all of it, all of me. She asked for it.

She loved it.

So I did what I had to do and kissed the top of her head, rolling off her bed so I could get rid of the condom, then ignored my reflection and left her bathroom.

She was already out of bed and half dressed, and it was exactly what I needed. She was right there with me during sex, but as soon as I was out of her bed, she wasn't waiting around and hoping I'd come back, begging me to stay, asking me for more than what we agreed to.

She didn't change the game. I did.

But I couldn't. I was leaving. She couldn't be mine forever. I already had the love of my life. Daisy was... second place.

She deserved better, and she knew it, so I had to go.

We dressed quickly and silently, grabbing our clothes and pulling them back on. I tucked my shirt into my pants and drew a breath.

She grinned and moved toward me. "Let me help you." She reached up and tugged on my collar. I felt it flip, a discomfort I hadn't realized was uncomfortable until her fingers brushed my neck and made it better. She smoothed her hands over the rest of the collar, then down my chest. She looked up at me, and my breath caught in my throat.

That was not love in her eyes. It couldn't be. She didn't want that from me. I was projecting. And I needed to get out of there before I said something we would both regret.

Because I was leaving.

"Thanks," I mumbled.

She smiled and stepped back, her hands falling from my chest. She unlocked her bedroom door and led the way to the front, not offering me any reason to stay longer than I already had.

Maybe she had plans. Maybe she had a date. Maybe Natalie would be home soon and still wasn't on board with us.

I wanted to ask, but I didn't deserve the answer. I was her summer fling, not her future husband.

I stopped at the door and turned to face her. She smiled up at me, and I reached to tuck a strand of hair behind her ear. I lingered, my fingers grazing her jaw.

Her eyes closed and the smile on her face turned liquid, like she was remembering my fingers on other parts of her body.

"I'm sorry I keep stopping by like this."

Her eyes flipped open, hurt in them for a second before she smiled. "You never have to apologize to me. We're having fun. We're enjoying the summer. And you have a daughter who needs you. I know whatever time we get is what you can afford, and I'm okay with it."

"That makes me sound like I don't care about you."

She breathed a laugh and shook her head. "I'm not your priority, Kingsley. I know that. And it's okay. I don't expect to be. That's not what this is."

"But you—"

She put her hand on my chest. "Don't tell me things that aren't true. This is temporary. That's what we agreed to. I'm not trying to change that. I'm not trying to ask you for more than you can give me." She blinked a few times and swallowed before she flashed a smile that didn't seem as bright as it usually was. "You're an amazing man. I am enjoying myself. I don't expect anything else from you. I'm not looking for promises about a future we'll never have. That's not what this is. We're good. I promise."

"Oh, okay." It was my turn to swallow, choking back my feelings and needing to get out of her house before I begged her to reconsider.

But why? What would change if she did? I wasn't moving to MacKellar Cove, and she wasn't leaving her store, her career, her friends. Nothing could change. Which meant nothing could change.

"I'll see you soon, I hope," she said, smiling again and taking a step toward the door.

"Yeah," I said. "Saturday? Are you free?"

She grinned. "I am."

"It's a date," I said, leaning forward to kiss her one more time before I left. "I'll see you then."

She nodded and held the door as I walked out. When I looked back, she was leaning against the side of the door, watching me. She waved.

I waved back, then got in my SUV and left. Because the other option wasn't an option.

A WEEK AND A HALF LATER, I left work early to pick up Isla from Finley and Trent's. My father was at work again, three days this week, and he insisted I leave.

Which meant he was at work with Sheila. Alone.

I wanted to fight him on it, but I couldn't stomach being around him and Sheila for another minute. The way they put their heads together to talk, the way she put her hand on his arm to get his attention, the way he looked at her.

I was done.

I seethed on my drive across town, knowing I needed to pull myself together before I got to Isla. She adored her grandfather, and just like I couldn't ruin his relationship with my mother, I couldn't ruin his relationship with my daughter.

I parked in the massive driveway leading to MacKellar Estates and headed for the door. There were more cars than usual there, but each week seemed to draw a different group of kids and parents. Most of them I recognized from guys' nights at O'Kelley's, something I'd become a regular attendee of.

Andrew opened the door when I rang the bell and welcomed me back. He nodded, knowing I knew the way to the crowd that always gathered outside for their Fridays of fun.

Trinity was leading the kids in a new craft, just finishing up from what I could tell. Two older girls flanked Isla, both helping her to perfect her creation.

"Hey, Kingsley," Finley said, the first to notice me. She approached with a hug, then led me to the other adults.

Isla looked up as I walked by and smiled, then focused on her task once more.

"Who are the girls with Isla? I think they were here the first week Isla came, but I never asked who they are," I asked Finley as we joined the others.

"The redhead is Ramsey and Melody's daughter, Amber. The brunette is Amber's best friend, Mikayla. Mom is Casey White, she works for the local paper. Mom and Dad got divorced about a year ago. Dad's still around, but Mom is primary. I've never met Dad," Finley whispered her words so the girls didn't hear her.

"They're really good with Isla. Always seem to include her," I said.

"They better," Melody said, joining us. "We've made it very clear to both girls that if they come here, they need to play with all the kids, not just hide in a corner together."

"Thank you. Isla has really enjoyed being the big kid, but I think she also likes having the big kids pay attention to her," I said.

Melody nodded. "They all realized they would be in school together. If you were staying. Fair warning, since I have a feeling it's going to come up tonight. Isla was telling Amber and Mikayla that she doesn't want to go back to her old school."

I groaned and wondered if that was my mother's doing

or just because of the fun she was having with her new friends. "Thanks for the heads up."

"Of course. We've never moved, but Casey was considering it when she and Kyle got divorced. Mikayla overheard Casey and freaked out. Refused to live anywhere else but in MacKellar Cove." Melody shook her head with sympathy. "Casey felt like the worst parent already for her marriage ending, and then to have her only child get so angry about possibly moving made her so sad. It's a struggle for her, though. Even with child support, things are expensive."

I nodded, understanding the struggle of single-parenting all too well.

"Daddy! Daddy!" Isla called, running across the yard toward me. "Look at what I made!" She stopped just short of colliding with me and held up her dream catcher proudly.

"Wow, Isla, that's beautiful. I love the colors you used. Pink and purple for you and Mommy?"

Isla nodded, a beaming grin on her face. "Yep. And blue like the water and yellow for the sun. It's going to make sure I have all good dreams. Can I hang it up in my new room tonight?"

"We can hang it up in your room at grandma's house."

The first hint of a fight showed in her frown. "Yeah. My new room."

"Well, that's only your room for now, Isla. We're going back home soon."

"But I like it here."

I glanced at Finley and Melody, catching Melody's silent sorry, then guided Isla to the side. I crouched in front of her, eye-to-eye. "I know you do, honey, but my job's back in Philadelphia. Your school is there."

"But I don't want to go back there. I want to stay here. I can go to school with Mikayla and Amber. And see George and Nina and Maddox. And live with grandma and grandpa." The whine was out in full.

"Honey, it's just not an option for us to move here."

"Why not?"

I sucked in a breath and again had to keep something from one of my favorite people on the planet. "Because it's not where we're supposed to be. This isn't home."

"But I want it to be home. I want to stay here. I don't want to go back to our stinky old house and my stinky old school. I want to live here!"

My heart cracked, splitting right down the middle. This could have been our life. Faith and I planned to raise Isla in MacKellar Cove. We wanted to be here. It was all we ever talked about.

But it wasn't our reality. It wasn't our future. I couldn't face my father after what I saw. I couldn't look at my mother every day and know I was keeping something from her.

And I still couldn't.

Years of lies, and I hadn't been able to change. Faith understood. She didn't like it anymore than I did, but she understood. She supported me leaving and never returning.

But now I was the only one making the choice. The only one breaking our daughter's heart and pulling her away from the friends she'd made, the first real friends she'd made.

"We should go, Isla," I said softly.

"No! I don't want to. I want to stay here."

"Let's go to grandma's house. Spend some time with her."

Isla threw herself on the ground and cried.

I closed my eyes. It had been more than a year since she threw a tantrum like that. There was nothing for me to do but let her have it. Let her get the emotions out and express her anger and disappointment and sadness.

I wished I could do the same. That I could throw myself on the ground and cry at the injustice of it all. At the heartache and pain and weakness.

Because I was weak. Too many years had passed for me to tell my mother what I knew. I should have told her the day I found out. The day I saw them kissing. But I kept the truth from her. I protected the man I thought was my hero and hurt the woman who truly was.

And now my child was suffering for it.

When Isla cried herself out, I scooped her up and thanked Finley for letting her stay. Finley apologized for not making sure Isla got a nap.

"None of this is your fault. She's upset with me, and to be honest, I am, too. This is where I always wanted to live, but it wasn't meant to be. If you'd rather she didn't come back next week—"

"Please, do not concern yourself with that. Every single one of these kids has had a meltdown like Isla just did. It's part of it, and no one here would ever ask her not to return."

I nodded. "Thank you, Finley. I'm sorry. I'll see you soon."

"Yes."

I nodded to the other parents and carried my passed out daughter to the SUV. I buckled her in and drove away, fighting my own tears.

At my mother's house, I carried Isla inside, finding only my mother.

"She wore herself out, didn't she?" Mom asked.

"She had a fit when I told her we weren't moving here. Did you tell her you wanted her to stay?" I demanded.

Mom backed up a step and crossed her arms. "I know

you're not coming at me like that in my own home, Kingsley Adam Harris."

I ground my teeth together and closed my eyes. "I apologize. I should not blame you for her behavior."

"You're damn right you shouldn't. And whether I told her I want you to stay or not has nothing to do with it." Mom's chin tilted up in defiance, giving me my answer.

I let out a sigh and shook my head. I turned and walked down the hall to my room, ignoring her requests to come back and her demands to know why.

I couldn't tell her.

I WAS A COWARD. A big coward. I stayed in my room all night, not coming out when I heard Isla leave her room and find my mother, not when Isla knocked on my door, not when my mother put Isla back to bed, and not when my mother said goodnight outside my door. I was a coward.

Even worse, after a shitty night of sleep, I snuck out of the house early in the morning, stopping by Cracked for breakfast to go before anyone else in my parents' house was awake.

I ate my breakfast in my SUV outside the clinic and wished I'd gotten an extra coffee. One didn't seem like it was going to be enough for the day, but too late now.

I opened the doors to the clinic and started my morning routine. I checked the schedule and got things ready for the day, letting the monotony of a routine calm me down.

I'd tossed and turned all night. In the moments I was honest with myself, I admitted I wanted to stay in MacKellar Cove. I wanted the friendships Isla and I had formed. I wanted Daisy in my life. I wanted to run my own vet clinic and live a life that was quiet and small and easy.

But every time I thought about choosing that option, I thought about my father. About the way he laughed before he kissed Sheila all those years ago. About the lies I told my mother when she asked why I couldn't come home for years. About the lies I was still telling her.

I didn't deserve to have the things I wanted. I deserved to be alone.

But being alone meant forcing the same thing on my daughter.

Round and round in circles my mind went until the alarm went off and I got up to leave for work.

Apparently, I was still going around in those circles because I didn't notice I wasn't alone in the building. A sound outside the office brought my head up as Sheila bent to pick up a tablet.

"What are you doing? Did you break that?" I spat at her.

She picked it up and smoothed her hand over the back and front. "No, it's fine."

"You need to be careful. You can't throw things around."

"I wasn't. I was—"

"What? Messing with something you have no right to touch?" I growled at her.

Her eyes went wide, and her gaze flickered to the side. She rolled her lips in, biting back a response.

Another noise drew me out to the hallway, where a mom and little boy were attempting to control a puppy that was squirming to get away.

"I apologize," the mom said. "He was about to jump out of my arms and Sheila caught him. It's my fault she dropped the tablet. I'll replace it if it's damaged."

"It's fine. Not broken or even scratched," Sheila said,

shooting me a look that reminded me of one my mother issued when she wanted me to agree with her in front of others.

"It's fine," I said, forcing the words out. I pressed my lips into a smile and tried to appear less like an asshole.

That was why I couldn't be there. Snapping at her in front of patients? Not paying attention to what was happening around me? I couldn't do it. Not as long as my father was there. And Sheila.

I went back into the office and ignored Sheila and the patient, needing a minute before I had to face them.

Two more weeks. Two more weeks and I would be gone from MacKellar Cove and never see Sheila again.

My phone buzzed. I debated ignoring it. It was going to be my mother asking why I snuck out so early. But it could be something about Isla.

I grabbed my phone and tapped to see the message.

DAISY

> Can't wait for our date tonight. Natalie's staying with Omar. And I bought a surprise.

> Wait, that's a swimsuit. I don't know the emoji for lingerie, but I do know what your face is going to look like when I model it for you. Come over early.

Daisy. Date night. Tonight.

My body reacted immediately, the thought of Daisy in lingerie for me... More than I could handle. But I was a married man. I vowed to love Faith my entire life. We made plans. We had a future mapped out.

And instead of honoring that, honoring my vows, I'd been falling in love with Daisy and forgetting about my wife.

I was no better than my father. It was my worst fear

come to life. I was the same as him. A man who couldn't stay true to his vows. A man who betrayed the one person he loved.

Four years. Faith had been gone four years, and in all that time, I didn't think about another woman even once. In only a few weeks of being around my father, I'd given my heart to another woman and betrayed my wife.

It had to end.

## 21

DAISY

I STARED AT MY PHONE AND WAITED FOR HIS REACTION. AND waited. And waited. That was weird.

Maybe he was busy. He said he was working, and not happy about it. That had to be it.

I stretched and rolled out of bed. I'd been up for a little while, but hadn't talked myself into actually getting up yet. My stomach rumbled. Breakfast was definitely in order.

I slid my feet into slippers, then headed to the kitchen. Natalie was still sleeping, so I was quiet as I made coffee and stared at the options for food.

My phone rang, and I answered it with a smile. "Hey. Good morning."

"Morning, Daisy," not Kingsley said.

I looked at my phone. Dick. The truck driver. Shit. "Um, hey, Dick. What's going on?"

"Sorry to call you so early, but it looks like no one's here."

"You have a delivery," I said, stating the obvious. Why else would he be calling me?

"Yeah. Scheduled for eight. I'm backed in and ready,

knocked on the door, but no cars are here. Any chance you just didn't see me pull up?" He chuckled like he already knew the answer.

"I'm so sorry. I'm at home, but my inventory manager was supposed to be handling deliveries." I rushed to my bedroom, kicking off my slippers and tugging my pajamas off.

"Yeah, this isn't like Wendy. She's been great."

"Wendy? No, Penny is the inventory manager." I stopped, half-naked, wondering why he thought Wendy was the inventory manager.

"Oh. Really? I... Uh, so..."

"I'm sorry, Dick. I'm heading out the door now. I'll be there in five minutes and get you unloaded." I yanked a tee over my head and stepped into a pair of shorts. I was grabbing my handbag and walking out the door before he replied.

"Thanks so much, Daisy. I'm sorry to bother you. I know you don't like deliveries when you're open, so I wanted to make sure I got this done now."

"It's not on you, Dick. I appreciate the call. I'll see you soon."

"Thanks, Daisy. Bye, hun."

"Bye," I said, hanging up and backing out of my driveway.

What the heck was going on? I was going to ask Dick before he left because if Wendy was covering for Penny even more than I thought, a change definitely needed to be made.

Dick met me at the door once I parked and rushed to get there. "Mornin'," he called, smiling like nothing was wrong.

"Hey, Dick. I'm so sorry, again. I know you take these deliveries so you can be home, and you've been sitting here all this time."

"It's okay, Daisy. We'll get it all set. Teri's going to have coffee and breakfast ready when I get home. She offered to bring something here for us."

"That's so sweet of her."

Dick chuckled. "Got me a good woman. Still don't know why she lets me in the door, but I'm smart enough not to ask and remind her she's too good for me."

I laughed with him. "Oh, Dick, she's smart to keep you. Not all men are as caring as you are."

"Sounds like you have some man trouble. You seeing someone, Ms. Daisy?"

"Oh, no, nothing like that."

"But it's something. Do I need to take care of someone for you? I can drive him to another state and leave him there. Give him something to think about on his trip back."

I laughed. "No, no. He's a good man. Just the right guy, wrong time."

"Ah. Fell in love with one who's not available."

I nodded, surprised by his perception. "Pretty much, yeah."

"Sorry, kid. Happens to all of us. Maybe he'll realize what a treasure he has in you."

I shook my head. "Not an option, but thanks. It'll be okay. There are other fish in the sea and all that, right?" I laughed it off, even though it hurt to know Kingsley was leaving in just two weeks.

"Yeah," Dick said, his tone telling me he wasn't believing my lies anymore than I was but wasn't going to call me on it.

"Let's get you unloaded so you can head home for that breakfast."

He nodded. "Thanks, Daisy."

The truck wasn't too bad, and I managed to get it unloaded fairly quickly. The storage area was still packed with boxes from the first delivery Penny ordered, and maneuvering everything around was a struggle, but I'd take care of that once Dick was on his way.

But first, I needed to find out why he thought Wendy was the inventory manager.

"Hey, before you go, why did you expect Wendy to be here?"

"Uh." He shuffled his feet and studied his paperwork. "I don't want to get anyone into any trouble."

"You're not going to. I promise. I just... I gave Penny the position after a few good suggestions, but I'm not sure it's working out for her. There have been a few times I found out Wendy was covering for Penny, but if you thought Wendy was the one managing inventory, it makes me think that's happened a lot more than I know about."

Dick sighed. "I used to see both of them, about equal, but in the last month or month-and-a-half, I've only seen Wendy. You mentioned Penny before, but I thought things had changed when I stopped seeing her."

I exhaled a long breath. "That's about how long it's been since Penny took the job. And you deliver to us more than any other driver, so that tells me Penny's not really doing her job."

"I'm sorry, Daisy. I thought for sure... I didn't mean to cause problems."

"You didn't. I appreciate you being honest with me. You get home. Thanks for the call."

"You'll get it all set. I know you will. Have a good one!"

"You, too, Dick." I waved as he climbed up into his truck. He drove off with a beep, and I went back inside to organize the mess of boxes because of my poor choice of inventory manager.

Jeff arrived thirty minutes after Dick left. He offered to

help me store boxes, but the store was opening soon and he had other things to do. Which meant I was exhausted and frustrated when Penny breezed in five minutes before the store opened.

She saw me on the forklift and waved, heading to the office and not stopping to speak to me at all. No explanation, no apology, nothing.

What the hell?

I finished what I was doing and parked the truck. I went to the office, finding Penny staring at the computer. A computer full of orders.

"What's that?" I asked.

"Orders I'm putting in. We're running low on some toys and I wanted to make sure we don't run out."

"We don't have space for that. The warehouse is full, Penny. Too full."

"Yeah, but everything will sell eventually."

"I hope so, but I can't accept new orders when the existing orders haven't sold yet. It costs me money to hold on to inventory like this. It's why I always managed things the way I did, with less-than-load orders that would fit on the shelves instead of filling up the entire space."

She spun to face me, defiance in her eyes. "Do you want me to do this job or not? Because you were the one who came to me."

"Are you doing the job, Penny? Because our truck drivers think Wendy's the inventory manager. And I'm here right now because no one was here to unload a truck two hours ago. He sat there for thirty minutes before he called me."

Penny scowled. "My... my alarm didn't go off." The words were fine but they weren't true.

"Your alarm?"

She shrugged. "It's not my fault."

I rolled my lips in, keeping the argument inside. She was lying. She was not doing her job. And the part she was doing was hurting my company. I couldn't afford the orders she was placing. Not at the volume she ordered.

"Penny, I think—"

A crash from the warehouse stopped my words. We both rushed out to find Jeff on the forklift, a pile of stuffed animals around him.

"I'm so sorry, Daisy. I was going to restock the bins and saw the box on top. I thought I had it, but I guess I didn't," Jeff said, looking around at the remnants of pallet and boxes.

"Are you hurt?" I asked him.

He shook his head. "I'm good. It fell in front of the equipment."

The forks of the forklift were speared through boxes instead of securely in the pallet the boxes had been secured to. The weight of the pallet and the forks through the plastic wrap must have been enough to tear through, and the pallet fell. Without the support, the boxes followed.

Thankfully, it was something soft and light, but it could have been worse.

"Let's get this cleaned up," I said. "Jeff, if you need a break, please take it."

He shook his head. "I'm good. I promise. Scared me more than anything."

"If you need a minute for that, it's okay."

He smiled. "I'm good, Daisy. Thanks. Sorry about this."

"It's okay."

Jeff and I worked to clean up everything, separating the damaged stuffed animals for disposal and stacking the boxes that didn't fall.

Penny helped for a little while, then returned to the office.

When Jeff and I were done, he went back to the floor, stocking the shelves and apologizing again. I assured him it was fine, then went to find Penny.

And discovered she'd already left.

I exhaled slowly, knowing I didn't want to make a decision when I was angry. I promoted her when I was frustrated, and firing her or demoting her in the same headspace wasn't good.

But this was not working. She couldn't keep skipping out on her responsibility and letting everyone else take the blame for what she was doing.

I had to check up on the orders she was placing. I didn't agree with how she was running things, but it had to be more than it was different. I needed proof, like Kingsley told me.

I spent the next two hours in front of the computer, going through all the data I had. In the end, I had my answer.

Penny was a great store manager, but she was a horrible inventory manager. Aside from not being present to do her job, she'd already cost me twice my normal budget for orders, and the warehouse was so full it was dangerous.

It had to stop. And Penny wasn't willing to listen to me if the order she placed while I was helping Jeff clean up was any indication.

I checked the schedule and saw Penny was scheduled for Tuesday. With Wendy. It was time for an honest conversation with both of them. And some changes.

Feeling better about my plan and knowing I was making the right decision, I checked in with Jeff, then headed out. I had to get ready for my date.

When I got home, I checked my phone. Still no reply from Kingsley. A tingle in the back of my mind tried to signal a warning, but I pushed the thought away. It was fine. We were fine. He didn't know I was in love with him, and no one was going to tell him. Two more weeks and I'd never worry about that again because I'd never see him again.

I rubbed my chest at that pain. It hurt a lot.

But I knew it would. I knew falling for him would mean pain when he left. Because he was always going to leave. Always. And I had no choice but to be okay with that.

I stepped into the shower and let the hot water run over my body. I washed my hair and body, shaved everything, and let anticipation build inside me.

It was going to be a great night.

When I got out of the shower, I slathered lotion all over myself, loving the gentle scent on my skin. I smiled when I opened my top drawer and saw the brand new blue lace lingerie. A treat for Kingsley, but a gift to myself. Something to remember him. Something to enjoy when he was gone and I wanted to feel beautiful and sexy and love myself.

It didn't matter that Kingsley didn't love me. He never said he would. He gave me so much more than love. He gave me a peek into what life could be like. How happy I could be. How it felt to love someone. What I deserved.

I would never be the same after loving Kingsley, and I took that as a win. I had always prided myself on knowing who I was, but I learned so much more with him in my life. And the lingerie was just one tiny piece of that.

I took my time with the lace, imagining the look on his face when I modeled it for him. It was going to be a good night. A really good night.

With my lingerie in place, and my boobs looking very perky and happy, I reached for the dress I picked up when I bought the lingerie. It was sexy without being too sexy. The dip in front was lower than what I usually wore but not indecent. The skirt fell almost to my knees, but the flirty bounce made it was much shorter when I walked.

Natalie knocked on my door. "I'm heading out soon."

I opened the door so I could see her before she left.

"Wow," she breathed, her gaze going right to my cleavage.

"Too much?"

Natalie shook her head. "Not when you're going out with the man you love. Don't let Omar see you."

I snorted. "Oh, please. That man only has eyes for you."

"I know, but he might demand you tell him where you got that and take me shopping on the spot."

I laughed. "Then maybe I should say hello to him. Give him a reason to treat you."

Natalie rolled her eyes. "Please. He doesn't need a reason. Every time I mention something I like, he buys it in hopes I'll moooo—"

"You'll moo? What does... Move? He asked you to move in with him?"

"Yeah," she said slowly. "I told him no. I'm not going to leave you."

"Yes, you are," I replied.

She opened her mouth to argue.

"Natalie, I love you, but you are going to leave me. You're going to marry that man because you love him and he loves you, and it would just be weird if he moved in here with us."

She chuckled.

"And I love that for you. I don't want to hold you back. I never wanted that. If you want to move in with Omar, you should."

"But we have a lease. And I pay half the rent. It wouldn't be fair to leave you to pay all of it."

"It also wouldn't be fair for me to keep you from doing what you really want to do. I might be able to afford the house alone. Or I can find another roommate. Move to a smaller place. I don't know. But first, you need to decide when you're ready to move in with Omar."

Her blush said she was past ready.

"Don't put your life on hold for me. Just promise we'll still see each other."

She hugged me tightly. "All the time. You can't get rid of me entirely."

I hugged her back. "I'd never want to."

Natalie stepped back and wiped the tears on her lashes. "Okay, I'm going to go so you can finish getting ready. I love you so much, Daisy."

"I love you, Natalie. Go see your man."

She grinned. "Have fun with yours."

"Thanks. See you tomorrow."

"Bye!"

Natalie walked out, and I realized she didn't even pack a bag. She was already moving in with Omar and either I didn't realize it or she didn't.

But she was happy. That was what mattered to me.

And for two more weeks, I was going to be happy, too. I was going to soak up every minute I could spend with Kingsley and love him enough to make him believe it was possible to find love again, even if it wasn't with me.

I finished getting ready and checked my phone. He was supposed to pick me up at six, but I told him to come early when I texted him in the morning.

A text that still had no reply.

It was okay. It was only five-thirty. He wasn't late. He was just busy. I was not going to panic. Not yet.

Five-forty-three.

Five-fifty-eight.

Six-oh-nine.

He was never late. Something was wrong.

I stared at the phone I'd been studying for forty minutes. Still no reply. I needed to know what was going on.

Easy breezy. That was best.

> Hey! I thought you were picking me up at six. Is everything okay?

I kept staring. Five minutes passed.

> I'm worried. If something came up, I understand, I just want to know you're okay.

Again, all I got was silence.

I grabbed my handbag and left, needing to see for myself that he was okay.

## 22

---

### KINGSLEY

My phone buzzed again. I was really tempted to ignore it. Every one of her texts was a reminder of who I was. Weak, wrong, a coward, a cheater.

I looked at my phone and stood.

DAISY

> I'm outside. I went to the clinic, thinking maybe you got stuck at work. No one was there, so I came here. Your car is here. I know you're here. Either you come out and tell me what's going on or I'm coming in.

Shit. Shit. She couldn't come in. She couldn't meet Isla. Even though they already met. She couldn't just show up.

But she did. And she was giving me a chance to keep her away from my life, from my family.

"I'll be right back," I said to no one, knowing my mother would watch Isla for me while I disappeared.

Daisy was still in her car when I walked out, but she got out when she saw me. Dammit, she looked good. The blue dress she wore hugged her breasts and appeared to offer them up. To me. For me.

My dick twitched as I grew closer to her.

Her skirt was long but moved with the slight breeze, lifting the edges and giving me a peek of thighs I knew well. Thighs I wanted to spend more time between.

No. I couldn't. I wouldn't. She wasn't mine. She never would be.

Her arms crossed over her chest, either in anger or to protect herself. My guess was the second one when I caught the pained look in her eyes. "Are you okay?"

I swallowed and nodded. "Yeah."

"So, you didn't show up because you're done."

It wasn't a question. She already knew me well enough to know what I was saying without saying it. "Look, Daisy, I know you're angry that I didn't call you."

"Didn't call... That's why you think I'm angry?"

"Well, yeah. I should have. It was wrong. I'm sorry. But I know—"

"You know. I'm glad you know. Or you think you know. But you have no idea what I'm thinking. Or why I'm mad."

"I... I don't?"

"No. I'm not mad that you didn't call. Or that you're done with this, with us. I'm really not."

"Then why—?"

"I'm not," she continued at the same time I started to ask. She stopped and rolled her lips in, looking up at me with so much pain in her gaze I almost reached for her.

Almost.

"I'm not even really mad. I'm hurt. I'm disappointed. We agreed we would talk. I always knew you were leaving. So I'm not mad you decided you were done a few weeks earlier than I expected. But for the last few weeks, you've shown me what I should be looking for. You've helped me in so many ways. You let me become the person I wanted to be but didn't know how to be. You showed me what it's like to have someone who cares the way you do. I know you don't love me, that you never will. It wasn't ever an option, but you showed me that there's better out there than I've ever known before. God, I was... I knew you weren't my future. You told me that. I accepted it. But what I can't accept is you treating me like this. You've never made me feel like I wasn't important to you, even though I knew you had more important people in your life. I was never going to be your priority, and that was okay. It's what I want, and what I need, from whoever I end up with. You can't give me that, and you never said you would. But I deserved better than you not showing up tonight. I deserved better than you not letting me know you were done. I deserve better than the way you treated me today, Kingsley. So I guess you did give me one more thing. You showed me, again, what I deserve. What I want. So..." She sniffed and wiped tears from below her eyes. "So, thank you. And goodbye."

She turned and walked back to her car, getting in and pulling away from the curb without looking back.

And taking a piece of me with her.

I stood on the grass and waited for her to come back. For her to tell me she was angry and that we would be fine. For her to yell, then forgive me for being an idiot, and to invite me back to her place so she could show me what was under that dress.

None of those things happened.

"Are you okay?" someone asked. A neighbor walking their dog.

I shook my head and stepped out of the sidewalk. "Yeah. Have a good night."

"You, too." He smiled and continued past me, not worried at all about me.

Why would he be? We were strangers. I'd never see the man again.

Just like I'd never see Daisy again.

It was how it had to be.

"WE NEED TO TALK," Dad said Monday morning, walking into his office before I got out. We'd been sharing the space since he came back, and it was getting way too tight.

I stood and moved the opposite way around the desk so I could leave. "I'm on my way out."

"No, you're not. Sit down," Dad said, his tone the same one he used when I was a teenager and he caught me trying to sneak out. I only did it once because I didn't want to hear that tone ever again.

I swallowed and moved to sit down, hating that he towered over me as I did.

"I don't know what your problem is the last few days, but you need to knock it off."

"Whatever," I said, full teenager mode coming out as I sat there.

"Don't *whatever* me. You're a grown damn man. You have a child. You don't get to act like one."

"But you do? You get to do whatever you want, but I have to be the adult? You're such a hypocrite! You walk around here like you're the fucking hero, but this place wouldn't still be here if it weren't for me."

"And this place would already be yours if it weren't for you!"

I shook my head and stood, pacing away from him. "Don't put that on me. That's not fair, and you know it."

"Why not? You're the one who chose to leave. Who couldn't stand to be around me."

"Do you blame me? Do you really blame me? You were the one having an affair. You were the one cheating on Mom with your tech. Does it get more cliche than that? I couldn't stand to look at you. I still can't."

"You can sit up there on your high horse and pretend you've never made a mistake in your life, but you will not speak to me that way. And you will not treat Sheila the way you've been treating her."

I rolled my eyes. "Whatever. Did she run to you and tattle on me?"

Dad moved toward me faster than I expected and managed to get in my face. "Don't you dare act like you know anything about what you're talking about."

"But I do," I growled at him. "I know all about it. And every time I see you, I feel like I'm going to be sick. I feel like I'm just as bad as you because I never told Mom what you did."

"She knows," he seethed.

"What? No. You're lying. She would have left you if she knew. Or told me. No."

Dad stepped back, head drooped. "I never told her you knew. I didn't want her to be upset that you didn't immediately tell her. But she knows. I told her. And she chose to give me another chance."

"Why?"

He shook his head. "Because your mother is a better person than I am."

I snorted in agreement.

"Every marriage is complicated, and ours is no exception. Your mother forgave me, and we've been in counseling for years to stay connected."

"You go to counseling?"

He nodded. "We do. Because we've changed since the day we got married. We've had struggles and good times and every day I wake up and am thankful for your mother."

"Except the days you're with Sheila," I snarled.

"Especially those days. What happened with Sheila was a mistake. We both knew it, and we ended it. But it's a reminder for me of what I have at home with your mother."

"Why does Sheila still work here then? If you're so in love with Mom, why keep your mistress around?"

"For one, it would be illegal to fire her. She did nothing wrong. If I let her go because we were together, that's sexual harassment and she could, and would, sue me. And she'd win. But the bigger reason is because your mother asked me not to."

"What? No. There's no way."

"Your mother likes Sheila. And like I said, she's a better person than I am."

"But you screwed around on her. You trashed your marriage vows instead of honoring them. You never should have been with Daisy!"

Dad's brows shot up. "Daisy? Who's Daisy?"

"I meant Sheila," I growled, my face getting warm.

"No, I don't think you did. And I'm not sure this conversation was about me after all. Who's Daisy?"

"She's not important."

"She's the woman who showed up Saturday night? The one you've been spending time with all summer and thought we wouldn't notice?"

I glared at him, and apparently that was an answer.

"You getting involved with another woman is nothing like what I did, Kingsley. Nothing."

"I made vows," I growled.

"Yes, you did. And as much as I hate it, Faith is gone. If you love another woman, there's no reason you can't be with her."

"I don't love her."

Dad looked at me closely, then nodded slowly. "Okay. But I think you're only hurting yourself and Isla by telling yourself that."

That hit me hard enough to take a step back. "How is it hurting Isla to honor her mother's memory?"

"Are you really honoring it? Are you really doing what's best for you and Isla by closing yourself off to love? By deciding Faith was the only woman you were allowed to love your entire life, and now that she's gone, you're done? What would you tell Isla if the same thing happened to her? If she married someone who was taken from her too soon? Would you tell her it was wrong to get married again? Would you tell her she was cheating?"

"No," I admitted, hating that he was right.

"Then why is it that way for you?"

"It just is," I said.

Dad nodded. He opened his mouth to reply, but a knock on the door stopped him.

Sheila stuck her head in. "Hey." She looked around and saw me, stopping and pulling back. "You're both here." Sheila's smile was tight. "We have patients if you're ready to start the day."

"We'll be right there. Thank you, Sheila."

She nodded and left without another word.

"I know I messed things up, Kingsley. I know I caused all this pain you're feeling. But I've been working to correct it for years. I started with your mother, but I haven't forgotten the damage I did to you. I just didn't realize it was so deep. For that, I am sorry. You have an amazing daughter, and you are an amazing man. And I'm sorry I didn't do more to help you become that man."

He didn't wait for me to reply before he walked out the door, leaving me in the office to stew on his words.

IT TOOK me two days to work up the nerve to speak to my mother about Sheila. I left work before Dad, who was back to full time and handling most of the patients, so I could catch Mom without him around. I needed to know the truth.

"I need to ask you about something," I told her. Isla was taking a nap, and Mom was getting dinner ready.

"Sure, honey. What's going on?"

"Dad said he told you about his affair with Sheila. Is that true?"

Her smile fell. She looked down at what she was doing. Her hands were still but trembling. "How do you know about that?"

"I... I've always known. I saw them. Years ago."

"That's why you left town. Why you never wanted to speak to him." She breathed a mirthless laugh. "I feel so stupid for not putting that together."

"You aren't stupid, Mom. I... He shouldn't have done it."

"No, he shouldn't have. And he knows that. We've been better. And his heart attack was a wakeup call for us. For both of us. I love your father. I've never wanted a life that didn't include him."

"Even after he cheated on you? Why? Why would you forgive him?" I barked at her.

"Kingsley Adam Harris, you do not get to speak to me that way. You and Faith didn't have long enough to go through the ups and downs of life. She was stolen from you far too soon. But marriage is complicated. It's messy. It's not perfect. And neither are we. Your father made a mistake, and it was a big one, but I forgave him for it. There are things you don't know, and they are none of your business to know, but you don't get to judge me for my actions."

"I'm not judging you, Mom. I'm judging him. He's the one who was messing around. It's not right. Vows are forever. Not just until someone else is more tempting."

"And our vows are still secure. I still love your father, and he loves me. You don't get to come in here and tell me I'm wrong."

"But Mom—"

"No, Kingsley. No. I'm not going to stand here and have you tell me how to act. I don't tell you what to do when you're spending half your free time out of this house instead of at home with your daughter. You were so annoyed when I called you because you had plans to do things with Isla, but every free minute you have, you're not here. You're somewhere else. And that's on you. I'm loving the time with Isla because I haven't gotten enough of it. I'll never have enough of it, but don't judge me for what I do and pretend you're perfect when you're not even living up to your own expectations."

"Grandma?" Isla said from behind me.

I hadn't heard her get up, and from the look on Mom's face, she didn't either.

"Come here, sweetheart. Are you okay?"

Isla shook her head and lifted her arms for Mom to pick her up. Isla was getting too big, but Mom lifted her up and immediately went to the rocking chair in the corner. She cuddled Isla on her lap and sang a soft song to her while Isla woke up.

I left the room, knowing Mom was right. I was only making things worse. I spent most of my summer with Daisy instead of Isla. I was not putting Isla first, even though Daisy said I was. I was putting my own selfish ass first.

And that needed to stop.

I grabbed the suitcase I'd used to carry my things to MacKellar Cove and tossed it on my bed. I went through the drawers and shoved everything I had into the suitcase.

When I was done, I went into Isla's room and did the same for her, packing up all her clothes except one outfit for the drive.

We were leaving. First thing in the morning. My dad was fine and could handle the practice. My mom would get her life back.

I could spend the last two weeks with Isla before she had to go back to school. We were only leaving ten days earlier than planned, but it was better. It meant getting back to our life. Getting back to the things we said we were going to do.

And it meant walking away from all the mistakes I made in MacKellar Cove.

I carried our suitcases out, setting them down so I could open the door.

"What are you doing?" Mom asked.

"We're going to leave in the morning. First thing. I'm getting packed up so we can be home by lunch."

"You don't have to do that, Kingsley," Mom said.

I shook my head and opened the door. "We do, Mom. You were right. This isn't the summer I wanted with Isla, so we're going to go home and have a few weeks of time together before she starts kindergarten."

"But I want to go to kindergarten here! I don't want to leave. I want to live with grandma!" Isla yelled and cried, her face crumbling.

Mom hugged her tight and whispered to her while I walked outside.

We had to go.

I put the suitcases in my trunk and leaned against the back of my SUV. I looked around the neighborhood. Faith and I wanted to buy a house on the street near my parents. Her parents were gone by the time we met, and she loved my mom. Faith wanted the life Isla and I had the last few weeks.

Aside from Daisy.

My throat tightened when I thought about her, but I pushed it away, just like I had since she walked away from me. It was for the best. She would move on with her life, and I would...

Stay stuck in mine.

I had no choice. I'd vowed to love Faith forever. I wasn't going back on that now. Or ever. So it was better to leave.

Isla was still crying when I walked back inside, so I went to my room and closed the door. Hiding from Daisy, hiding from my mother, hiding from Isla.

Hiding from it all.

Because they all deserved better than me. Leaving would give Daisy that option. Same for my mother. Isla would eventually have better than me. And until then, I would make sure she knew how much I loved her.

## 23

DAISY

THERE WERE FEW TIMES IN MY LIFE WHEN I FELT COMPLETELY hopeless. When I couldn't see the light or know where to go. The week after things ended with Kingsley was one of those times.

Not entirely because of Kingsley, but that was a huge part of it. I finally understood why Natalie was so worried about me getting involved with him. Love did funny things to a person, even when I was prepared for it.

Love made me ache for him to call. It made me cry for him to come back. It made me want to stay in bed all day and never change out of my pajamas.

But I couldn't do any of those things the week after things ended because my inventory manager was on vacation. And forgot to tell me about it.

Ugh.

It was a good thing, sort of, because it meant I had no choice but to get out of bed and go to work. I couldn't wallow in my misery and wish my days away. I had to function and be human and take care of things.

It reminded me of what I'd worked so hard to accomplish. Even though I'd wanted Kingsley in my life, and knew I'd never have him, I had other things. Good things.

Without Penny around for a week, and with me running the inventory again, I knew the decision I made about taking the job from her was the right one.

I took the time during the week to watch Wendy and Jeff and figure out what the right move was. By the time Penny was supposed to return, I knew the answer and had already made moves to put things in place.

Wendy was cautious about accepting Penny's job before I'd had a chance to speak to Penny, but I assured her it was a done deal and that it would be up to Penny if she took her old job back or left, but neither of those had anything to do with Wendy. If Wendy declined the job, I would be looking elsewhere for someone because Penny running things was not sustainable.

Wendy finally agreed. She was excited about the opportunity. And she started learning how I did things and understanding why, with lots of questions, instead of just doing it the way she wanted without regard to why I managed inventory how I did.

Penny could have gotten it eventually, but she didn't seem to want to, and then not showing up multiple times and passing the job on to others. I couldn't overlook all of it.

Wendy and I were in the office Tuesday morning, the latest delivery unloaded, reviewing the upcoming orders, when Penny arrived for the day. An hour later than she should have been. Plus ten days.

"Good morning!" Penny said, smiling like nothing was wrong. "How is everything?"

"Good," Wendy said, quickly vacating the seat she was in. "I'm going to go check the floor."

I nodded to Wendy, then focused on Penny.

Penny watched Wendy leave, then turned to me. She sighed and sank into the seat Wendy left. "Are you firing me?"

I shook my head. "I don't want to, but I think it's up to you."

"I know I haven't been any good at this new job. You should give it to Wendy. She's been covering for me. The only thing I've been doing is placing orders, and even that I'm not very good at. I don't see things the way you do."

"Why didn't you tell me any of this when I offered you the job?"

"Because you seemed so overwhelmed and stressed, and I didn't want to let you down."

"But you did by not doing the job."

She sighed and nodded. She swallowed roughly, then looked up at me with watery eyes. "I'll get my things."

"I'm not firing you, Penny."

"Why not? I was really bad at the inventory job."

"Yes, you were. But you were really good at the store manager job."

Her head snapped up. "I can have my old job back?"

"If you want it."

"I do. I'm so sorry, Daisy. I... I really like working here, and I screwed up so many things, and I know I should have talked to you, but I didn't want to put more on you when I was supposed to be taking things off your plate and—"

"Let's get something clear, Penny. My first job is to make sure this place is successful. If that means I have to work extra hours or do more, that's okay with me. I'm the owner. The risk is mine. And so is the reward. I'm very aware of that. I want to surround myself with the best people possible because I know that's essential to success. But those people have to be honest with me, too."

Penny nodded. "I will be. I'm really sorry I wasn't before." She stood to leave, then stopped and faced me. "For what it's worth, I think Wendy was really good at this job and you should give it to her. She's smart and talented and loves this place as much as you do. The only parts where I succeeded were because of her."

"Thank you for telling me that. And I've already asked her to take the position. You two will be swapping, and Jeff will stay as the other store manager."

Penny chuckled. "That's a great idea, Daisy. Thank you for giving me another chance."

"I know you won't screw it up. Everyone who works here loves this place. We're all in this together."

"Yes, we are," Penny said.

I smiled, and she left the office, leaving me to my thoughts.

Which were just as bad as they'd been for the last ten days. My fingers itched to call Kingsley. To tell him things were finally resolved with Penny and that his suggestion was a good one.

But I couldn't call him. Not anymore. He made it clear he was done, and I was not going to be that crazy ex who kept calling when the other person made it very clear things were over.

Kingsley and I were done, and the sooner I moved on, the better.

I WAS NOT ready to move on. A cute single dad came into the store with his little boy, and I couldn't bring myself to flirt back when he made it clear he was interested. I was polite, but it was exhausting to resist the man.

After my day, I went home and decided I was done wallowing. Kingsley had no issue ending things, and I owed myself the same release.

My friends had been great, trying to get me to forget Kingsley and offering to set me up with other men, but I wasn't looking for that. I just wanted to feel normal. To feel like myself again.

So when Natalie suggested dinner at O'Kelley's, I agreed. We hadn't talked about her moving out again and I wanted to ask her about it.

We found a table and ordered drinks and dinner before I had a chance to ask her. "So, when are you moving in with Omar?"

She huffed a laugh. "Not anytime soon."

"What? Why? What happened?"

She looked at me like I was crazy for asking the question.

"Because of me? And Kingsley?"

"Well, yeah. I'm not going to leave you right now when you're heartbroken."

"No. Let's go," I told her, standing up.

"Where are we going?"

"To pack your shit so you can move."

"Sit down," Natalie said, grabbing my hand and pulling me back to the table.

"You're moving in with the man you love. I'm not going to be the reason you aren't happy."

"I am happy living with you. And I'll be happy when I move in with him. But now isn't the right time."

"It'll never be the right time. Not if you wait for everyone else's lives to be perfect."

"Not everyone. Just you."

I snorted and leaned back. "Natalie, I love you, and you are always going to be there for me. You have no choice. And you're moving in with the freaking mayor, so I know you're not leaving town. But you can't put your life on hold for me. You have to live it for you."

"Daisy—"

"Natalie! Hey!" a man said, stopping next to our table.

"Andre! Hi. How are you?" Natalie said, smiling. Andre maintained the landscaping at Mountain View Retreat for Natalie and owned his own company. Natalie had been singing his praises all summer.

"I'm good." Andre turned to me and offered his hand. "Andre Davidson. I'm not sure we've met."

I shook his hand, noticing there was absolutely zero spark there. "Daisy Lincoln. Nice to meet you."

"Daisy's my roommate, and she owns Lincoln Toys," Natalie explained.

"Very nice place. I've been in a few times to get things for my niece and nephews. Nice to meet you." Andre's smile was kind and friendly, but still did nothing.

"Thank you. I love my store. Bringing childhood to all kids."

"That's perfect. As the youngest in my family, I got a lot of secondhand toys."

"If you could bring back one toy from your childhood, what would it be?" I asked him before I had time to process that it was the first thing I asked Kingsley, too.

"Ooh, favorite toy?" Andre asked. He rubbed his chin while he thought for a minute. "I think I'd bring back my toy cars. I loved playing with those. The ramps and things they have now are pretty awesome, and I'd love to be able to run my cars all over some of those."

I nodded. "Nice. It's crazy the way toys have changed in only a few decades."

"Yeah, it really is." Someone called Andre's name and drew his attention from us. "Nice meeting you, Daisy. Natalie, I'll see you soon. Have a good night."

"You, too," Natalie said. She waved as Andre walked away.

"Did you set that up?" I asked her.

Natalie sipped her drink as studied me over the edge of her glass. She set it down slowly. "No. I promise you, I did not. I don't know if Andre is single, and if he is, it's up to you if you want to date him. I wouldn't try to force a man on you. For both of your sakes."

I nodded. "Okay. Thank you. And sorry I asked."

Natalie shook her head. "It's okay. I want you to be happy, but I know that's not going to happen until you're ready."

"I'm ready, but I'm also still a little broken."

"I know." Natalie reached for my hand and squeezed when I took hers.

We spent the rest of the night talking about her moving in with Omar, and by the end of it, I had her convinced to start making plans.

At least someone was getting their happily ever after.

Labor Day weekend was a quiet one at the store. I learned that my first summer. Families were out getting school supplies before classes started the following week or taking one last vacation before summer was over.

Summer camp was officially done and Natalie was spending the weekend with Omar, their first weekend living together. She still had things at our house, but she'd started moving. I was casually looking for a roommate, but I hadn't found one yet.

And I was working. I gave my employees the weekend off so they could go out of town or see their families or do whatever they wanted. I knew the store would be close to dead, and there was no reason to make everyone work when I was looking for a distraction anyway.

It had been three weeks since I'd seen Kingsley. More than two weeks since he'd left town. Not that I was told he was leaving, but he called Trent before he left, and Finley told me.

Three weeks of missing him wasn't long enough to move on. And going into the winter season when things were much quieter was not going to make it all easier.

But I had to do it.

I'd never known heartbreak, and it sucked. I felt like I saw him and heard him all the time. Hell, I even thought I heard Isla, and I'd only met her twice.

"Daddy, can I get this?" the little girl said.

I couldn't see them, but I smiled.

"Yeah, Isla. You can get that."

My heart leaped. It sounded like Kingsley. And the daughter was Isla. What were the odds? High apparently because Kingsley was gone, and Isla was gone, so the little girl in my store had to be a different Isla.

I waited at the register for the two of them to come to the front. Probably with a significant other. It didn't matter. They were just there to shop.

Too bad my heart didn't get the memo. It galloped while I waited for Isla and her daddy to wander the store. When they finally made their way up front, I forced myself to smile.

Until I saw them.

Oh, God, it was them.

"Hello, Daisy," Kingsley said, as if we saw each other all the time.

"Hello. Welcome to Lincoln Toys. Did you find everything you were looking for?"

"Daddy said I could get a new dollhouse for my room!" Isla shouted.

I smiled at her, keeping all my focus on her and not on the man who shredded my heart. "That's so nice of him. You must have a very kind daddy."

"He moved here because I wanted to stay. I wanted to live near my grandma and grandpa, so Daddy said we could."

I sucked in a breath, fighting the tears in my eyes. And my throat. "That's... That's really nice for you."

"Daisy," he started.

I shook my head, keeping my head down instead of looking at him. I couldn't. I couldn't look up and see the answer in his eyes. And I couldn't ask the question either. Not when I knew the answer was that we were still over. "I'm happy for you. It sounds like you're getting everything you want. That's all I ever wanted for you."

He reached over and put his hand on mine.

I sucked in a breath, those tears I was holding back coming faster than I could suck them in. I pulled my hand from under his and wiped at my tears.

"Look at me, Daisy."

I squeezed my eyes shut and willed the tears away. It was no use. I blinked my eyes open and let the tears fall. It's not like he didn't know they were there.

"We need to talk."

"No, we don't. You said everything you needed to say. I am not going to get in your way of living your life here."

"You won't."

I sucked in a pained breath. I swallowed and nodded, focusing on the task once more.

"What I meant is you'd never be in the way. You are my life here. You're the reason I came back."

"No. You can't say something like that. I know what we were, I know what you wanted. I'm not going to press for something else."

"Okay, but I am." He shifted closer, the checkout belt keeping him from getting to me. "Can I come back when you're done for the day? Take you to dinner?"

I shook my head. "You don't have to do that. You don't have to explain anything to me. It's all good." I wiped at the tears and forced a smile for the little girl who had no idea what was going on. "Your total is nineteen-seventy-one."

Isla handed over a crumpled twenty. "Why are you sad?"

"Sometimes people get sad when things don't happen the way they hoped for."

"Like when you miss someone?"

I nodded. "Exactly like that. I missed someone, but the way I missed him is different than the way he missed me, and I am sad that things can't be the way I hoped."

Isla looked up at her father. "You should make Ms. Daisy happy. You said you loved her. Why don't you make her smile?"

I gasped, dropping the change I was going to hand her. I scrambled to pick it up, apologizing the whole time.

"Daisy," Kingsley said, putting his hand over mine again. "Please, let me take you to dinner tonight."

"You don't..." I nibbled my lip and looked at Isla. "What..."

"Yes. What she said is true. But I wanted to tell you a little more eloquently than that. If you'll let me."

Tears rolled down my cheeks, and I knew there was only one answer I could give him. "Yes."

## 24

KINGSLEY

I couldn't stop my smile when she breathed that one word. That was all I needed to know. She was in, and I was going to make sure she knew I was, too.

Leaving MacKellar Cove was the hardest thing I'd ever done in my life. It was hard the first time, after I caught my father and Sheila. Leaving the second time, after destroying Daisy, was worse. I knew it was the wrong choice, but I had to do it. I didn't deserve her.

I still didn't, but I was going to fight for her anyway.

Isla and I left Lincoln Toys and went to my parents' house. We moved back in with them until we found a new house. Somewhere we could potentially grow. Maybe one day have Daisy move in, maybe one day have siblings for Isla.

But first was getting Daisy to agree to give me another chance.

"How did it go?" Dad asked when we walked in.

Isla ran to Mom to show her the toy we bought. It was a small excuse to see Daisy, but it was also a bribe for my daughter. Not that she needed it. Isla was a nightmare when we went back to Philadelphia. She stomped around the house and told me she wanted to move in with grandma again because she was nicer than me.

It all came to a head when Isla cried. It wasn't anger. It was gut wrenching sadness. And it told me I wasn't alone in that feeling.

I still had to pull my head out of my ass and realize I'd made a lot of decisions that were wrong, but it was the first step to moving back home. For good.

"She agreed to dinner," I told Dad.

Dad smiled. "That's all you need. A chance to tell her you love her."

"Isla already told her that part."

Dad snorted a laugh. "Leave it to that one to make sure you're not leaving again."

I nodded. "Let's hope Daisy sees it the same way."

"She will, son. She will."

I hoped so.

Daisy was off in another hour, but she asked if I could pick her up from home so she could change. I wasn't expecting her to make an effort, and totally expecting her to make me work for her forgiveness, but I agreed. And hoped it wasn't a ploy to get away from me before I could talk to her.

Just in case, I was waiting in her driveway when she arrived home from work. She got out of her SUV with a smile. "I need time to shower and change."

"I'll wait. I'm not going anywhere."

"Why don't you come inside?"

"Are you sure?"

She nodded. "You don't have to sit out here. I'll try to be quick."

"You don't have to be quick. Take your time." I followed

her in, moving to the couch before temptation had me following her to her room.

The door closed down the hall and a minute later, the shower came on.

I looked around the living room, noticing there was a lot less stuff than the last time I was there. Like Daisy was leaving.

My throat tightened at the thought. Was she moving? She was the only one at her store earlier. Did she close it and was leaving the area? Isla and I moved back, but Daisy wasn't staying?

No. I had to convince her to stay. She was my future, but that future was in MacKellar Cove.

"Are you okay?" she asked from right behind me.

I spun on her, startled. "I didn't hear you."

"Sorry?"

"It's fine. It's..." I looked at the living room again. "Are you moving? Because Isla wasn't lying when she said I love you. Being with you, being here, it's everything I wouldn't let myself want for so long. Is there anything I can do to convince you not to move? I know that's a lot to ask, but Isla loves it here, and I'm going to take over my father's practice, and I want you with me. I love you, Daisy. And I know it's fast, and I know you're not at the same place as me, but—"

"I love you, too," she whispered.

"You... Do?"

She smiled. "You silly man. Of course, I love you. I've loved you for weeks, but that wasn't our agreement so I didn't tell you."

"But you... I wasn't very nice. You said you deserve better than me."

"Oh, I do. Unfortunately, our hearts don't listen to reason."

I breathed a laugh. "Where does that leave us?"

"Well, I thought you were going to take me to dinner." She spun, and I finally saw what she was wearing. The same dress she wore the night I didn't show up. "I figured I'd give the dress another chance."

"And me?"

"We'll see." She grinned.

I shook my head and moved toward her. "God, I love you. I never thought I'd fall in love again, but I do."

"I can't live with a ghost, Kingsley," she said, nibbling on her lower lip.

"You won't. Faith was... I loved Faith. I always will. She's Isla's mother, and she was the first woman I ever loved. If you can't accept that, I don't know—"

"I understand you have a past. You had a life before us. I would never expect you to tell me you don't still love her. But I also can't have you comparing us or wishing I did things like she did."

I shook my head. "Never. I... I know I was doing that before because I was struggling. With so many things. You're the first woman I've been involved with since Faith died, and there were times when I had to remind myself you weren't her. But that's part of why I love you. You don't have to be. You shouldn't be. I don't want you to be."

"But you still love me?"

I smiled, nodding when I couldn't squeeze words out past the lump in my throat.

"And you're moving to MacKellar Cove?"

"Already moved. I resigned from my clinic in Philadelphia last week."

"Where are you living?"

"With my parents for now. I'm going to look for a house,

but I wanted to get Isla started in school before I worried about that.”

“Any interest in a two bedroom on a quiet street that comes with a renter already?”

“Well, I... Wait. This place?”

She shrugged.

“You’re not moving.”

“Natalie is moving in with Omar.”

I chuckled. “And you were just going to let me believe you were leaving.”

“You didn’t really let me get a word in.”

I nodded and took a step toward her. “You’re right. I didn’t.”

She took a step toward me. “I know it’s fast, but I’ve been looking for a roommate. Natalie is going to be gone by the end of September.”

“That’s a month from now.”

She nodded. “It is. Too fast?”

I shook my head. “Not fast enough for me to get you in my arms.” I yanked her to me.

Her hands went to my chest, and she breathed a sigh, like she was still waiting for me to tell her it was all a joke.

“Are you really here for good?”

I nodded. “I’m really here for good.”

“And you really love me?”

“I really love you.”

“And you’re not going to stand me up again?”

I sighed, and she tried to take a step back. I held tight. “When I was in vet school, my dad had an affair.”

“What?”

“I idolized him. He was my hero. I wanted to be like him when I grew up.”

She led me to the couch and sat next to me, holding my hand.

"I saw them together one day, and I confronted him about it. He asked me not to tell my mother, and I left. I left town. Moved away and couldn't come back. I couldn't face her knowing what he was doing, and I couldn't be around him. So, I left."

"Oh, Kingsley, I'm so sorry."

I nodded. "Thanks. Faith and I always talked about living here, raising our family here and me taking over his practice. It all ended that day. I couldn't do it. She understood, and when I was done with school, I found a job wherever there was an opening. It was fine, but it never felt like the right place for us. Then she died, and I couldn't think about anything. I was so lost in grief and over my head with raising Isla all alone, and survival was my only goal."

"Until your dad's heart attack. You came home to be here with him."

I shook my head. "No. I... My mom called. I felt like I owed her. All the years of not telling her about Dad's affair had me drowning in guilt where she was concerned. I came because she asked me to."

"That was still good of you."

I breathed a laugh. "I was a jerk to my father. But he told me my mom knew about the affair. He told her years ago but never told her I knew. She forgave him, and they stayed together, and things ended with Sheila."

"Sheila? The tech that works for him?"

I nodded. "Yeah."

"That's why you would come over after work," Daisy whispered.

"Sometimes, yeah. It wasn't fair to you, but I needed... Well,

I needed you. Your sunshine and happiness. It erased all the bad in my world. Working with my father's mistress, working with my father, being in his home, feeling like I was lying to my mother. It was all too much sometimes. Unless I was with you."

"That kind of thing would mess anyone up."

"You're being too nice to me. I was an asshole. The week... The week I didn't show up, I saw my dad and Sheila together."

"No."

"Not like that. But it was too close for me. I thought it was still going on. I lost it on Sheila one day, and everything felt like it was closing in on me. Dad was cheating, and I felt like I was cheating on Faith with you."

She inched away from me with that confession. "Oh."

"That's why I didn't show up that night. I knew I was in love with you, but I thought I was like my father. That I was no better than him. I couldn't do it."

"Then why are you here now?"

"My father ripped me a new one. It was after that night that he told me things were over with Sheila and Mom knew. And he asked me about you. Said he knew we were together and told me what I did was nothing like what he did."

Daisy didn't comment, just stared at me, keeping her distance.

"He was right, but it still took me leaving for it to sink in. It took me leaving and knowing I left my heart here with you for me to accept that falling in love with you wasn't wrong. That I could love two women at the same time and miss one while I was loving the other."

"I can't compete with Isla's mom, Kingsley. I won't."

"You're not. You never were. I was twisted up in my mind because of everything with my father. I was... I was scared.

Isla doesn't remember her mom. She has no memories of Faith at all. I worried if I didn't keep her alive for Isla, Faith would just disappear. That wasn't fair to her, but keeping her in the center of my world wouldn't be fair to you."

"So what do we do?" Daisy whispered.

"I'm going to start with counseling. My parents have been going to someone, and I reached out to her and start seeing her next week. If you're open to it, I'd like you to meet her at some point."

"Counseling? Really?"

I nodded. "I never dealt with all the things in my past. Dad's affair, Faith's death. I need to if I'm going to be a good husband for you."

Her brows shot up. "Husband?"

I chuckled. "I didn't mean to confess that, but I'm hoping one day, yeah."

She eased closer. "I think I can get onboard with that."

"Yeah?"

She nodded and reached for my hand.

I couldn't wait another second to have her back in my arms. I scooped her up and brought her onto my lap. "I don't know how I managed to get so lucky to find you, but I'm really happy I did."

She scrunched her face and winced a little. "Well, you know it was actually your mother who found me."

I groaned. "I finally got you back in my arms and you bring up my mother?"

She laughed. "Well, she is the one I matched with on Book Boyfriends Wanted."

"No, sweetheart, that was all us. And you are all mine."

"Yes, I am."

I leaned in to kiss her, then pulled back. "Wait a minute. Why are you not punishing me for what I did?"

"What do you mean?"

"I was horrible to you. You deserve so much better than me. Why in the world are you not throwing me out right now?"

She shrugged and smiled. "Because I'd much rather be kissing you."

I nodded slowly, bringing her lips to mine. She sank into me as soon as our lips touched, her arms sliding around my neck. I kissed her softly and knew there was nowhere else I'd rather be than in her arms, on her couch, with my future in her hands.

"I love you, Kingsley," she whispered against my lips.

"I love you, Daisy."

"Do you still want dinner?"

"Dinner can wait. I want you first."

She scrambled off my lap. "Good answer." She reached for the hem of her dress and pulled it slowly off her body. Inch by inch, revealing blue lace and creamy skin.

"Holy fuck."

"I was hoping that would be your reaction," she said. Then she turned and walked away, leaving me to chase her to the bedroom.

# EPILOGUE
## ANDRE

I parked my truck and grabbed the sling Molly slept in. Never in my life did I expect I'd be a cat guy, but the little thing had me wrapped around her paw tight. So tight I bought a sling online so she could ride with me while I worked all day.

My mom joked that if I didn't give her human grandchildren, at least I brought home the sweetest feline grandchild ever. Everyone fell hard for Molly.

Including my stubborn and allergic best friend. Not that he'd admit it to me.

"Yo! Landon!" I called out as I let myself in the back of Blossom & Grow. The nursery was both the best and the only place in town to get plants and flowers. But even if there were other options, I'd go to Landon.

"Where are you?" I yelled as I continued through the shop.

Molly meowed to help draw attention to us, but Landon wasn't around.

"Hello?" a man called from up front.

I'd been in the store more than anyone else besides

Landon, so I headed up to the front to see if I could help his customer. "Can I help you?" I asked. "Oh, hey, Kingsley!"

Kingsley smiled and reached to shake my hand. "Andre. How are you?" He reached to pet Molly, and his grin widened. "And how are you, Molly?"

Molly responded with a nudge to his hand and a meow that I chose to believe was her hello.

"That's a nice sling. Obviously she's doing well."

I nodded. "Yep. All cured from her surgery, but she screams bloody murder when I try to leave her. My neighbors said she didn't stop all day. Sofia, she does maintenance in the building, she even had to go into the apartment to make sure Molly was okay because she was screaming so loud."

"Oh, jeez. She just adores you."

"Yep. Feeling's mutual. But you're not here for a check in. What's going on, Kingsley?"

"I was hoping to grab some flowers. Natalie moved in with Omar, and Isla and I are moving in with Daisy this weekend. Isla's spending one last night with my parents, so Daisy and I have a full night together. For the first time ever. And I don't know why I'm telling you all of this."

I chuckled. "It's all good. I'm sure you get all sorts of weird confessions in your job. Landon does, too. I think it's the magic of a flower shop. Something about the anxiety of what you're about to do. But it's a good kind of anxiety, right?"

"Yeah, it is," Kingsley said.

"All right, well, let's see what we can come up with. Did you order something or just going with what inspires you?"

"No, I didn't order. Was driving by and thought it would be a nice touch."

"Well, I'm assuming she either hates daisies or loves them."

"She loves them," he said.

"Okay, maybe start with those? Some of the Gerbera ones?" I pointed to the case with the large, colorful daisies.

Kingsley nodded. "Yeah, I like that."

"Perfect. So, we'll grab a few of those." I plucked a yellow one, added a hot pink and a soft pink. "Good?"

"Nice."

"What else?" I asked Kingsley.

We walked around the store and added flowers that worked well with the Gerbera daisies without getting lost in the bouquet or overwhelming the daisies. When we were done, I talked him into a vase to hold the bouquet of a dozen flowers.

"That's perfect. Thanks, Andre."

"You're welcome. Any time. And enjoy your night."

Kingsley smiled like a man who couldn't get any happier. "Thanks."

I waved at Kingsley, then turned to go back to find Landon. Fifteen minutes of abandoning his store wasn't like him.

I paused, then went to the front and flipped the sign on the window so no one else came in unattended. I almost reached the stairs to Landon's apartment when I heard footsteps coming down.

"Where were you? You had a customer. I took care of it, by the way, and you're welcome," I said.

"Sorry, Andre," Reegan said, brushing past me.

"Oh, shit. Sorry, Reegan. I thought you were Landon."

"He's... he'll be down in a minute." She rushed outside, letting the door close behind her.

I stared after her, wondering why she was acting weird. And why Landon wasn't down right after her.

They'd been together for years, six or seven, so as I'd gotten to know Landon, I got to know Reegan. We weren't as close, but she was good for him, and he talked about asking her to marry him.

But something was off.

When Landon didn't come downstairs within a few minutes, I went up, bracing myself for what I was going to find. I knocked on his door when I made it to the landing. "Are you dressed? I saw Reegan leave. She wear you out?"

He didn't answer, so I knocked again. "Landon. What's going on? Are you okay? Answer me, dude."

The door swung open as I knocked, and Landon stood in front of me. His hair was a mess, his shirt wrinkled. I wouldn't have thought much of it except the look on his face was one of shock.

"Are you okay?"

He shook his head. "I... I don't know."

"What happened? I saw Reegan leave. I figured you two were up here having sex in the middle of the day."

Landon snorted. "Nope."

"Okay. Then what were you doing?"

"Breaking up."

"What?" I had to have heard him wrong.

"We're... I asked her to move in with me. Her lease was coming up for renewal. She said she'd think about it. We've been together forever. Our families are friends. We know all the same people. It makes sense to move in together. To get married."

Not the most tempting offer in my opinion, but I kept that part to myself. "So, what happened?"

"She signed a new lease."

"What?"

He shrugged. "She was supposed to move in this month. Her lease is up, and she was going to move in. But she signed a new lease. She's staying in her apartment. She doesn't want to live with me."

"She ended things?"

He shook his head. "No. I did."

"What? I thought you loved her."

"And I thought she loved me, but she doesn't want to live with me. She just... Why are we together if we don't really want to be together?"

"Is that what you want?"

He shook his head again. "I... I don't know what I want. All I know is it doesn't make sense to keep dating if there's nothing else. So I said we should take some time apart. Figure out what we both want. And if it's not each other..."

"Dude, I'm sorry. That... That sucks."

He shrugged. "Yeah." He drew a breath, then looked at me like he was seeing me for the first time. "You didn't come here for all that. What's going on? Oh, your order for MacKellar Cove Inn. I can get you all loaded up."

"Thanks. And I'm sorry about Reegan."

He nodded, then sneezed. "Ah, man, you brought her into my apartment?"

"What else was I supposed to do with her?"

"Leave her in the truck!" Landon yelled as he scratched Molly's head.

"You love her, and you know it."

"Patient Zero does not need to be in my living space."

I covered Molly's ears and followed Landon downstairs. "Don't call her that. You'll hurt her feelings."

"She doesn't have feelings. She's a cat."

"So uncultured."

Landon snorted. "Says the man with a cat in a sling and jeans that are more dirt than fabric."

"Because you're so clean and perfect," I teased him back.

"Yeah, well, at least I'm not sin—"

Shit. He was about to say single. I clapped him on the back. "Want to get a beer tonight? Get out of the house?"

"I'm not looking for a hookup the day things end with Reegan."

"I wasn't suggesting one. I said a beer."

Landon took a minute, then nodded. "Yeah. That sounds good. Thanks, Andre."

"Anytime."

"Cats not invited!" he called after me as I went to back my truck up to the door.

"Yeah, yeah!" I called back. I rubbed Molly's head. "Don't worry, he loves you."

She meowed up at me and snuggled in tighter. She knew who kept her litter clean and her food bowl full.

And I knew Landon and Reegan would find their way back to each other. They were too good together not to.

If they couldn't make it work, I had no hope of finding my one and only. So they had to figure it out.

THANK you for reading Daisy and Kingsley's story! When Daisy first walked into this series, I fell hard for her. She was the light I needed in my world, a brightness that made me smile through every word of this book. And who better for her than a grumpy single dad who needed that same joy in his world.

The next book in the series is Andre and Joelle's story. Joelle runs from her wedding... for reasons... and ends up stranded on the side of the road. The man who offers her a ride brings her to MacKellar Cove Inn, and she finds herself unable to stop watching the hot man cutting the grass... with a cat in a sling? Preorder His Curvy Fascination now and start reading on June 3!

WANT MORE from Daisy and Kingsley? Getting forgiveness from Daisy was easy, but Sheila might not forgive and forget quite so quickly. See how Kingsley makes up for his attitude to Sheila now. Bonus epilogue is only available to subscribers. Sign up now!

WHEN DEX IS CALLED in to work as private security, Taylor is less than interested in his assistance. Until it's clear her life, business, and employees are in danger. He doesn't let her out of his sight, and he doesn't mind the duty one bit. Read Future now!

# ABOUT THE AUTHOR

*USA TODAY* Bestselling Author Mary E Thompson spent most of her childhood wishing she had a few less curves. She hid in the pages of books because her favorite characters never cared what size her clothes were. Now, neither does Mary, and she writes stories that celebrate women like her. Real women who have curves, chase dreams, and find love, because we should all be happy, no matter our dress size.

Mary spends her non-writing time with her husband and two kids, watching too much TV, cheering for her hometown football team (Go Bills!), and hiding chocolate from her family.

Visit https://MaryEThompson.com/ to sign up for Mary's newsletter, **Romancing the Curves**. Subscribers get free ebooks and other fun stuff, like exclusive, members only content and giveaways, plus are the first to know about new releases and sales!